FEAR

A Medical Thriller

A Dr. Powers Mystery

H.S. CLARK

Immortal Fear is a work of fiction. Names, characters, places, organizations, and incidents either are the product of the author's imagination or are used fictitiously. Any resemblance to actual persons, living or dead, events, organizations, or locales is entirely coincidental. *Immortal Fear* does not endorse or discourage any consumer product, professional service, or medical treatment.

Published by Grand Media
Puyallup, WA
www.grandmediacompany.com
grandmediacompany@gmail.com

ISBN: 978-0-9884274-9-5
eBook ISBN: 978-0-9884274-6-4
eBook: ASIN: B00SD3GL2W
LCCN: 2015900272

For Luba, my wife,

still the best thriller

"We labour against our own cure,

for death is the cure of all diseases."

-SIR THOMAS BROWNE

Religio Medici, 1643

PROLOGUE

London, September 30, 1888:

FOG DRIFTED UPWARD off the cold cobblestones of Mitre Square in the heart of the city, heavy with the musty smell of fresh blood. It dripped from an open neck wound and flowed through the mortar joints, tracing rectangular lines along the surface of the street. The crimson lines spread out in all directions from the crumpled body of a young woman, her once pretty red dress shredded and darkened by her own blood. Tangles of fiery red hair covered her mangled face like a woven hood. Her wraith-like body was parchment white, drained of all color.

A circle of City Police in uniform held back the growing crowd of gawkers.

"Everyone keep back," said the Constable to the growing mob. He drew his nightstick and slapped it into his hand, with his broad shoulders facing toward the crowd. Feet planted firmly, he held his ground.

Gossip passed like contagion among the onlookers, the murmur of voices merged into a constant hum. A tall man in a dark overcoat walked toward the crime scene. Grey hair circled the edges of his tweed cap, and he badly needed a shave. He approached the Constable, parting the crowd and police line like Moses crossing though the Red Sea.

"Thanks for coming Inspector," said the Constable. The duo stood over the body. "She beds at the doss down the way. Landlady says she goes by Catherine Eddowes. Ghastly bit of business, but you know what this means."

The Inspector nodded and put on black leather gloves. "Bloody hell. First time the Ripper struck within the city limits. So now these deaths are no longer just a Whitechapel problem. And we found another, Elizabeth Stride, less than an hour ago, on Berner Street. Jack's hard at work."

"Are you sure he's responsible for both murders today?" asked the Constable.

"I'm afraid so," said the Inspector. "Too many details we never released." He knelt by the body. With gloved hands, he parted the bright, red hair, and turned the head to face upward. The girl's lower jaw dangled loosely.

"Lower jaw sliced ear to ear, that's his mark. Note the many stab wounds. Entrails in the street. He preys on the poor, the destitute, and the harlots. Diabolical, methodical, pure evil. A kind of evil I've never encountered before. It's Jack alright. Blood's still tracking on the road. Another fresh one."

A gust of wind blew through the square. Orange and yellow leaves swirled around the lifeless corpse. Autumn had arrived in London. Low grey clouds hung overhead, so close you could touch them, continuous with the fog below.

"I pledge the City Police to the Met," said the Constable. "We'll do whatever it takes to catch this Ripper. But two murders, close together, different territory. I'm thinking we may have more than one killer."

The Inspector stood up and rubbed the palms of his gloves together, as if trying to wash off the blood. "Hard enough to face one Devil," he said. "God help us if there's another."

USA, Present Day:

Pong was eight years old and the youngest member of the family. She played with her brother on the flatbed of an old pickup as it flew down Interstate Highway 90. The two children sat facing each other on the humps over the rear wheels, giggling every time the truck bounced them off their seats.

Long, black bangs churned in a whirlpool on Pong's forehead. Her big brown eyes squinted into the wind as she walked to the rear window of the cab. With her finger she traced the mountain picture on the white and blue license plate taped to the inside of the window. She had seen this mountain, and hoped to visit it someday. She traced the word: *WASHINGTON*, and then peeked in the window.

Her father smiled, he loved driving the old truck. On the bench seat, her mother sat with eyes closed, hanging on to the dashboard as the truck bounced down the highway. Pong wondered if her mother would ever learn how to drive.

The engine coughed loudly, and Pong coughed, too. Her brother laughed. She turned around, her back to the wind, grabbing the side of the flatbed for support. A large piece of crumbly orange metal broke off in her hand, and she fell onto the flatbed, laughing. Her brother laughed, again. The metal crumbled to dust in her hands. She knew the truck had been brightly colored, long ago, like the new cars passing on the highway.

How proud her father had been when he took her to the big city, Seattle, to buy the truck. It cost two-hundred dollars, the entire family savings from four months of picking vegetables and berries. Many times her father had told her: "In America, I am a wealthy man."

The family had always lived off the land in Cambodia. In America, they still foraged. They picked watercress from storm runoff ditches. They caught ducks at a town park in Issaquah, until the King County Sheriff told them to stop.

Mushroom hunting was Pong's favorite. Today, she would hunt for chanterelles and shaggy mane. She loved to eat them alone, or added to mother's bai sac mon.

Pong sniffed and looked up. The sun had not yet risen and the sky was dark. She felt it wouldn't rain. A dry day in September was a good omen.

The truck slowed. "Nuu," she shouted, pointing at an old logging road that disappeared into the woods. The pickup turned off the freeway, and down the gravel road. Half a mile later, the truck stopped.

She listened. This was a quiet place where few people had been, and a good place to find mushrooms.

The children leaped out of the flatbed, their thongs sinking into the soft mud. A fine mist arose from the forest floor, sparkling with the first light of the new day. The family spread out in different directions and combed a wide area.

Pong was proud of her ability to find food in the woods. She knew how to read the forest floor, to look for the dead vegetation that supported the growth of mushrooms. Walking silently with her head bowed, she traced the patterns created by the fallen leaves. This was her secret to mushroom hunting. While others saw only mud, she studied patterns on the forest floor.

Ten minutes later, the pattern of leaves was interrupted by five, round, gray objects. Pong smiled and squatted, her face inches from the ground. Carefully, so as not to break any fragile stems, she removed a few leaves, revealing the fingertips of an open human hand. A mound of muddy leaves formed the outline of a body.

She remembered being very little, in the old house. Men with guns had beaten her mother and taken Pong's older sister outside. Pong cried for her father to come home. Through the doorway of the old house, in the driving rain, she saw her sister screaming and her clothes being torn off. Pong never saw her sister again.

She stood up, spit, and then called for the others, "Munee! Kaymunee!"

The entire family gathered around the limp hand and the mound of leaves. Pong looked up at her father. He frowned and shook his head.

A burst of cold wind howled through the dark forest. They'd come to America to get away from the killing. America was supposed to be different.

o o o

The Jeep Cherokee was unstoppable, easily overcoming mud, potholes, and rocks, even at thirty-five miles per hour.

"You probably know this as the old Brewster logging road," Jackey McCann told the Sergeant.

"You know, Jack," said the Sergeant, "I'm not as old as I seem."

Jackey smiled. She felt like an involuntary celebrity. She was the youngest female deputy in King County. This was her first week on the job, not counting orientation. She'd hoped the first week would be a quiet one. But as she drove Sergeant Frank Roberts deeper into the woods, she tried to prepare herself for the worst.

Frank rolled down the window. He looked into the wind and squinted. Wrinkles spread from the corners of his eyes like cracking ice. He turned his head back and looked Jackey over, trying to make the motion seem natural.

Jackey didn't mind the attention, she felt confident in her appearance. Physically, she was Frank's equal. Six feet tall, she was broad shouldered, and all muscle. Keeping up with men in the department did not come easy to her. Her daily workouts at the gym were grueling.

Her most singular feature was her deep tan, a rarity in the overcast Pacific Northwest. Maintaining her tan required frequent visits to an ultraviolet tanning bed.

"I've been a cop for ten years since the Marines," said Frank. "And heading up the Task Force has been my worst job so far. You wouldn't believe some of the stinking corpses we've pulled out of the slime."

Jackey shuddered, flipping her short, brown hair. Her only close encounter with death had been her father. A good cop, young and strong, he had collapsed in her arms, dead from a heart attack. She was nine years old at the time. The intervening years had not helped her to understand the loss.

She knew, someday, she would have to face death again. She felt sick. "Doesn't look like this road gets much use," she said.

"How did a tough gal like you get such a sweet voice?"

"I've been asked that before. My voice just doesn't go with the rest of me."

Jackey wanted to investigate this call alone. But Frank happened to be nearby when the homicide report came in. It was bad luck, because Frank might insist on conducting the investigation himself.

"I'm going to let you handle this one," Frank told her. He reached into the back seat and retrieved a nylon shoulder bag. "First authority on site for homicide. That's good experience for you."

"And a hell of a lot of paperwork," said Jackey.

"That's good experience, too," said Frank. She detected a faint smirk on his face. "Besides, someone has to keep the record." He pulled a video camera from the nylon bag and snapped a fresh data card into position.

"There's the marker," Jackey shouted, as she stopped the Jeep, and backed up a few feet. In a mound on the passenger side of the road, two pine tree branches were lashed together with a frayed scrap of rope to form a crude wooden cross.

Jackey jumped out of the Jeep, and searched in a wide semicircle, using the cross to mark the center. She remembered her training exercise, to avoid traveling a direct route, so clues remain undisturbed. Frank followed Jackey closely, videoing her progress.

Fifty feet from the road, she saw the hand protruding from a pile of muddy leaves and twigs. She approached the pile from the point farthest away from the road. Frank continued filming, as she bent over and removed a leaf from what appeared to be the head.

"Aren't you forgetting something?" said Frank, as he switched off and lowered his camera. He reached into the left pocket of his long, green coat and pulled out a pair of latex gloves and a small plastic bag.

"Oh, of course," she said, setting the leaf back onto the pile. She put on the gloves and took the plastic bag. Starting over, she carefully placed each leaf and twig she picked up into the specimen bag. More than before, she felt the scrutiny of Frank's camera.

Soon, she had removed enough of the foliage to reveal the deathly gray face of a young woman. Her mouth had been slashed from ear-to-ear. Her lower jaw dangled freely, disconnected from the upper face and head. Blood had drained from diagonal cuts across her forehead, and pooled within the eye sockets.

There was a loud ringing in Jackey's ears, and the ground did not seem solid. Nausea grew rapidly in a tight knot that was once her stomach. She spun around and staggered past Frank, back toward the Jeep, clutching at a fir tree to steady herself. The sound of her labored breathing filled the woods.

"You gonna make it, Jack?"

"Just got a little lightheaded, that's all. It's a young girl. I've never seen anything like that."

"It's all right, Jack. Take a break. I can handle this one."

"Thank you, sir, but I'd like to continue."

Jackey knelt and finished uncovering the head. Frank leaned over, recording her every move. Some of the leaves were covered with a thin layer of mud. "Must have happened late yesterday," said Frank. "Otherwise, yesterday's early afternoon rain would have washed these leaves clean."

The woods were silent. "Multiple stab wounds," said Jackey, "blow to the head, body disposed of near the road. Is it the Cascade Killer's work?"

"No doubt. Victim number fourteen. Freshest corpse we've ever found. The Task Force will have a feeding frenzy."

"Is the ear-to-ear slash typical?"

"We call it the smile cut. Every victim's had one," said Frank. "Now finish it."

Jackey continued to examine the body. Lifting both eyelids revealed blank, glassy eyes, and dark, midsized pupils. She placed the first two fingers of her gloved right hand on the limp neck.

Cold, penetrating the latex fingers, sent a chill up her arm. A light wind rustling through the evergreens made goose bumps erupt on her neck. For a minute, she knelt like a sinner in Church, praying for forgiveness. Suddenly, she stood up. It was like she had just realized the entire congregation was standing.

"What is it, Jack?" Frank asked, lowering his camera.

She didn't answer. She was already halfway back to the truck, pulling off the gloves as she ran. Reaching through the passenger window, she grabbed the radio microphone.

"King County base, McCann."

"Spiker, dispatch. Hey, Jack. What have you found, out there?"

"I have a white female, about twenty years old, multiple stab wounds, head trauma, probable sexual assault. Must have happened last night. Looks like the Cascade Killer was here." Frank was now leaning on the hood of the Jeep.

"Got it. I'll have the Task Force there in thirty minutes."

"Dammit!" Jackey yelled, staring beyond the microphone into Frank's eyes. "I don't need the fucking Task Force. I need an ambulance. I need it now."

CHAPTER 1

AT UNIVERSITY HOSPITAL in Seattle, Dr. Paul Powers was finishing his post-operative rounds and hoping to go home. He never made it past the ward secretary.

"Dr. Powers," said the secretary, flashing a cute smile, "Your lawyer is on the phone. Line three."

"More good news?" Paul sighed.

The secretary shrugged and began chewing on the top of a plastic pen.

Paul picked up the phone in the corner of the nursing station and tried to tune out the rest of world. "Hello, this is Dr. Powers."

"Milton Freeman here, and I've got bad news. You ready for this?"

Paul massaged his temples with his left hand. "Give it to me quickly, it's cheaper."

"Anne won't settle. She wants more. I'm afraid you're in for a long, expensive fight."

"Forget it. I'm through fighting. Just give her everything."

"Everything?"

"Yes, everything. Except for the old pickup truck and my sailboard. They're of no use to her." If he could only be at the Columbia River Gorge right now, sailboarding the wide channel, wind at his back, alone. He saw the sailboard bouncing through the whitecaps, water spraying over his feet.

"Doc? Are you still there?"

The vision faded. "I'm here, Milton."

"You sure you want to give her everything?"

"All I want is for this to be over. If we fight any longer, you lawyers will get it all anyway." Paul slammed the phone onto its base, and noticed a nurse standing silently at his side.

"Yes? What's the problem?"

The nurse hesitated. "It's Ms. Hackler ..."

"The gallbladder?"

"Right. She's back from recovery and complaining of a severe sore throat. Could you take a look at her? She's right here at the desk."

"Sure."

Paul walked around the high counter. Upright on a gurney, with the back of the cart raised for support, was a huge woman. She was rubbing her throat and whimpering. Paul leaned over the railing of the gurney. A pale, fleshy face looked back at him, with no sign of recognition.

Paul usually had about ten minutes before surgery to explain the anesthetic choices, risks, and side effects. It was no wonder that a terrified person, who was about to be dissected, might forget the preanesthetic consultation.

"I don't have much pain from the gallbladder," croaked Ms. Hackler, "but my throat is killing me. What did you do to it?"

In spite of the patient's hoarseness, Paul could sense anger. Obviously, Ms. Hackler did not remember what he had told her about the need for a breathing tube, and the possibility of a sore throat. Anesthetizing this woman had been a difficult job. Her cigarette smoking and high blood pressure were bad enough, but she was also three-hundred and sixty pounds. Placement of the breathing tube had been difficult.

"I'm sorry your throat is so sore," he consoled Ms. Hackler. "I'm sure it'll be fine in a few days. As you may recall, I mentioned to you before surgery that a sore throat and a hoarse voice are common after anesthesia. During surgery, I have to place a breathing tube in your throat, to give anesthesia gas and oxygen."

"Yes, now I recall. I had no idea my throat would be so painful. It's terrible! Is there anything you can do for it?"

"Time will take care of it," Paul replied. He could tell that Ms. Hackler wasn't happy with his answer. She wanted an instant cure for what she undoubtedly viewed as a horrible anesthetic complication.

"I'm pleased with your progress." Paul continued, changing the subject.

A nurse ran past the ward secretary. "Has anyone closed the windows in the west end?"

The secretary pulled her pen from between her teeth. "I haven't seen anyone go down there."

Many days he had seen the nurses run to close the windows, to dampen the roar of a helicopter landing. He was the only anesthesia resident currently available, everyone else was in surgery. That was the problem at a regional trauma center, the chopper could come at any time. "I hope you're feeling better, soon," Paul told Ms. Hackler, as he left the gurney and circled around to the secretary's station.

"What's falling from the sky today?" Paul asked.

"I don't know," she said, pointing her finger toward the ceiling, "but here it comes."

A fierce repetitive chopping sound increased until it drowned out all other sounds. The hospital ward shook. Somewhere, a loose window banged in the mechanical wind. The vibration diminished, indicating the helicopter had touched down at the hospital.

The phone rang and the secretary answered, "He sure is, I'll tell him." She hung up. "Guess what? They want you STAT in the ER."

Paul sighed. He walked rapidly through a maze of halls and stairwells. He could travel these passageways blind. While he walked, he was preoccupied with thoughts of Anne. She was still his wife. They'd been separated for four months, and the divorce would soon be final.

He tried to use his busy anesthesia residency as a tool to take his mind off the pending divorce, but this mental technique just increased his mounting stress. His five foot, nine inch frame stooped beneath the weight of his dissolving marriage, and his heavy work load at the hospital. Gray hairs replaced the brown ones, at an enormous pace. The edges of his mustache were overgrown and neglected. Work was an incomplete escape from reality.

He was exhausted, and thoughts of his failed marriage haunted him during every free moment. How many nights had he come home late from work and fallen asleep on the couch, with his coat on? How often had he declined sex, due to fatigue? Anne was so beautiful. How could he have been that tired?

Paul collided with two large Seattle policemen at the emergency room entrance.

"Can I see your hospital ID?" asked one of the policemen.

Paul wore his ID badge on a lanyard around his neck, beneath his white coat. He retrieved the ID badge and flashed it to the policemen.

"I'm sorry," said one of the policeman. "The ER is on lockdown, and you're not authorized to go in." The two officers blocked Paul's path.

"But I'm Dr. Paul Powers, the anesthesiologist on duty. I'm needed in there."

The two policemen looked at each other. One of them left, returning with Wendy, the emergency room secretary. She smiled, revealing a mouthful of braces. "It's OK, he's the anesthesiologist," she said.

The policemen stepped aside, and Paul entered the orderly chaos of the trauma room. A naked, bloody, and unconscious woman lay on the emergency room gurney, her legs raised in stirrups. Dry mud and leaves stuck to her skin, and a large plastic tube protruded from her mangled mouth. Connected to the tube was a bag full of oxygen. A respiratory therapist assisted the victim's breathing by squeezing the bag.

Dr. Christine Mason, the chief neurosurgery resident, stood at the head of the gurney examining the patient. Christine didn't acknowledge Paul's arrival. She continued her neurologic examination with robot precision.

Paul marveled at her immaculate grey pant suit and crisp makeup. He wondered how she could always look so fresh. She was excessively thin. Her auburn hair was pinned into a tight ball, except for two fine wisps left deliberately dangling in front of each ear.

Paul grabbed a stethoscope from a peg on the wall and listened to the chest of the trauma victim. As he leaned over, he looked down at the young girl's face. Her disconnected lower jaw lay flat against her chest, so she appeared to have no neck. He watched Christine wipe blood from one eye of the victim in order to examine the pupil with a penlight.

"Breath sounds are decreased on the right," he said. "I need a chest tube."

The nurse brought him a set of surgical instruments and a garden hose sized plastic tube. He put on a pair of latex gloves and washed the patient's right chest with Betadine solution. He slid a scalpel blade onto a handle he held in his right hand. With his left hand braced against the patient's chest, Paul lowered the blade toward the skin. A brown hand grabbed Paul's wrist.

"The pneumo is on the left," said Dr. Benga, a cardiothoracic surgeon, currently doing a trauma fellowship. He was East Indian, bald, and short. The top of his head only reached up to Paul's nose. Benga put his arm around Paul. "Hey, Pauley," said Benga, "you can't always tell just by listening, especially in multiple trauma. When all else fails, look at the patient. The entry wounds are on the left."

Paul looked at the naked chest of the woman on the gurney. Benga was correct, the chest wounds were all on the left. It was the left lung that was deflated and needed a chest tube for reexpansion. Paul set down the scalpel and removed his gloves, trembling. If Benga hadn't intervened, Paul realized he might have placed the chest tube on the wrong side. He could have collapsed the good lung and killed the girl.

Benga slapped Paul lightly on the back, and turned to the nurse. "Get me a chest pack. I'll put the tube in, on the left."

Christine looked at Paul with piercing green eyes and almost laughed. It was the first indication he'd ever had that she was anything more than a robot.

Benga effortlessly inserted the chest tube. Paul wondered how many years it would take to accumulate a similar degree of clinical judgement and technical skill. He was a thirty-one year old baby in the eyes of the medical staff. Three years of anesthesia residency was his only clinical experience.

"Why all the security?" he asked everyone.

"She may be the first living victim of the Cascade Killer," said a nurse at the foot of the bed, between the victim's raised legs. "I've got the vaginal and rectal washings," she said, holding up two fluid filled plastic containers. "Rectal temperature is sixty-five degrees."

"Sixty-five degrees!" said Paul. "At sixty-five degrees, the textbook says she should be dead."

"Obviously," said Benga, "she hasn't read the textbook."

Laughter erupted in the trauma room. It ended quickly when Paul noticed a sudden change on the heart monitor. "She's in V-fib." The irregular, squiggly line across the EKG screen would mean death to this woman. Her heart was now quivering uselessly in her abused chest, her circulation at a standstill. Ventricular fibrillation was exactly what the human heart was supposed to do at temperatures below eighty-five degrees. "Defibrillate, two-hundred watt-seconds," he ordered.

A nurse peeled off the foil wrappers from two slimy, rectangular electrode pads. She positioned them on the woman's upper, middle and lower, left chest. The electrode pads stuck to the woman's skin, blue jelly from the pads channeling its way through the dried mud and blood.

"Two-hundred watt seconds, charging," Paul shouted, as he plugged the connector wire from the electrode pads into the defibrillator. "Stand clear."

A vacant ring formed, as everyone in the room jumped away from the gurney. The defibrillator broadcast a soft hum that grew quickly into a loud whine. Paul leaned his hips away from the patient, and pressed the button on the defibrillator. The woman's chest jumped off the gurney in one convulsive spasm, and then slapped down against the thin mattress with a loud thud. Her arms flew off the cart, hanging by the shoulders. The room was silent.

"Sinus rhythm, heart rate thirty-five," said Paul. "Too slow. Get some atropine."

"Forget the atropine," Benga ordered. "Set up the heart room. She'll never make it out of the regular OR. Let's be on bypass in ten minutes. Send the blood to surgery as soon as it's ready. We can give it faster through the pump. Dr. Norton is in the house, tell him I need an assistant. OK with you, Pauley?"

"It's a good plan," Paul agreed. "We can rewarm her on bypass, while you patch the leaks."

"That's the whole idea," said Benga, "but don't rush to warm her up. The cold is the only thing keeping her alive."

CHAPTER 2

PAUL WALKED behind the head of the trauma victim, as the cart rolled foot end first through the double doors of the emergency room, into the wide hallway. He squeezed the breathing bag with one hand and pushed the gurney with the other. Off to one side, a television cameraman paced the gurney, filming the trauma victim as she was rushed around the corner to the elevator. The camera made Paul nervous. He wondered if he'd be on the evening news, and then wished he'd worn a surgical mask.

The victim was covered with a white sheet, except for her head. Bloody spots soaked through the sheet. Bags of intravenous fluids were swinging from a pole on wheels. The nurse pushing the pole was having a difficult time keeping up with the gurney. A crowd of people in white coats followed.

Paul felt good leaving the television cameraman at the door of the elevator. A strange silence began with the shutting of the elevator doors. Thankfully, when the elevator doors opened, the quiet continued, because the curious hadn't yet reached the hallway to the operating area. Inside the operating room, the familiar sight of an anesthesia machine further boosted Paul's spirits.

Numerous gauges and dials adorned the towering, black console of the anesthesia machine. Three vaporizers the size and shape of coffee cans hung from the front of the console. They contained liquid anesthetics. Above the console, on a shelf, sat a large LCD monitor connected to several modular boxes on either side. Wavy, green lines flowed across the screen.

Attached to the rear of the anesthesia machine were three metal tanks, two green and one blue. Each cylinder-shaped tank was three feet long. The green tanks contained oxygen, and the blue one laughing gas.

Two chrome pipes jutted out of the side of the anesthesia machine. Attached to the chrome pipes were twin corrugated plastic tubes. They hung down several feet, almost to the floor. The twin tubes merged into a single connection from which an anesthesia mask dangled.

Paul disconnected the anesthesia mask and set it aside. He removed the manual breathing bag from the patient's breathing tube and attached the corrugated tubing from the anesthesia machine.

After switching on the mechanical ventilator of the anesthesia machine, he watched it pump oxygen under pressure into the patient, rhythmically inflating and deflating her lungs. Both he and the patient breathed a little easier.

The patient was transferred to the operating table, and a nurse gave Paul the chart. It was only a few sheets of paper. The lower, left hand corner of the record sheet contained patient ID numbers, the medical record number, and the name: Jane Doe. Paul tossed the paperwork aside.

First, he paralyzed the patient with an injection of a muscle relaxant. She was now paralyzed, but was she completely unconscious? He needed to be sure, if she regained consciousness, she would not be in pain. So he began a slow infusion of a potent narcotic.

He pumped salt water fluids and heart stimulants into her veins, trying to keep her alive long enough to get her on the heart-lung machine. The nurse brought him several antibiotics, and he gave these, too.

In the center of the room, the bloody woman lay exposed on the operating table. Everywhere, electrical cords and tubing hung down from the ceiling and disappeared into various pieces of machinery. Some of the cords and tubes ended in midair, dangling like snakes poised to strike.

The heart-lung machine was a box shaped device as large as the operating table. The machine could temporarily assume the functions of the patient's heart and lungs. On top of the main console were several circular pumps. Metal rods arose from the rear of the machine. Odd shaped plastic devices hung from the rods, interconnected by a tangle of tubes and wires. A perfusionist, the specialist responsible for operating the heart-lung machine, was busy checking all the connections.

The two circulating nurses began to rapidly scrub the patient up to her neck using a Betadine solution. Muddy leaves stuck to the wet sponges or fell to the floor. Paul retracted the patient's lower jaw, so her neck could be washed. A gold chain on her neck was in the way and had to be removed. The two nurses had to keep their gloves sterile, so Paul removed the chain and put it in the right pocket of his white coat.

Under the patient's ankles, a metal rack temporarily held the legs elevated, allowing the nurses to wash both sides. Bloody, brown Betadine solution ran down the legs from numerous wounds. Paul placed a wire cage over the patient's head to protect it and to serve as an instrument table. Two scrub nurses covered the patient and the cage with light blue paper drapes. The two surgeons entered the room and hurried into their OR gowns.

Paul examined a slip of red paper brought to him by an orderly. "Hemoglobin four grams," Paul announced.

"Jesus," said Dr. Norton, the chief surgery resident. "Hasn't she gotten any blood, yet?"

"Here's the blood," answered a nurse.

"Prime the pump with it," said Paul.

"Let's get her on, now," Benga demanded, as he ran a scalpel deep along the patient's breastbone. "Saw," said Benga, and a mechanical compressed air saw appeared instantly in his hand. He positioned the serrated saw blade at the top of the breastbone.

The saw ripped loudly through the breastbone, kicking up a cloud of bone dust, and filling the room with the stench of burning flesh. A rib spreader was placed in the newly created gash. Turning a large screw on the rib spreader forced apart two steel jaws and pried the chest wide open. Benga slipped his fingers into a hole in the thin membrane covering the heart.

"How about that. The left chest stab wound entered the pericardium. They don't come any closer than that."

Working scissors between his fingers, Benga slit the membrane. He examined the slowly beating heart.

"The ventricle looks OK."

He quickly placed a collection tube into the heart to drain the patient's blood. Then he inserted an inflow tube into the aorta, the largest blood vessel in the body. "Heparinize her," he ordered.

Paul had never given heparin, a potent blood thinner, to a patient that was bleeding to death. He felt uneasy. But he knew heparin was essential. Without it, blood would clot in the plastic tubing of the heart-lung machine, leading to certain death. He had already drawn the massive dose of heparin into a syringe. He pushed the plunger and wondered if he had just signed the patient's death certificate. "heparin going in."

"Ready?" Benga asked the perfusionist.

"Ready," he said.

The tubes were connected, and the new pump heart gradually took over the continuous job of pushing blood through Jane Doe's body.

Inside the centrifugal pump, in a sealed plastic chamber, a paddle wheel smoothly rotated. Driven by invisible electromagnetic force, the blades of the paddle wheel gently propelled the life-giving blood forward.

Along the way, blood journeyed through the membrane oxygenator lung. Wound tightly inside this melon sized plastic cassette, were forty square feet of hollow polypropylene fibers. Billions of oxygen starved red blood cells rushed past the semipermeable fibers, but could not enter them. Pure oxygen flowed continuously through the fibers, enriching the passing blood.

Paul turned off the mechanical ventilator and the anesthesia machine. He breathed a sigh of relief. For now, at least, Jane Doe did not need her heart or lungs to survive. The cold Northwest weather had saved Jane Doe, by putting her body into a slow metabolic state, not unlike hibernation. She would live for at least a few hours more because the heart-lung machine was supporting her circulation. He expected the excitement to peak when it came time to remove Jane Doe from the heart-lung machine. He wondered if she would ultimately survive.

Ice cold potassium solution was pumped into the tiny arteries of the heart. Flooded with potassium, the young heart that had pumped seven-hundred million times, stopped instantly. To cool the heart further, Benga filled the chest cavity with crushed ice.

The LCD screen over the anesthesia machine showed the heart to be at rest, with no electrical activity. Benga placed another tube into an artery, and an electrical transducing system displayed the patient's blood pressure on the LCD monitor. Her temperature was also displayed. The perfusionist began to raise the patient's temperature very slowly by warming the blood as it passed through the heart-lung machine.

The two surgeons now concentrated on repairing the numerous stab wounds. Benga worked in the chest, while Norton addressed the many abdominal injuries. The perfusionist regulated the heart-lung machine.

Paul sat in the operating room at the anesthesia machine and began the drudgery of completing the computerized anesthesia record. After bringing the record up to date, he started planning for the end of the operation. The patient would be fine as long as she remained on the heart-lung machine. But in a few hours, he'd have to take her off the machine. Restoring her own circulation might be difficult.

"Paul, go home," said Dr. Beck, a tall, scrawny man. "You look exhausted, and we need you alive tomorrow. Go home. I'll get Jane Doe off bypass."

"Thanks," said Paul. Beck was an excellent anesthesiologist and a good colleague. Grateful for the relief, Paul could leave the patient in good hands and go home, finally.

He left the operating room and stopped at the control desk, a high square counter that partitioned off the corner of the surgical complex located nearest to the main doors. In the corner alcove, he found the next day's schedule on the surgical secretary's desk. Sitting down at the desk, he closed his eyes, thinking how good it would feel to get some sleep. A wave of dizziness hit, so he folded his arms on the desk and put his head down.

He tried to get a few minutes of rest, but couldn't stop thinking about Anne. Four months ago, he'd been given the day off after night call. Although he would normally have spent the time sleeping, on that day he prepared a surprise for Anne. She'd been late getting home from her shift as an agency nurse, but Paul didn't care. When she came in the door, he gave her a bouquet of long stemmed red roses. He kissed her on the lips, but she didn't kiss back.

"I know I've been distant, lately," said Paul. "I want to make it up to you. Starting today, I'm going to take the time to show you how much I love you."

Anne's brunette hair was disheveled, her makeup smeared, her white uniform shirt untucked. She took the roses and frowned.

"Paul, you should ..."

"Shhhh. Come into the dinning room."

Anne followed him. A lively fire burned in the fireplace. The cafe style table was set for two with white linen. On the table, a champagne bottle chilled in a bucket. The sweet aroma of chicken and wine floated in from the kitchen.

Paul picked up the champagne bottle and scraped off the foil wrapper. He wrestled with the cork until it exploded and bounced off the ceiling. He filled the two wineglasses on the table and handed one to Anne. She took the glass in her right hand. She still held the roses in the other.

"Here's to us," he said, smiling, as he raised his glass. "Let me take the roses."

"Here, have the roses," said Anne, and she threw them into the fire. They began to smolder. "And the fucking champagne, too." There was a crash of breaking glass and a puff of smoke as Anne's glass landed in the fireplace.

"Anne. What's the matter? What did I do?"

"You stupid shit. Where do you think I've been tonight?"

He set down his glass and picked up the champagne bottle. Grabbing the stone mantle above the fireplace with his left hand, he leaned over and stared into the fire. The rose petals curled and turned black. A wave of heat blew up into his face. He tilted his head backwards and took a big swig from the champagne bottle. Then he wiped his mouth on his sleeve.

"So, where've you been tonight?"

"With my boyfriend."

"Boyfriend?"

"Don't give me that innocent routine," said Anne. "I work at a hospital. I know what goes on. I know why you come home so tired."

"I don't believe this. Anne, I've never cheated. I just work too hard. How could you?"

"I got tired of waiting for nothing."

"Who is this guy? A doctor?"

"He's a forest products manager for Weyerhaeuser."

"Great. A fucking forest products manager, with a sawdust brain and a Douglas Fir in his pants. What could you possibly have in common?"

"We're both good in bed," said Anne. She stomped out of the apartment, and slammed the door.

Four months later, Anne was still living with her lover, and Paul couldn't bear it. He loved her too much. She'd been a marvelous companion: intelligent, beautiful, and energetic. She'd encouraged him to work hard and to play hard, to enjoy life to the fullest. But he hadn't been able to keep up, that's why he'd lost her.

Exhausted, he raised his head off the secretary's desk, stretched his stiff arms, and then left the corner alcove. Walking out of the operating area through the main double doors, he passed two Seattle policemen. They paid no attention to him. On his right, a line of TV and radio reporters broadcasted the news, while a crowd of people watched.

Paul overheard bits of the news: "... unknown woman ... victim of the Cascade ... Task Force trying ... found in the woods ... possibly a teenage prostitute ..." He walked quickly through the crowd and turned left down the hallway, worried the media might detain him with questions. But they let him pass unscathed.

A woman wearing a long, yellow raincoat blocked Paul's path. Thin, disheveled hair stood out almost horizontally on both sides of her wrinkled forehead. She looked startled. "Excuse me," said Paul, but the woman didn't move.

A man grabbed her arm. "Marilyn, sit down, please," said the man. On his navy blue shirt was a Boeing company ID tag with the name "William Walker."

"Bill, I'm going to ask the doctor. He may know," the woman insisted. She refused to budge.

"Marilyn, it can't be Jenny," said Bill. "Please, sit down." He tried to drag her out of Paul's way.

"Doctor," she said, holding up her left hand. "May I have a word with you?"

"How'd I ever let you drag me here?" said Bill, releasing his hold on Marilyn's arm.

Paul was trapped in the middle of the argument. More than anything else, he wanted to go home. "I'm Dr. Powers. Is there something I can help you with?"

"Were you in there with the young girl from the woods?" Marilyn asked.

"Yes, I'm one of her anesthesiologists."

"Did she talk to you? Did she tell you her name?"

"She's not able to talk to anyone, yet. Why?"

William Walker ran his fingers through his graying hair. "I'm Bill Walker, and this is my wife Marilyn. Jenny, that's our only daughter, ran away last year. This young girl they found, she's about Jenny's size, the same hair color. They say she was a prostitute, well ..." Bill looked at his wife.

"We don't know about that," she said, looking at the floor.

"My wife is convinced that young girl in there is Jenny. I know it's crazy, that girl could be anybody. But Marilyn had a strong feeling ..."

"I know she's Jenny," Marilyn scolded.

"The girl can't talk to anyone," Paul repeated, "She's unconscious."

Marilyn opened a black vinyl purse and removed two photographs. "Please, look at these," she said, thrusting the pictures into his right hand.

He looked at the photos. In one picture a smiling girl in a team uniform held a baseball bat, and in the other photo a beautiful teenage girl blew out the candles on a birthday cake. Paul was amazed at Jenny's resemblance to his own younger sister. She'd had the same smile, until she was raped. The experience had driven her inward until she couldn't get close to anyone, not even him.

Saddened, he returned the pictures, shaking his head. "Look. The woman is badly disfigured. I can't help you." Marilyn took the pictures and backed away, with moist, dark circles around her eyes. He put his hands in his pockets and shrugged his shoulders. "I'm sorry," he said.

"Thank you, doc," said Bill. "Sorry to bother you."

As Paul walked down the hallway, he felt something odd in his right pocket and pulled it out. It was the gold chain. He'd forgotten all about it. He turned around.

"Mr. and Ms. Walker, I just remembered. I took this off the girl before surgery."

Paul held up the fine, gold chain. For the first time he noticed, hanging on the chain, a golden charm, a small heart with a purple stone. The heart spun around, and the purple stone twinkled as it caught the light. Marilyn's eyes opened wide.

"Oh, Bill. It is Jenny," Marilyn wailed. "That's the heart I gave her last year for her sixteenth birthday."

CHAPTER 3

EARL SWORE he wouldn't kill anyone today. Today would be different. He dusted crumbs off his white shirt and straightened the badge. It said "Golden Cup, Earl Dobbs, Assistant Manager." An old man approached the counter. "How was everything?" Earl asked.

"It's always good food," said the old man, handing Earl a slip of paper and a twenty dollar bill. "You remind me of my son. He's a tall, clean cut boy, like you."

"Thanks," said Earl, returning the smile. He held the change in his outstretched hand. A slight tremor made the change rattle, a warning that he was about to kill again. The old man took his change, sifting briefly through the coins. He left the restaurant.

Earl closed the register. He grabbed a damp towel and wiped the imitation wood linoleum countertop, keeping an eye on the Seattle policemen seated at the corner table.

The 24 hour restaurant always had a table with police, and they made him nervous. A man wearing a cowboy hat, sunglasses, and a long overcoat sat alone in another corner. He was a regular customer, staying for hours, drinking coffee. Earl wondered if the lonely cowboy was waiting for someone.

A bleached blond approached the register and handed Earl a credit card.

"How was everything?" he asked.

"You've got the most beautiful eyes," said the blond. "Anybody ever tell you that?"

"They say I've got a baby face."

"And they're right," she said, signing the credit slip.

"Come back, soon," Earl said, handing the woman her receipt. As she took it, she stroked his hand.

"Sure thing," she said.

He slammed the drawer of the cash register shut and brushed white donut frosting off his black polyester pants. Sweat soaked through the armpits of his shirt. His right eye twitched and he rubbed it to quiet the spasm. Running his fingers across his forehead, he wiped away a trickle of warm sweat.

A wall phone next to the register rang, but he didn't answer. The shrill cry of a child arose above the babble of the restaurant patrons. The din came from far away, like many distant screams echoing through a tunnel. A young man held a slip of paper up to Earl's face. "Can you ring me up? I'm in kinda a hurry."

Earl took the paper in his moist fingers and laid it on top of the cash register. He picked up the wall phone, but the ringing continued. It was coming from inside his head. After hanging up the phone, he turned and ran through a swinging door into the restaurant kitchen.

He staggered through the kitchen to the employee rest room. Once inside, he locked the door. He stood in front of the toilet expecting to feel pain like he'd felt many times before. But the pain didn't come.

At the sink, after washing the sweat off his face, he checked the mirror cautiously. It was like looking through a doorway, not knowing what he might see in the other room. He pulled down the skin beneath his eyes to examine the whites. Today, they looked normal.

He loosened his tie, stood up straight, and dried his head with paper towels. After running a comb through his hair, he headed for the manager's office in the back of the restaurant.

Behind a desk in the small office sat a fat, middle aged man, punching numbers into a beeping calculator. A long ribbon of paper flowed out of the calculator. The paper strip fell over the back of the desk, curling into a heap on the tile floor.

"Don, I need the day off."

The calculator stopped beeping. "What? Again? Earl, you can't keep runnin' out on me like this. You're the best help I've got. You ain't been the same since Trudy died. You look awful."

"Just some bug I picked up, I'll be OK. But I need the rest of the day off."

"Earl, this is a full time job. If you expect to go up in the company, you've got to do your share. Look, I know a good counselor ..."

Earl pounded his fist on the desk. "I don't need a shrink. I just need the day off."

"Aw-right, go." The manager sighed. "And I hope you snap out of it."

Earl knew he didn't need to kill, he just hadn't tried hard enough to stop. Today, he would prove he was in control. He drove his aging Chevy sedan to the Eastlake Health Club. While changing, he planned a strenuous workout. He thought twenty-five repetitions on twelve progressive resistance machines ought to be enough. Halfway through his workout, while pushing 220 pounds on the overhead shoulder press, pain pierced his stomach. The weights crashed down.

Unable to complete weightlifting, he ran on the indoor track. After seemingly endless circles, he headed for the showers. Ice cold water poured over his body for an hour, but the pain in his gut persisted.

As Earl left the shower, pain arose from the center of his gut and reached out like an open hand. It consolidated into one giant cramp, doubling him over. He staggered to the sink. Acid burned his throat.

"Please God. Not again."

Earl turned the cold water on and bowed his head. Stomach acid stung his nostrils. He sneezed. The acrid odor preceded a wave of nausea. Cupping both hands, he dowsed his face with the frigid water. A familiar face looked back at him from the mirror. It was not his face.

His eyes were tiny, red, and intense, with pinpoint pupils. His lips formed a thin line. A greasy black mass of hair and a stubby beard seemed to grow as he watched. He needed to drive into the countryside to escape.

The white shirt, tie, and black pants stayed at the health club. Wearing the blue jeans and flannel shirt he always kept in his locker, Earl fled Seattle. He traveled east for over an hour on Interstate Highway 90. He was startled by his image in the rear view mirror, a pale man with a stranger's eyes. He changed the angle of the mirror until it faced the roof.

He turned the mirror back. Had he seen a familiar face in the car behind? Was it the man from the corner of the restaurant, the man in the cowboy hat? Earl took another look, the driver in the car behind was a total stranger. He kept close watch on the rear view.

The bitter taste of bile lingered at the back of his throat. At a familiar exit sign, he left the highway and turned down a gravel road. Beads of sweat dripped off his forehead. A dry, furrowed tongue pushed against the roof of his mouth. His heart pounded. Panting, he stopped the car and jumped out into the thick evergreen forest.

The soft crunching of his heavy shoes filled the forest. He looked up at the tall trees and stumbled blindly. Abruptly, he stopped, both feet frozen to the mulch. Saliva poured from the right side of his mouth.

Falling to his knees, he clawed at the ground. His rapid panting sounded like an engine. He stopped and scanned the woods. Had he heard a car? But there was nothing now. He continued digging on the floor of the forest, creating an airborne cloud of leaves, bark, and soil. Skin tore from his knuckles, and his fingernails cracked while scraping at the larger rocks. The dark hole grew to an arm's length, and then something shone at the bottom.

More carefully, Earl removed the soil from a silvery object trapped in the earth. He ran the fingers of his right hand along a cold metal surface. Digging his hand beneath the metal, he wrapped his fingers around the object and wrenched it from the earth.

In his hand was a knife, ten inches long, with a serrated edge. Gently, with the fingers of his left hand, he stroked the knife. A wave of warmth radiated from his hands into his gut. He pulled the blade across the open palm of his left hand, watching as the tiny teeth disappeared into his flesh. Little rivers of blood ran from the wound. Raising the cold knife to his lips, he kissed the bloody edge of the blade. He felt good.

CHAPTER 4

DR. CHRISTINE MASON had been on call for over 24 hours, but she refused to give in to fatigue. She walked through the hospital hallway, looking forward to a full day of neurosurgery. Before surgery, there was a diagnostic procedure to supervise. And this morning was the weekly Grand Rounds lecture. She didn't want to miss it.

She made sure her makeup was fresh and not one hair was out of place. Her immaculate white coat ended in a pair of neatly pressed slacks, and polished shoes.

Several sleepy male residents passed her in the hallway and looked her over. She made eye contact, and they quickly looked away. That was her usual effect on men. She wondered if her traditionally male role scared them off. A female neurosurgeon was an oddity, at best. The demanding job did not allow much time to develop a social life. She felt capable of achieving anything, except love.

A female medical student positioned the patient as Chistine arrived in the treatment room for the early morning procedure. The patient was all skin and bones, and covered only by an open-backed hospital gown. Christine introduced herself to the patient: "I'm Dr. Mason, and you must be Ms. Schmidt."

"Doctor, I'm so scared."

"Everything will be fine," said Christine, reaching for the patient's hand. "We'll use local anesthesia, you'll hardly feel a thing."

"Thank you, Dr. Mason." Christine gave the patient's hand a brief squeeze.

Then Christine turned her attention to the student, a freckle faced woman. Her white coat pockets bulged with manuals. "How old is Ms. Schmidt?" Christine asked.

"Forty," said the student.

"What procedure are we doing, and why?"

"We will be putting a needle directly into the brain to get a sample of spinal fluid. We hope to make the diagnosis of Multiple Sclerosis by measuring the level of protein in the spinal fluid."

"Why not draw some spinal fluid from her back?"

The student hesitated. "I don't know."

"You didn't do your homework. Ms. Schmidt has metal rods in her back, put there to correct her severe scoliosis deformity at age fourteen. Why don't we do an MRI scan of her brain?"

"Its been done, but it didn't show anything definite."

"Very good." Christine smiled. She didn't want to come across as being too mean. The eager young student reminded Christine of herself years ago. She checked her watch, it was 7:29 AM. Dr. Swan, a junior neurosurgery resident, would arrive punctually at 7:30. She could always depend on him.

Swan entered on long strides, his brilliant blond hair blazing. Green operating room scrub clothes showed beneath his white coat. His strong, angular jaw sported a friendly smile. The air smelt of fragrant aftershave. After scanning the room, he raised his white eyebrows. "Is Rupp going to show?"

"I don't know," said Christine. "But let's give him a few minutes."

Dr. Thomas Rupp, the other junior neurosurgery resident, dragged himself into the room followed by a locker room odor. His filthy cover coat, one size too small for his tall, muscular body, could hardly qualify as white. The wrinkled coat and a five-o-clock shadow made him look like he'd last slept weeks ago, in his current clothes.

"Swan will do the cisternal puncture," Christine announced.

Rupp shot her an angry look, but she pretended not to notice. She was grooming Swan for the position of chief neurosurgery resident, in July. George Delianis, the Department Chairman, was fond of her and unlikely to veto her choice.

The neurosurgery training program was the pyramid type. No one could graduate from the program without spending a year as chief resident. Rupp had already been passed over, last year. He'd lost the position to Christine. If Swan became the new chief resident, Rupp would have to wait another year.

Swan repositioned the patient carefully on the treatment table, on her right side. The woman's head rested on a pillow, with her chin against her chest. Wearing gloves, Swan shaved and sterilized a small area on the back of the patient's neck, just below the base of the skull.

"This will sting," Swan said, using a fine needle to numb the skin. He looked at the medical student. "I'm aiming for the largest collecting area of spinal fluid in the brain. Give me the name."

"The Cisterna Magna," the student answered.

"Right. With two fingers, I straddle the base of the skull. Using my fingers as a guide, I insert this needle toward the skull. It passes through skin, a thin ligament, and into the bone. I walk the tip of the needle off the bottom edge of the skull, and enter the brain." Clear fluid flowed from the end of the needle. "I'm in. It'll take a few minutes to collect the fluid."

"Dr. Rupp," said Christine, "why don't you finish collecting the specimens. "Then you can run the samples to the lab. I need Dr. Swan to get started in OR six."

"No problem," said Rupp. "Is there anything else?"

"Go to OR six when you're done. I'll scrub in after Grand Rounds."

Rupp put on a pair of gloves and took over the menial task of collecting several containers of spinal fluid. Christine and Swan left the treatment room. They stopped together in the hallway.

"Rupp could be the new Dr. Otto," said Swan. "The perpetual junior resident."

"I've heard the Otto story," she said. "Fifteen years to finish a seven year residency."

He raised an eyebrow and smiled. "Right, but I heard it took twelve. The story keeps getting better."

"I'm worried," said Christine. "Rupp doesn't seem to care anymore."

Swan's smile collapsed into a thoughtful line. "He's obviously depressed and probably unsafe."

"We have to keep him out of trouble, somehow," she said.

"Right. Give him only scut work, for awhile," he suggested. She nodded. They walked down the hallway in opposite directions.

Over one hundred physicians, nurses, and medical students already filled the staff auditorium by the time Christine arrived for the Grand Rounds lecture. She grabbed a printed announcement from the desk by the door, and signed the roster.

Luckily, she found a seat on the left end of the last row of the auditorium. Sitting down felt good, in spite of the hard, barely padded seat. Silently, she read the announcement: "Today's Grand Rounds Speaker; Dr. Arens, M.D., Ph.D.; Professor of Surgery, Emeritus; Topic; Update on Clinical Biogenetics."

"Who's the speaker?" asked the man in the next seat.

She realized he was the anesthesia resident from last night's emergency room trauma case. He offered his right hand. "Paul Powers, anesthesia," he said. "I know you're Dr. Mason, but we've never been introduced."

She shook his hand. "Call me Christine."

"Have you seen the girl today?" he asked.

"No, I haven't been to ICU yet. But the TV news this morning said she was still alive."

"Funny how we get our information. Who's the speaker?"

"Dr. Arens, Clinical Biogenetics." She handed Paul the announcement paper."

"Sounds boring," he said, yawning. "Maybe I'll take off."

"He's an excellent speaker," she insisted. "I've attended several of his lectures in medical school and previous Grand Rounds. And he loves to answer questions, about anything. He's well read. Spends a lot of time in the Stacks, the old library, reading. You might learn something."

"No thanks." Paul rolled his eyes. "I need a little more clinical experience."

"Don't let Benga's ego get to you," said Christine, patting Paul on the back. "I think you did a great job last night."

A man stood up for a minute on the wooden stage in front of the room and introduced Professor Arens. The Professor slowly rose from a seat in the first row. He shuffled his bent frame up to the podium carrying a stack of papers. Standing behind the podium, his face barely reaching over the top, he checked his notes. A spotlight glared on the Professor's pale, bald head. Black, half lens bifocals slid down his nose to the bulbous tip and stopped. He looked into the audience and grabbed a microphone attached to the podium by a flexible tube. Pulling the microphone down to his mouth, he cleared his throat and began. "Thank you for that wonderful introduction. I've been retired from clinical practice for eleven years now. The worst thing about being retired is that you can't quit your job." The audience laughed. "Today I will update you on the progress of genetic testing, treatment of genetic disorders, and family genetic counseling."

He lectured for forty-five minutes and answered questions. At the end, he received loud applause. Christine and Paul rose to leave. The crowd slowly filed out through the exits. Paul stretched his arms. "Did you doze off?" she asked.

"You were right," he said. "Arens is an interesting speaker. Such a nice old guy. Brilliant, too."

She felt relaxed talking to Paul, he spoke freely. Unlike most men, Paul didn't seem to be intimidated by her professional stature. She didn't want the conversation to end. "I'm going to visit Jenny Walker in the ICU. Would you like to join me?"

Paul scanned her from the ground up, finally settling on her eyes. "Let's go," he said. They strolled leisurely toward the intensive care unit through the old hospital hallways. Paul was silent.

"Are you thinking about Jenny Walker?" Christine asked .

"What? Oh. Unfortunately, I've got a habit of thinking about my wife when I'm walking through the hallways. Actually, she's my ex-wife. But it's not official."

"Divorce among doctors is epidemic," said Christine, hoping to draw his feelings out into the open. He bowed his head and walked faster. She matched his pace. "What's it like?" she said.

His face spasmed like a surgical patient in response to the probing of a raw nerve. "It's torture, to live with the memory of someone who hurt me. I mean really hurt me, in an intimate way. It's like living in hell." She felt like she'd pressed on a painful wound, and didn't know what to say, so she said nothing.

When they arrived at the door of the intensive care unit, a Seattle policeman checked their ID badges. "I barely got into the ER with this ID yesterday," said Paul.

"OK. Go on in," said the policeman, his face rock hard.

In Jenny Walker's huge bed was a small form that looked vaguely human. Shock had caused her blood vessels to leak fluid, and her body had swollen into a grotesque, amorphous lump. She was covered with surgical dressings, and plastic tubes protruded from everywhere. Motors, hissing gasses, and electronic alarms blended to produce an intolerable cacophony. The air smelled like curdled milk.

Marilyn Walker sat by the bedside crying into a pink handkerchief, her head bowed. Bill Walker stood behind her with his hands on her shoulders.

"I'm telling you, Bill, something evil has happened to Jenny," said Marilyn.

Bill rubbed his wife's shoulders. "Of course, what's happened is terrible. I can see that."

"You don't see, you never see. I feel it."

"You feel what?"

"The evil. Like, like a presence."

Paul interrupted. "Mr. Walker?"

The man raised his head and wiped tears from his eyes. "Dr. Powers, will Jenny make it?"

"I don't know any more than you."

Christine assumed Mr. Walker was Jenny's father. A tall woman in a sheriff's uniform approached the bedside. "Dr. Powers," said the woman, "I want to thank you again for helping me with this investigation." Christine was puzzled. She wondered if everyone in Seattle knew Paul Powers.

Paul introduced the policewoman. "Dr. Mason, this is Deputy McCann. She's part of the team that recovered Jenny Walker. I helped her identify Jenny. "

"Actually, I'm now part of the Cascade Killer Task Force," said Jackey. "The governor has authorized more staff since we found Jenny Walker."

"Mr. Walker," said Paul, nodding toward Christine, "this is Dr. Mason, a neurosurgeon."

"Does Jenny need neurosurgery?" Mr. Walker asked.

"Not at all," said Christine. "I'm just following her progress." Christine looked at the young girl. Her breathing tube was still in place, and she was unconscious. Lines of black stitches covered in greasy ointment criss-crossed her face.

Christine put on gloves and pried open Jenny's badly swollen right eyelid. The pupil was open wide, and little of the blue color of her iris could be seen. Through an ophthalmoscope, a small flashlight with an assortment of magnifying lenses on one end, Christine looked at the retina lining the back of the eye. As the light of the ophthalmoscope shone into the eye, the black pupil constricted slightly.

An eerie red glow emanated from the retina and sent a cold chill down the back of Chrisitine's neck. The red glow was reflected light, the red reflex, a normal phenomenon. Examination of the left eye gave her the same unnerving feeling. But the blood vessels in both eyes looked fine, and the examination was normal. She felt uneasy, but didn't know why.

At the foot of the bed, she scraped the bottom of each foot with a pointed stick, and the toes curled downward. "It's too early to tell if there's been any permanent brain damage." she said.

"She'll never be the same," said Marilyn. "Evil is in her."

Bill blushed. "Marilyn, please. Such nonsense. Please excuse my wife. She's very upset." He pointed at his daughter. "Maybe you can tell me why Jenny's doing that."

Jenny kicked, and punched her chest. Her head thrashed, and a terrible grimace contorted her swollen face as sweat poured from her forehead. Her lips formed silent words, as if she was screaming.

Marilyn sobbed, burying her head in the handkerchief. "Jenny wants to tell us something," said Marilyn, "but she hasn't spoken."

"The breathing tube goes through her vocal cords," said Paul. "She won't be able to talk until it comes out."

"She's unconscious, anyway," Christine added. "It's impossible to say what's going on in her head."

"Evil, evil, evil," Marilyn chanted.

Bill sighed. "Dr. Mason," he asked, "if Jenny ever wakes up, will she remember what happened?"

"I don't know," Christine admitted.

"I hope so," said Jackey.

"I hope not," added Paul.

CHAPTER 5

JENNY STUCK OUT her thumb to the interstate traffic and waited for the perfect ride. She couldn't recognize individual cars. She saw only a blur, the cresting of waves on a busy ocean. The waves occasionally slowed down to look her over, and she felt confident and sexy enough to get a ride. Sooner or later, some man would decide she was worth the trouble. A cute, seventeen year old girl would always turn someone on.

Even at sixty miles per hour, the drivers would notice her skinny waist and her chrome studded, black leather pants. Her short sleeve blouse billowed in the wind, braless. The cold made her nipples erect, and they poked through the lacy fabric. She played with the golden heart on the chain around her neck, a birthday present from her mother. It was Jenny's only reminder of her former home.

She was heading for Spokane, Washington, hitchhiking her way to freedom. The move from California to Washington State at age fifteen had ruined her life. She'd never adjusted to Seattle. Her parents had always debated what was best for her, but they'd never asked her opinion. The move was supposed to put some distance between her and her uncle. He'd abused her when she was too young to protect herself. Where had her parents been in those days?

One year ago, she ran away, deciding to live on the streets of Seattle. There, she found drugs and an endless supply of cigarettes. To pay expenses she found prostitution. After one year on the streets of Seattle she discovered competition, drug addiction, and an intolerable police presence. Worst of all, she was pursued by her parents.

She wondered if her parents would follow her to Spokane. She hadn't spoken to them since running away. A private detective had found her in Seattle at the sleazy boarding house. Three months ago, her father came to take her home, but she refused to speak with him. He sat in his car all night, watching her sell herself on the street.

Information travels quickly through the streets. A rumor said Spokane was a land of opportunity. The word was that in Spokane, street people don't fight for territory, customers are as plentiful as drugs, and police look the other way. She hoped the rumor was true.

Evergreens towered over her, forming a barrier surrounding the freeway. It was cloudy and always drizzled lightly west of the Cascade Mountains. She missed the California sunshine, and she'd heard Eastern Washington was sunny. Standing on the shoulder of Interstate Highway 90, she wanted to be swept away to the east by the strong current of cars, and carried over the mountains to the sun.

Glaring at the traffic with blue eyes, she turned her smile on. The baby face had never failed. Her swollen feet ached inside her brown cowboy boots. Slung over her left shoulder was an old camouflage jacket. She held out her right thumb, following the passing cars. Blond hair fell across the jacket. Hours passed, no one stopped, but she didn't care. A pocket full of amphetamines helped to pass the time.

An ancient, blue Chevy, two door sedan slowed down. She couldn't guess it's original color, or how many times it had been repainted. It had no hubcaps, and the right front fender was crushed and rusted. The passenger door was red, a junk yard replacement. Four snow tires with oversized tread adorned the greasy rims. She noticed cakes of dried mud around the wheel wells, hinting that the car had been off road. She wondered if it had ever been washed.

Passing her, the Chevy pulled off beyond the shoulder of the highway, onto the struggling grass, and waited. She hesitated, afraid, though she'd spent many evenings in worse looking vehicles. She approached the passenger side, opened the door, and climbed in.

The driver had two small, red eyes sunk into dark sockets. Black, greasy hair fell across his unshaven face. She shuddered and looked away, wishing she'd waited for the next ride. "Are you going all the way to Spokane?"

"Not that far," he answered. "But, I can take you in that direction."

"Thanks," she said. There was no easy way to leave now. They were back on the highway, traveling seventy miles per hour.

Twenty minutes passed, no one spoke. She studied the driver's face, and started to shiver. There was no exit in sight, no gas stations, and no buildings, just the evergreens along the freeway. The car slowed.

"Hey, why are we slowing down?"

"Got to get some gas. I'm almost out."

She looked at the gauge, it was half full.

"Gauge doesn't work," he said, nodding toward the instrument panel. "I go by mileage. There's an old gas station off this back road."

"I'd like to get out here."

"Sure."

The car slowed to a crawl on the shoulder of the highway, but didn't stop. She saw evil in the man's eyes, evil she'd never forget. She pressed her body against the door, fumbling for the handle. He pulled a crowbar from beneath his seat, and swung.

She awoke curled in a ball, on her right side. Reaching out, she felt gravel beneath her and saw the red passenger door overhead. The door was open. Her head ached and she rubbed it, discovering a tender lump on her forehead. A pair of boots appeared and she looked up. The driver towered over her, tall, solidly built, and at least 200 pounds. She was too terrified to speak.

He picked up her jacket from the passenger seat. Rummaging through the pockets, he found a handful of loose change, and a vial of pills. He opened the vial, pouring the pills out in his hand. "Good!" he said, as he returned the pills to their container and tossed it into the glove box.

Jenny tried standing, fighting a wave of dizziness. He pushed her down, onto her back, and dragged her clear of the car.

Screaming, she punched and kicked, getting a smile in return. Reaching down to his tall right boot, he pulled out a knife. It was a survival knife, ten inches long, with a serrated blade.

She tried again to get up, to run, to crawl, but he held her down and cut off her clothing, slashing leather, lace, and skin. She screamed each time the knife descended, felt the white hot pain, and screamed again. A pile of torn clothes lay next to her bleeding body. He placed the knife back into his boot and lit a cigarette, smoking as she sobbed. He spoke to the cigarette: "I'm really sorry. I don't want to hurt you. If I could make you understand. Too late. Who would understand? Even I don't understand."

He smoked the cigarette to the filter. "But you're like all the others. Gone, like all the others," he said, flipping the butt into the woods. He opened his flannel shirt and unbuckled his belt. A partly open zipper revealed a bulge, struggling to escape his blue jeans. A large, metal buckle with an engraved portrait of an elk dangled against his thigh. She tried to get up, but he dropped down and pinned her.

"Please don't," she said. Too small to fight back, she cried. So often men did this to her, but that was business. On the street, she was never beaten for sex, and she was always paid for it. He would finish, she hoped, and let her be. He entered her forcefully, and the pounding began.

Pounding and pounding. Gravel on the road dug into her back, and still the pounding continued. Beads of sweat poured off his body, his thrusting intensifying to a rhythm more violent and primitive than anything she had ever felt. Blood, mud, sweat, and grit mixed between them, forming a vile paste. He didn't stop.

She couldn't breathe each time he crashed down, so she took quick breaths as he rose. She heard her ribs snapping, the pain was unbearable. She whimpered, and saw within the madman's eyes an alien presence incapable of remorse. It was like a horror movie, but closing her eyes didn't help. He no longer seemed aware of her, the road, or the world. Like a puppet, mindless, in a choreographed dance, his right hand moved down to his boot.

The knife traveled to the hilt through her chest. It was a strange sensation. It was not pain, just a warm rush as the blade withdrew and blood flowed from the wound. Again and again, the blade penetrated. It passed through her chest, abdomen, face, groin, arms, and legs. Both the knife, and the murderer's body, stabbed at her with the same rhythm and fury.

The killer screamed a primeval cry, as he ejaculated into her. The sky darkened, and a pleasant chill replaced the warm rush.

"Jenny, Jenny it's me, your father."

"Dad?"

"My God. Marilyn. She's talking."

Out of nothing, three faces came into focus. One was Jenny's mother, and she looked 20 years older. Next, Jenny's saw her father, at least he looked the same. Maybe I'm dreaming, Jenny thought. Maybe I wasn't raped. Maybe it was all a dream.

"Dad?"

"Yes, Jenny. It's me. You're in the hospital."

"The hospital?" *So, it wasn't a dream.* "How long?"

"Three days."

"That's not Jenny," said Marilyn "Look at her eyes."

A tall, tanned woman looked down at Jenny from over her father's shoulder. "Who are you?" Jenny asked.

"I'm Jackey McCann, and I need to ask you some questions."

CHAPTER 6

Four months later:

PAUL POWERS PULLED himself out of bed and swatted the snooze button on the alarm clock. He looked at the dial, it was 7:10 AM. He wondered how many times he'd hit the snooze button. The alarm had been set for 6:30.

He'd worked until 3:00 AM, and hadn't bothered to go home. Home still reminded him of Anne, even after eight months of separation and divorce. He took a deep breath. The bunk bed in the resident's call room smelled like old fish. There was no time for coffee, so he quickly brushed his teeth. Foul breath would not be an asset for his first patient interview of the new day.

He hurried from the call room through the underground tunnel and wound his way to the surgical complex. The scramble to get the morning cases going had already begun. On the tops of gurneys, frightened looking patients covered with thin white sheets rolled through the electric double doors.

Inside the doors, to his left, nurses and doctors crowded into the corner behind the high counter of the control desk, making last minute changes to the schedule. Conversations merged into unintelligible babble and phones rang constantly.

On the wall behind the control desk, an LCD monitor listed the cases of the day. A nurse was busy making changes on the board. Paul walked up beside her to check his assignment. His first case was an abortion on a eighteen year old girl.

Some of the anesthesia staff refused to participate in abortions for religious reasons. Although he had no religious objections, he found participating in abortions disturbing and had asked to be excluded, whenever possible. The anesthesia assignments were normally made at random, but next to his name was a notation: "req." It indicated the patient had requested him. He saw her name: Jenny Walker.

"Are you all right," said the nurse by his side. "You look like you've just seen a ghost."

"I think I just did." He pointed to Jenny's name. "That's the teenager who was raped by the Cascade Killer. I helped resuscitate her."

"I vaguely remember," she nodded. "When was that?"

"Four months ago," he said.

"Oh. No wonder she wants an abortion. The schedule info says she's sixteen weeks."

He visualized a grotesque form in an intensive care unit bed. The din of a hundred strange machines roared in the background. The room smelled like air freshener had been used in an unsuccessful attempt to conceal a rotten stench. By the bedside, a man watched his wife cry into a pink handkerchief.

The nurse stepped closer. "Are you sure you're all right?"

Paul shuddered. "Just missed my coffee, that's all. I'll be fine, thanks." She squinted at him like he was an unusually interesting tissue specimen. "Really, I'll be OK." She shook her head and resumed entering scheduling corrections into the computer.

As soon as Paul entered the outpatient holding area, he recognized Bill and Marilyn Walker. Marilyn was leaning over the side rail of a gurney, wearing a black overcoat and gloves. A black scarf covered her hair. Bill stood behind her, his blue shirt sleeves rolled up above his elbows into tight rings.

Bill ran around to the opposite side of the gurney, thrust out a callused hand, and shook Paul's hand firmly. One corner of Bill's mouth smiled. "Dr. Powers, I'm glad you're here."

Marilyn was motionless, her head bowed. The sheet was pulled up over Jenny's mouth. Paul saw a thick mass of criss-crossing scars, and two sunken eyes. Looking into her eyes, he shivered, something evil was looking back. He remembered the pictures of the beautiful teenage girl who looked like his sister. One bad experience had ruined his sister's life, how could Jenny ever recover from such a brutal mutilation.

"She's carrying the bastard's kid," said Bill. "She's miserable, in a fantasy world. Look at her." Bill leaned on the side rail of the gurney.

Jenny appeared almost catatonic. Paul pulled back the sheet to her waist. The hospital gown fit loosely, she was excessively thin and obviously pregnant. Soft restraints bound her wrists to the gurney. Except for the silent rising and falling of her chest, she was perfectly still.

"Is she always like this?"

"Oh, no," said Bill, gripping the guard rail as if he wanted to break it. Marilyn raised her head for the first time, her eyes stained with tears. Bill released the railing and ran his hands through his thin hair.

Paul put the sheet back across Jenny's lips. "I assume ..."

Jenny sat up on the gurney, her arms thrashed. She kicked the mattress. Marilyn backed away. "I'll kill you if I have to," Jenny shouted at Paul. "Take it, take it ... don't come near me, any of you ..." She pulled against the restraints, her eyes bugged out, red. "No, Nooooo ..." She fell back on the gurney, weeping. "Momma, make it go away. Please Momma."

"I'm here Jenny," said Marilyn, reaching for her daughter's restrained hand. Marilyn ran her other hand through Jenny's hair. "It's all right, sweet cake, mommy's here. We'll make it go away, we will."

"What can I do," said Bill, "argue with her psychiatrist? He tells me Jenny's like an Afghan War vet. Post Traumatic Stress Disorder. He says she's got to have an abortion, or else she'll never make any mental progress. She can't survive the stress of having this baby."

"I understand," said Paul. A diagnosis of Post Traumatic Stress Disorder meant her outburst was probably a flashback. He recalled the incident in the intensive care unit, when she had seemed to reexperience the attack. "I'll take good care of her."

"I know you will. That's why I want you."

Paul waited. There was something more on Bill Walker's mind. Paul could feel it.

Wrinkles appeared in Bill's forehead. "Jenny's all I've got left. Please help her." Marilyn gently stroked Jenny's hair.

Aside from a caring and vigilant anesthetic, there was nothing Paul could do for Jenny. The best anesthetic could not cure the patient.

In the midst of Jenny's dazzling high technology resuscitation, no one had adequately addressed the possibility of pregnancy. It should have been dealt with immediately. This wasn't the first time Paul had seen modern medicine perform the impossible and neglect the obvious. Specialists, trained to examine the parts, often ignored the whole.

"I'll do my best," he said, and then hurried to the operating room.

He went through his preanesthesia checklist, preparing the machine and drugs. In the small holding area outside the operating room, Jenny waited, quiet. A bag of salt water hung beside her on a metal pole. Plastic tubing from the bag ended in a vein on the back of her left hand.

He rolled her into the operating room and transferred her to the operating table with the help of a nurse. The nurse fastened a strap across Jenny's waist, and slid two padded arm supports into brackets on opposite sides of the table. Paul positioned Jenny's arms on the supports and retied her wrist restraints.

On the index finger of her left hand, he placed a pulse oximeter probe. This clothespin like device measured the amount of oxygen in her blood, by means of an infrared light. Her pulse was signaled by a shrill beep that would change to a lower pitch if the oxygen level in her blood decreased. Around her right arm, he wrapped an automatic blood pressure cuff. To her chest, he pasted three electrode pads attached by wires to a LCD screen that displayed her EKG, the electrical activity of her heart.

Oxygen flowed through corrugated plastic tubes from the anesthesia machine to a mask that fit snugly on her face. He was getting ready to paralyze her, to stop her breathing. A few initial breaths of oxygen would protect her from brain damage for a few minutes, in case he had trouble restarting her breathing.

Into a rubber access port on the plastic tubing of the intravenous line, he injected Propofol, a sedative, to render her unconscious. Next, he injected succinylcholine, a muscle relaxant, but it flowed backwards in the plastic tubing. He checked her left hand, she had bent it upwards at the wrist, kinking the tube in her vein and blocking the flow. Bending her hand down solved the problem, and the paralyzing drug entered her system.

Twitching started in her face and spread downward through her entire body, a sure sign the paralyzing drug was working. After the muscle spasms, her breathing stopped, she was motionless. He stuck his gloved fingers into her mouth, opened it wide, and inserted a laryngoscope, an "L" shaped flashlight with a dull metal blade. With the help of the laryngoscope, he saw her vocal cords and passed a breathing tube between them.

The breathing tube connected to the mechanical ventilator of the anesthesia machine. He restarted her breathing by turning on the ventilator, pumping oxygen into her lungs, and then added anesthetic gases to the oxygen.

The nurse put Jenny's legs up in stirrups, and washed her vagina, lower abdomen, and inner thighs with a Betadine solution. She was covered with paper drapes, and then the surgeon started.

He opened the vagina with a speculum, and passed a series of progressively larger metal rods into the cervix. A sharp scoop was used to remove the fetus from the womb. In a stainless steel basin on top of the instrument table, Paul saw a fetus the size of a small lemon, doubled over, mangled, and covered with bloody strings of fibrous membrane. The heart was beating, but it wouldn't for long. Paul felt sick, and turned away.

He hated abortions. He wasn't sure abortion could ever be justified morally or legally. This kind of abortion, after a rape, raised even more questions. The phenomenal yearly number of abortions worldwide was a disgrace. Thankfully, he'd helped on only a few.

The surgeon picked up a hollow plastic wand and passed it through the cervix. The other end of the wand was connected to a tube that ran into a glass jar. The jar was set into a machine on the floor. "Suction," said the surgeon.

The powerful suction machine came alive, hissing and slurping the remaining bloody contents of the uterus into the jar. As the vacuum was removed from the womb, it sucked air, clearing itself with one giant sigh. The machine stopped, and the room was quiet.

Dr. Melvin, a pathologist, entered the room. Dumpy and awkward, he struggled to pull latex gloves over his fat fingers. He picked up the fetus, holding it up to the light, blood and fluid dripping off his gloves. Melvin seemed to be admiring the fetus. He put it in a container of salt water, capped the container tightly, and left the operating room. The surgeon followed.

Paul was glad to see Melvin leave. The man was weird. Rumors said he had greater rapport with dead tissue specimens, than with live humans. Paul believed the rumors. He'd seen Melvin examining raw tissue without gloves, as if he wouldn't mind catching a disease. Paul wondered if Melvin believed in hand washing.

As Paul reversed the anesthetic, the nurses removed the drapes and washed Jenny off. Ragged scars formed an ugly web all over her body, and he realized her mind was mutilated in the same way. The heroic rescue of Jenny Walker had left her with a grotesque body, a scrambled mind, and a dead baby.

CHAPTER 7

PAUL ENTERED the outpatient holding area, and the memory of yesterday's grisly abortion returned. He thanked God there were no abortions on the schedule today. Instead, he'd be working with Christine Mason. Ever since their conversation after Grand Rounds four months ago, working with her had been a pleasure.

Like many neurosurgeons, Christine was busy and often aloof. But she always had a smile and greeting for him, and the courtesy to say "thank you" after each anesthetic. She took the time to discuss clinical problems with him. He admired her extreme confidence and her quiet, controlled beauty. She was a talented neurosurgeon, the perfect resident, and one hell of an impressive woman.

Paul's first patient of the day, a powerful looking man, was lying on a gurney in the outpatient area. Standing beside him was a black haired, husky woman, holding his hand. The pair made a perfect couple, Paul thought, as he accessed the online chart.

The chart said Joe Tyce was an unemployed lumberjack, thirty-nine years old, six feet tall, 220 pounds, and on no medications. His only prior surgery was an extensive reconstruction of his left knee years ago, after a tree had fallen on him. The consent for surgery had been signed, along with a living will, and an organ donor form. He noticed, clipped to the top of the thin paper chart, an envelope that read: "Northwest Organ Procurement Agency Family Donor Cards." The organ procurement agency maximized efficiency by signing up family members along with patients going to surgery.

Paul approached the patient. "Are you Joe Tyce?" The man did not respond.

"This is Joe," said the woman, with a deep voice. "He can't talk much anymore."

"Are you family?"

"Bertha, I'm a friend."

"I'm doctor Paul Powers, the anesthesiologist who'll be taking care of Mr. Tyce in surgery." Joe was bald, except for three white buttons sewn to his scalp that formed the corners of an imaginary triangle. His blank face looked like it was carved from stone. He opened his almost toothless mouth and then curled his lips together, sucking at the air. Joe's muscular arms, folded across his chest, trembled. The tremors traveled in waves down to his large hands.

Paul grabbed one of Joe's arms and tried to lift it off his chest, but it was stiff as a board. It yielded after many jerky movements. The harder Paul pulled, the more the arm jerked. "How long has Mr. Tyce had Parkinson's Disease," he asked.

"Ten years," said Bertha. "Shakes got worse last year. Couldn't even feed himself. Can barely move. They say it's brain damage from boxin'."

"Boxing?"

"Yeah. We're from Forks, originally. Came to Seattle for work. Not much for lumberjacks to do, anymore.

"Professional boxing?"

"Ha. You kiddin'? Boys rigged a ring out behind the bar. We won a lot of money. Joe was good. Could've been a pro."

"He's not taking any medication?"

"Not no more. We tried it all. Either the damn stuff didn't work, or he's allergic. That's why we're here."

"Do you have any questions?"

"Yeah, will it work and how long will it take?"

"Those are questions better answered by the neurosurgeon. As you know, it's an experimental procedure. There are no guarantees, but we've had some excellent results. I expect the operation to take at least four hours."

"Thanks."

In the operating room, Joe Tyce was anesthetized and prepared for surgery. An x-ray was taken of his head. Paul sat at the anesthesia machine, feeling a lot better than yesterday morning at Jenny's abortion.

Covering Joe from the neck down was a tent, the roof supported by a large instrument table. Only his head protruded from beneath the tent. Sparkling stainless steel instruments lay in rows across the instrument table. The pointed metal pincers of cranial tongs immobilized his head in an upright position. A sticky, plastic wrap covered his smooth, white scalp, making it look like the bottom of a glazed ceramic bowl.

A massive chair, called the "Throne" by the house staff, faced Joe's head. An operating microscope hung between the chair and the prepared scalp. Next to the chair, Dr. Swan, the junior resident, waited in sterile attire, his white eyebrows like check marks below his blue cap. Christine entered the room with her hands dripping wet. She carefully picked up a towel from the instrument table. "Good morning Dr. Swan, everything ready?"

"Right. All set."

She looked around. "Where's Rupp?"

"God knows," he said.

She shook her head and walked behind the drapes to the anesthesia station. "Is that Dr. Powers behind the mask?"

"Good morning," said Paul.

"How's Joe doing?"

"Never felt better."

"Excellent anesthesia, as usual."

"Dr. Mason," said Swan, "We have a medical student today."

A young woman approached, her mask and thick red glasses taped to her face. "This is my week on neurosurgery," she said.

"Ah. A whole week. That ought to be enough to learn everything," said Christine, winking.

Christine wasn't facing the door as Rupp entered, unsteady looking, and without a mask. A nurse tugged on her mask, but Rupp didn't take the hint. Christine slid her arms into an open backed gown and pulled off one end of the paper belt. She turned to wrap the belt around her waist, and then she saw him. "Glad you could make it," she said, "Now leave, and get a mask." Rupp staggered from the room, returning with a face mask.

"Dr. Rupp," she said, "since you're so late today, don't bother to scrub in. You can keep our medical student company. Today, we're going to introduce her to the frontiers of neurosurgery. Let's get started." Rupp took the undignified position of observer next to the medical student.

Christine carefully squeezed through the maze of equipment, wires, and hoses cluttering the room. Like a queen she ascended the Throne, Swan at her side, like a squire. Her hands and feet activated control switches on both sides of the Throne. It came alive, quiet electric motors adjusting the chair's position. She reached overhead and drew the microscope downward, so it hung between her eyes and the prepared scalp. A large LCD screen, hanging from the ceiling, provided everyone present with a view from the microscope. "Is the computer active? Have you x-ray localized the markers?" she asked, focusing the microscope on the scalp, on one of the three plastic beads.

"We're active," came over the intercom from a radiologist in a remote computer room. "Markers have been x-ray localized. I have the light coordinates of the first marker. Please continue." The second scalp marker came into focus, and then the third. "Localization complete," said the radiologist.

"Now, the fun begins," Christine said, focusing the microscope on the left side of the scalp. "Start the overlay. Tell me when I have control."

"Superimposing, now. You have control."

The monitor showed a cross sectional x-ray view of the patient's brain, superimposed on the scalp. The x-ray view moved with the microscope as Christine flipped through the x-ray sections, cutting imaginary slices through the brain. She took her face from the microscope. "Perhaps our student can explain to us what just happened."

"Uh, Yes," said the student, her eyes magnified, swimming behind her glasses like goldfish in a bowl. "You just located the position of the patient and the microscope in space using infrared lights on the microscope and the x-ray we took before you arrived."

"Very good, but how do we generate the two-dimensional x-ray images in the microscope?"

"Uh, yesterday, you attached three markers to the patient's scalp and x-rayed him with the CT scanner. The digital information was stored in the computer. Today, you fed the new coordinates into the computer so the images can be recreated in the light microscope."

"You did your homework," said Christine.

Rupp was leaning against the wall, eyes closed, beads of sweat across his forehead. A strong scent of alcohol came from his direction.

Swan made a small incision into the scalp and turned back a flap of skin to expose the skull. A nurse gave him a drill filled with oil, powered by compressed gas, and capable of spinning 75,000 times per second. The diamond tipped burr instantly turned bone into dust. A steady stream of water running over the drill bit prevented it from burning the patient. A small hole formed in the skull, exposing the membrane covering the brain.

Rupp began snoring loudly, his head bobbing against his chest. "Dr. Rupp," said Christine, "Will you tell our student what we usually do now?" Rupp continued snoring. "RUPP! WAKE UP!" Rupp awoke, trembling, and struggled to attention. "Go home, Rupp. You're finished here. And don't bother coming back." Rupp stumbled out of the room, mumbling unintelligibly. The words sounded like garbled obscenities.

"What are you going to do?" asked Swan.

"I'm going to tell Delianis the truth. Rupp's been showing up late, dirty, and drunk. He should be expelled from the program."

"Right. I'll certainly back you up."

"OK, everyone," said Christine, "Show's over. Let's get back to work."

She used the computerized x-ray pictures to guide her microscopic dissection through Joe's brain. After an hour, the surgical site was exposed, deep within the brain.

"Name this structure," Swan said to the student.

"That's the caudate nucleus."

"Right. Why do we care?"

"The patient has Parkinson's Disease."

"What's that?"

"Parkinson's is a movement disorder caused by lack of dopamine, a neurotransmitter in the caudate nucleus."

"Right."

Dr. Melvin, the pathologist, entered carrying a small specimen cup. Fumbling with the lid, he removed it and held the open container over the instrument table. The nurse put a Petri dish, half filled with salt water, on the edge of the table. Melvin dumped a small clump of dark tissue from his container into the dish.

"What have you got for me, Dr. Melvin?" said Christine.

"Ah. Only the finest for you, Dr. Mason. Substantia nigra from a very mature fetal brain. Prepared to perfection. Mmm." He kissed his fat fingers like a gourmet chef with a tasty meal, and then left the room.

"Dr. Melvin is our transplant coordinator," Christine told the student. "He brought us some fetal tissue. Can you tell me why?"

"Uh, you're going to implant the fetal substantia nigra into the patient's brain to produce dopamine. It's a treatment for his Parkinson's."

"Yes," said Christine, "and I hope it's the cure."

Paul knew where the fetal tissue came from. It bothered him to see medical technology running so far ahead of morality. Maybe the neural transplant was part of a divine plan to mitigate human hardships. A child conceived in violence was being used to save a man's life.

CHAPTER 8

JACKEY MCCANN TUCKED her nine millimeter Beretta into the holster above her buttocks. She stepped out of her CR-Z sports car, faded blue jeans straining against her muscular thighs. The drive south from Seattle had taken over two hours due to the evening rush hour. Dark, unbroken clouds over her head seemed within reach.

Frank's urgent and unexpected phone call had left her no time to change into uniform. Her brown leather jacket hung to midthigh, concealing her gun. Long leather fringe under the jacket's sleeves remained in constant motion as she approached the scene of the investigation.

"Sorry to drag you all the way to Tenino," said Sergeant Frank Roberts, wrinkles heaping together on his weather-beaten forehead. He looked Jackey over. "Even though you're off duty, I thought you'd want to see this."

He led her to the middle of a cow pasture, surrounded by a yellow ribbon. In the center was a blue Chevy, a four door sedan, with a red passenger door in the front. Two policemen stood by the car taking photographs, and a third dusted for fingerprints. Several others took measurements on the muddy grass. Inside the Chevy, on his hands and knees, another man vacuumed the carpet.

"Just how Jenny described it," said Jackey. "Anything inside?"

"Nothing. Stripped clean," He ran his fingers through his hair. "No prints."

"How about fibers?"

"We're checking, but I'll bet he vacuumed it."

A small crowd behind the yellow police line grew larger. At the front of the crowd, Jackey noticed a man with a cowboy hat and a long overcoat. It was odd he was wearing sunglasses on such a dark day. "How'd you find the car?" she asked Frank.

"An anonymous phone call." He tilted his head to one side. "Are you still having nightmares?"

She blinked, and her eyes lost their focus. "Yes, and always the same one. I see the killer's face reflected in a knife blade. Only it's distorted, like a fun house mirror. The knife moves closer and closer to my face ..."

"And then?"

She put her right hand on her hip, lightly touching the butt of her Beretta. Then she shook her head, the world came back into focus. "That's when I always wake up."

"Don't worry. It won't be long. We know what he looks like, how he operates, and how he kills," said Frank. "Old man Walker just offered a $10,000 reward for information."

"Frank, even with everything Jenny told me, its taken four months to find the damn car. And what good is it?"

"Look, Jack, I need you back here at first light. It's too late for me to head back to the city." He looked into her eyes. "I'm going to find a place near here tonight. We could have a drink. The department's paying. How about it?"

It was a tempting offer, she'd like to know Frank better. "I don't think so," she said. "I'm heading back to the city, tonight."

"All right," said Frank, "If anything more turns up, you'll know."

"Thanks."

Jackey squeezed herself into the small CR-Z. Damp, forty degree air followed her into the car, and a light drizzle coated the windshield.

As the ride back to the city began, she felt wet to the core. A mildewed copy of the Seattle Times lay on the passenger seat, open to a composite photograph of the Cascade Killer. She switched on the interior light, studied the picture, and then shut the light off.

She'd looked at the picture hundreds of times, and knew every feature of his face. In her patrol car, clipped to the visor, she kept a list of information about Jenny's attack. Jackey knew the list by heart. From the limited amount of data, she reconstructed the Killer's personality, projecting herself into the Killer's mind. She took the Killer to bed with her every night.

It was late, and she was hungry. After driving for fifteen minutes, she saw a tavern she'd passed on the trip out. It had looked like a friendly place in the daytime, but was less inviting at night. The simple wooden building resembled an oversized hut. Spotlighted above the door was a hand painted sign: "A-Frame Tavern-Good Food." She hoped it was true.

In the dim light, she barely saw the potholes in the gravel parking lot before they swallowed the small tires, bouncing the Honda CR-Z. She parked the car between two pickup trucks, an old full size pickup, and a brand new mini-pickup. The old, beat-up truck was crammed full of tools, ropes, and ladders. The new truck had a KISW rock station decal on the tailgate, and a bumper sticker: "Excuse me for not working." She smiled and thought about the variety of characters she'd be likely to find here.

Inside, country music blasted from four overhead speakers. To her right was a curved bar with a fat, middle age women behind the counter. The bartender wore her ratty brown, shoulder length hair banded behind her head. She leaned over the counter and flirted with a man seated at the bar. She flirted like it was part of her job, but the man didn't care, he was enjoying the attention. He paid for another beer with a large bill, and the bartender kept the change.

More men sat at the bar drinking beer, or eating hamburgers. About a dozen people sat at several tables. "Way to go," one man shouted. Over in the corner, Jackey saw a couple on a long bench seat, embracing. She watched them sink below the table surface, and out of sight.

The dimly lit bar area contrasted with a brightly lit game room, complete with pool table. A skinny youth in a rainbow colored T-shirt completed several difficult pool shots before yielding his turn. She wondered how much money rode on the game. Besides the pool table, there was a dart board, three video games, and an old fashioned pinball machine. She pulled up a stool at the bar and sat down where she could best watch the room, and the door, while she ate.

"Hey, what's a nice kid like you doin' in a place like this?" the bartender asked.

"Hungry, I guess."

"For food or guys?"

"Food first."

"Food, I got. My name's Rose." She handed Jackey a one page cardboard card. "Look it over, best grub in the Northwest. Anything ya want, just ask, except for men. Unless ya wanna divorce one, I'm an expert three times over."

"I never married one, but thanks, anyway," said Jackey.

"You're a smarter girl than old Rose, that's for sure," she said, and left the counter to tend the tables.

Jackey was amazed at the uncanny ability of bartenders to rapidly break down social barriers. She scrutinized the short menu.

"If ya study the food so long, you'll never get to the men," Rose scolded. "What'll it be? It's all great, anyway."

"Uh, the New York steak and fries will be fine," Jackey replied.

"I can give ya a baked potato with that steak, with all the trimmings," said Rose.

"OK, I'd like that," Jackey agreed. "And a Rainier Light, please." Rose nodded, and ran off to the kitchen. Jackey saw the top and bottom of the cook through the saloon style swinging doors, as they closed behind Rose's sizable bulk. A few moments later, the double doors flew open, and Rose returned. She scooped a frosted glass mug out of a freezer along the back wall, and filled it to overflowing with fresh beer from the tap. In one smooth movement, she slung the beer a few feet along the counter. It stopped in front of Jackey, without a drop spilling.

The golden liquid felt cool and refreshing on her lips. She swiveled to watch the progress of the pool game. The young player supported himself on his pool cue, as his opponent, a man of nearly 300 pounds, took careful aim. The youth stood in the corner, alone. A man drinking beer at the counter looked her over. He was undoubtedly young, but balding in the front. She named him "Baldy."

Hot food appeared in front of her, it tasted great. She was hungrier than she'd expected, and ordered a second beer to wash the food down.

Another man entered. He was large, very solid, and familiar looking. Neat, black hair complemented his evenly trimmed beard and mustache. She couldn't place him, but she felt she'd seen him before. The newcomer chose a seat at the opposite end of the bar, nearest the door, and ordered a beer. She was strangely curious about him and tried to make eye contact, but he just stared into his beer.

She walked slowly toward the opposite end of the counter, her beer mug in tow. "This seat taken?" she asked, with her sweetest voice.

"Help yourself," the stranger replied, coolly. His head turned briefly in her direction, but he returned his gaze to the beer mug without making eye contact.

She grabbed the barstool next to him and sat, sipping her beer, and watching him closely. His heavy coat was made of polar fleece and tightly zipped. He looked rugged, and she wondered if he worked outdoors. After finishing his beer, he pulled a pack of cigarettes from his coat pocket. Jackey drank the rest of her second beer. "Another one for the man," she called to Rose.

Rose winked and replaced the man's empty mug with a fresh beer. "I think she likes ya," said Rose. "Why don't ya introduce yourself?" He put a cigarette between his lips. "No smoking in here. Government rules." He pretended to take a long drag and blow the smoke in Rose's face. She shrugged, and walked away.

Jackey extended her hand. "My name's Jackey. Most people call me Jack." He removed the cigarette from his mouth, shook her hand and smiled. "OK, Jack." He took back his hand and grabbed the beer mug. "I'm Fred, and I'm a little shy, in case you didn't notice." He took a drink.

"It's real obvious," said Jackey. "But I'll take it easy on you." He laughed into his beer, choking and coughing. With his coat sleeve, he wiped his wet beard, and then looked at her face. She saw striking eyes, small and red, desperately crying for compassion and somehow familiar. She had to know more. "This is the oldest line in the book," she said, "but haven't I seen you somewhere before?"

"You might have. I've helped manage several restaurants in the Seattle area. You might have been a customer."

"Very likely. What restaurants?"

"I came here to forget the past," he said, and then drained his second beer with a loud gulp. He stared at the empty glass.

Talking about the past had been a mistake. She didn't buy the restaurant story, she'd known him from somewhere else, she was sure of that now. He unzipped his coat and put the cigarette box into the front pocket of his checkered, flannel shirt. From the other front pocket he pulled a ten dollar bill and tossed it on the counter.

"If you stay awhile," said Jackey, "I promise not to ask about the past."

"Thanks, but I need to leave." His face spasmed and turned red, sweat dripping off his forehead.

"Hey. You all right?"

"Just some bug I picked up, I'll be OK. But I need to leave."

As he stood up she saw his belt, the large buckle engraved with an elk. She watched him go, and then thought of Jenny's list. He had the right height, weight, hair color, flannel shirt, elk, and was a smoker. He could have grown the beard. She swallowed hard, took a few deep breaths, and wondered if her obsession had finally taken over. Was she starting to see the Killer everywhere?

Jackey had more doubts. Could she handle him alone, or should she call for backup? She was off duty and drinking. Would Frank stand by her if she arrested an innocent man? If she took the man in for questioning, could Jenny identify him? Then Jackey remembered why he was so familiar. He had Jenny's eyes.

"Dammit, call the Sheriff," Jackey shouted. "Tell them Deputy McCann needs backup, right now. And have them contact Frank Roberts." Rose hurried toward the phone. Jackey ran into the dim parking lot as a dark sedan sped away, tossing gravel behind. She couldn't see his license plate, so she jumped into her CR-Z and went after him. She chased him at over sixty miles per hour along the blacktop road that led east, out of town. With her little CR-Z, she cornered tightly and accelerated quickly, until she was tailgating, and wondering what to do. She hit her bright lights, but he didn't stop.

The road was one lane in each direction, undivided, and unlit. The night offered no additional light, and rain reduced the usefulness of the headlights. It was impossible for her to see more than a few car lengths ahead. The road twisted and turned, disappearing into an inky black abyss.

She held her breath and prayed no one was coming in the opposing lane of traffic, as she swerved to the left and accelerated. The small engine screamed, filling the car with the smell of burning oil. How much more could her little CR-Z take? She pulled up to the rear door of his car, and turned the steering wheel hard, to the right. Glass sprayed over her hood as her right headlight shattered. His car skidded sideways, but stayed on the road. She nudged it right, again, just as the road turned sharply left. His car went flying off the right side of the road, and crashed into a tree.

Front wheel drive pulled her around the sudden left turn, hurling her into the opposing lane of traffic. The bright lights of a semi truck shone down at her from dead ahead. She turned her steering wheel hard, to the right, and closed her eyes, tensing in a futile attempt to brace for the impact. The bellow of the truck's horn became a shriek. Her car spun as it passed through the breath of the enormous truck. The truck's horn became a distant sigh, and the spinning stopped. She opened her eyes, surprised to be alive.

Slowly, she drove back, her remaining headlight cutting a narrow path through the darkness. She saw his car wrapped around a tree, the doors crushed. He was trapped inside, struggling to get out. She left her car and drew her gun, holding it with both hands as she approached. Standing in the beam of her headlight, ten feet away, she waited for him to get out.

He did. His bulk was more impressive in the bright headlight beam. A Godzilla sized shadow grew behind him, dissolving around the edges into the misty darkness of the night. Jackey was standing in a muddy drainage ditch, and he towered above her on the embankment. "Police! Freeze! You're under arrest!" she shouted, trying hard to make her voice sound tough. He didn't move.

She stepped backwards to get out of the ditch, and the muddy bank slid, taking her down with it. He rushed toward her. She got up on her knees, the tip of her gun hovering a few feet from his chest. He hesitated, but so did she. She couldn't shoot, he was unarmed, she had no proof he was a criminal. She'd had a few drinks, harassed a man at a local bar, chased him out of town, run him off the road, destroyed his car, and claimed to be a policewoman out of uniform. If he's not the Killer, she'd be charged with murder.

He jumped on top of her and tried to wrestle away the gun. Pinned beneath him, she fought in total darkness, below the corridor illuminated by the headlight. The gun was sandwiched between them, pointed at their feet, with her finger on the trigger. His right hand suddenly released the gun, but he still held on with his left.

An enormous knife sparkled as it caught the beam of the headlight high above her head. Like a flashbulb exploding in a dark room, light bounced for an instant off his face. His features looked dark and distorted, like in her nightmares. She bent her wrists, tilting the barrel of the gun upward, and pulled the trigger. He roared in pain, rearing backward, and landed in the ditch, sitting. With both hands he grabbed at his crotch. His lower right leg made an odd angle with the upper portion.

She sat up in the ditch, a few feet from him, her hands still fused to the gun. It was aimed, once again, at his chest. He remained seated, moaning. It seemed like an eternity until she heard a patrol car siren, and longer before the flashing lights became visible. It was a Jeep. She couldn't imagine a more glorious sight.

Bright lights shone in her face as the Jeep approached, a spotlight on the driver's side sweeping the area. Sergeant Frank Roberts got out, carrying a flashlight and a gun. Her four month long nightmare had ended.

"Are you wounded, Jack?" Frank asked, scrutinizing her with the flashlight. She remained seated in the ditch, her gun raised.

"No, Frank, I'm fine. But I think he's been hit."

Frank pointed his flashlight at the man. "Looks like you broke his leg. Hands on your head, mister." The man's hands stayed on his crotch.

"He had a knife, Frank," she warned.

Sweeping the beam of light across the ground, Frank located the knife well out of the wounded man's reach. After looking him over carefully, Frank put his gun away. Flashlight tucked under one arm, he put on a pair of latex gloves. From his belt he pulled a pair of handcuffs, and then reached down. "Easy fellah," he said, soothingly, "let me take a look at that."

He slapped on the cuffs in one smooth motion, and then searched the man quickly. Frank found a wallet, took out the driver's license and read, "Earl Dobbs, Seattle."

Gloves off, Frank pulled a handkerchief from his pocket. "Here, put direct pressure on it with this," he said, offering the handkerchief. "It'll stop the bleeding."

Earl took the handkerchief and pressed it between his legs. Sirens could be heard in the distance. "Would you mind telling me what this is all about?" said Frank. The crevasses on his face looked bottomless in the dim light.

"Well ... I ... I think I've just captured the Cascade Killer."

"The Lord works in mysterious ways. I think you also castrated the man."

CHAPTER 9

Three weeks later:

JACKEY RETURNED to duty, fully exonerated, after enduring a long mandatory administrative suspension and internal affairs investigation for the shooting of Earl Dobbs. Now, she was fighting another battle to get Dobbs out of the hospital and into lockup. She thought by now the University would be only too happy to get rid of a psychotic murderer, but apparently the main worry was adverse publicity.

Jackey walked around the corner of the hospital hallway just in time to see Dr. Arens disappear into the Cascade Killer's room. She'd been warned about Arens, a prestigious Professor Emeritus and surgeon, a major alumni fund-raiser, dragged out of retirement to handle the press and the police. A well founded worry, since up to now the press had treated everyone like hell.

"I'm here to arrange the transfer," Jackey told the two Seattle policemen that stood guard outside the room.

"Good luck, Jack," said one of the policemen. "Doc just went in, and he didn't look happy."

"He's been in and out all day," said the other.

Jackey entered the room, and immediately knew something had gone wrong. The Cascade Killer was bound to his hospital bed by leather restraints. The man kicked wildly and bellowed: "Gone away ... gone away ... no one knows ... help me go ..."

"Remember me, Earl?" said the doctor, leaning over the bed. "I'm Dr. Arens. I want to help you."

Earl sneezed violently. Foamy saliva poured out of his mouth and nose. He struggled against the arm and leg restraints.

"You ... take me away ... go back home ... home ... now ..."

Arens took Earl's blood pressure. The doctor's hands, covered with age spots, trembled slightly. Earl wept, and then yawned, his red face drenched in sweat. A wave of muscle spasm traversed his abdomen, and he screamed in pain. Arens examined Earl's abdomen, his skin looked like a plucked turkey. Using a reflex hammer, Arens struck Earl's kneecaps, eliciting a brisk response.

"How's he doing, doctor?" Jackey asked.

"Obviously, terrible," said Arens, wrinkling his bald forehead. "His blood pressure is 210, systolic. His heart rate is 160, and irregular. The antibiotics haven't touched his fever. His reflexes are hyperactive. Clonidine and methadone haven't helped. His electrolytes are unbalanced. He's acidotic. To put it bluntly, he's a mess, and getting worse." Arens frowned and shook his head. A nurse entered the room. "Call ICU," he said to the nurse, "I'm going to transfer him down." She acknowledged with a nod, and hurried out of the room. Arens and Jackey followed her.

At the least, Jackey felt entitled to an explanation. She stood in Arens' path. "Dammit," she said, "it's taken years to find this maniac. I want to transfer him to Walla Walla as soon as possible. You can't keep him in the hospital forever. The DA has a trial to schedule, and the media are pounding on us. The hospital board agreed Dobbs would be transferred today." Nurses and visitors appeared from both ends of the hallway to witness the confrontation.

"Look, young lady," said Arens, "the hallway is not the appropriate place to have this discussion. Let's go to a conference room, please."

Arens led her through the hospital to a door marked: "Rainier Conference Room." Inside, the room was paneled with dark walnut and had plush carpeting. Sixteen heavy, straight backed chairs surrounded a huge, oval shaped table. On one wall hung pictures of past members of the hospital board, all deceased. The opposite wall was cluttered with pictures of former members of the medical staff, also deceased. The third wall contained the door, a telephone, and a brass plaque that read: "This room given in loving memory of Mark and Sarah Gladson."

In place of a fourth wall was a ceiling to floor picture window. Jackey wondered if Mt. Rainier would be visible through the window on a clear day. She would probably never know. It was raining, and the rooftops of the buildings surrounding the hospital appeared gray and indistinct. She pulled out a chair, and sat down at the table. Arens sat opposite her, separated by the wide oak surface.

"First of all, young lady, the hospital board has many other priorities. They dragged me out of a comfortable retirement to handle this case. Publicity is bad enough without policemen spreading rumors in the hallway. If you have any questions, you'll direct them to me. Is that clear?"

"Yes, sir."

"Good. Let me summarize. Transferring Dobbs now could be fatal."

"I don't get it," she said. "He was all recovered from the gunshot wound. That's ancient history. Now, I hear something about drug withdrawal."

The bags underneath Arens' eyes bulged. He rubbed his bald head. "Dobbs is severely anorectic," said Arens. "He hasn't eaten anything for three weeks."

"A hunger strike?"

"No, he's sick."

Jackey clasped her hands on the table. "So, what do you know?"

"When Dobbs first arrived three weeks ago, one of his early problems was drug withdrawal."

"From what drug?"

"I don't know," said Arens. "Initial tests showed amphetamines, but this is not a case of amphetamine withdrawal."

"How can you be sure?"

"Try to understand. Amphetamine withdrawal causes fatigue, prolonged sleep, and depression. Dobbs has been in an excited state for several weeks, more like the withdrawal seen after morphine and heroin."

"What did he take?" she asked. "Some new semi-synthetic, designer drug?"

"No, the timing and severity of symptoms are all wrong for narcotic withdrawal, and he would have responded to treatment." Arens placed his hands on the table and leaned forward, peering over the edge of his half lenses. "All I know for sure is that Earl Dobbs is dying."

The dead hospital board members smiled across the room at the dead medical staff. "Do what you can to save Dobbs," she said, poking her finger in the air after each word. The room filled with loud chirping, and Arens pulled a smartphone from his coat pocket, looked at the display, and frowned.

"Wait a moment," he said, rising from the table. "It's my emergency code." He called back. "Arens, what's the problem? ... I see, thanks ... I'll be there shortly." He hung up the phone. "Dobbs has arrived in the intensive care unit and he doesn't look good. We'd better go."

They left the conference room while an overhead page echoed ominously: "Code 99 ICU, Code 99 ICU." Hurrying through the hospital hallway, Jackey had little doubt the cardiac arrest code was for Earl Dobbs.

At the door of the intensive care unit, two Seattle policemen looked bewildered as

Jackey, Arens, and a dozen people in white coats ran inside. Earl Dobb's room overflowed with people and equipment. At the head of the bed, Paul Powers squeezed a breathing bag and held a plastic mask on Earl's face. A nurse pumped rhythmically on Earl's chest with both of her hands, dripping sweat from her forehead.

Jackey watched as Paul pried open Earl's jaw with a laryngoscope, slipped a tube down his throat, and hooked the tube to a breathing bag. A nurse squeezed the bag as Paul listened with his stethoscope to Earl's chest. "Tube's in," said Paul.

"What happened?" asked Arens.

"I responded to the Code 99," said Paul. He was asystolic when I arrived."

"No heart activity at all? Not even an arrhythmia?"

"Nothing. I gave him epi. I shocked him twice."

"Shock him again."

"There's nothing to shock."

"Do it anyway."

Paul administered the electric shock. It had no effect.

"That's enough," said Arens. "I'm going to call it."

The nurse pumping on Earl's chest stopped. She closed her eyes and panted. At the head of the bed, the other nurse disconnected the breathing bag and bowed her head. She reached for the bed sheet and pulled it over the corpse. Jackey swallowed.

"Cause of death?" asked the nurse.

Arens scratched his head. "Cardiac arrest due to drug withdrawal."

The room emptied fast. Only Arens, Jackey, Paul, and the dead man remained. "Drug withdrawal?" said Paul. "From what drug?"

"None that I could find, young man," said Arens. "But I have to put something on the death certificate."

Paul shook his head. "Drug withdrawal without drugs? That doesn't make sense."

"The man's entire life doesn't make sense," said Jackey. "He was a model citizen until his wife died a few years ago. Must have taken it hard. That's when bodies started showing up."

"The important thing is the Cascade Killer is finally dead," said Paul. "Let's leave the academic debate to the profilers and historians,"

"You're right," Jackey agreed, "but it's a damn shame. I needed Dobbs alive to face the death penalty."

CHAPTER 10

One month later:

JACKEY SHUDDERED, examining the dead woman. She was slashed from ear-to-ear, her body laying in the heart of Waterfront Park, covered only by blood and the early morning drizzle. A circle of policemen, squad cars, and spectators surrounded the scene. A ferryboat whistle hooted, and a flock of seagulls took to the air. Dawn tried desperately to slice through the low cloud cover and the tall buildings to the east.

"Block off the entire area," said Sergeant Frank Roberts "Nobody gets in or out."

"But the businesses ..." a Seattle cop protested.

"Give them all the day off," said Frank, his face like taut leather. "I'm running the Task Force. I've got jurisdiction here."

"All right, we'll block 'em off," said the cop.

A woman approached Jackey. "Deputy McCann, I'm Elizabeth Caldwell with the Seattle Times. Recently, there have been three similar murders in the city. Is this one the work of the same man?"

"The investigation has just begun," Jackey replied, "so I can't say for sure."

"Are you any closer to finding the killer."

Jackey smiled, white teeth showing off her dark tan. She put her right hand on the butt of her Beretta. "We're always getting closer."

"Jack, I need you," said Frank.

"Gotta go," she said, walking away.

The police erected a barrier of wooden sawhorses and yellow ribbons as the crowd grew. She noticed a man behind the police line in a long overcoat with a cowboy hat and sunglasses. Where had she seen him before?

"Get in the Jeep," said Frank.

She did. "I hate reporters," she said.

"Watch what you tell those vultures," he said softly. "Close the door, Jack, and tell me what you think."

She shut the door. "It's authentic in every detail," she said.

"I knew it," said Frank, "but I wanted to hear it from you. How come that Dobbs bastard dies over a month ago, and now he's out killing again?"

"Yes. That's the spooky part." Jackey scratched her head. "Unbelievable. It's stuff we never released. The facial slashes, the exact knife, the head trauma."

"That stuff leaks. I've got someone tracking the data, but it doesn't look promising."

"Frank, what if ..."

He held up his hand. "Don't say it. Someone on the inside, from the Task Force? OK. I'll consider it, I'll check it out, quietly."

"Maybe we're going about it all wrong," she said.

"I'm listening."

"Maybe we need to examine what this killer does that's different. It's not just teenage prostitutes and run-a-ways he's after. The first three women were solid citizens, and they disappeared from all over the city, one a week at the present rate."

Frank nodded. "We know he's full of energy. Kills them somewhere else and dumps them in City parks. At least we find the bodies before they rot."

"That's the problem," she said, "the high visibility. The media loves it. We've got a publicity minded killer on our hands."

"So, what do you suggest, huh?" he asked, with a smirk on his face. "A talk show appearance? An advertising campaign?"

"Why the hell not? At least admit we're hunting for a copycat of the Cascade Killer. They're going to find out, sooner or later."

Frank sighed. "You're right. I'll call a press conference.

CHAPTER 11

PAUL'S CELL PHONE SQUEALED, but he was already running. The text had been preceded by a call from the emergency room to the operating area requesting an anesthesiologist. Someone had been stabbed, that was all he knew. He arrived breathless.

"Trauma room one," said Wendy, the secretary, smiling, her braces sparkling.

Paul didn't need directions. A crowd overflowed from the main trauma room. He saw Christine's slender figure slipping through the door, disappearing from sight. Some of the personnel gathered around the door yielded when they saw his face, but others he jostled out of the way.

A young woman lay on the gurney, her face hidden by long blond hair covered with blood. She was receiving heart massage, a burly nurse pumping hard on the girl's chest.

The heart monitor displayed a straight line. An intern attempted to hold pressure against the bleeding neck wound, but blood spurted between his fingers each time the nurse pumped. From within the clump of bloody blond hair poked a breathing tube, and a respiratory therapist squeezed the attached bag full of oxygen.

"What happened?" Paul asked.

"It's a suicide," said the burly nurse. "Young girl slit her wrists and stabbed herself in the neck."

"That's a tough way to kill yourself," said Paul.

"I suppose so," the nurse admitted.

Four plastic tubes dangled from bags of salt water on the ceiling and ended in the veins of the victim. The fluid poured in rapidly. Her wrists were wrapped with tight bandages. "Looks like you have enough lines," he said. "Is blood coming?"

"On the way," said the nurse.

He listened to the girl's chest with a stethoscope. "Good breath sounds on both sides." Christine stood next to him, and he spoke to her quietly. "What more can we do?" She shook her head.

She walked to the head of the gurney and put on a pair of gloves. Parting the bloody blond hair uncovered a face criss-crossed with ugly scars.

Paul froze. "Ever get the feeling you've been here before?"

"You knew her?" asked the nurse.

"She was my patient, more than once," he said. "Jenny Walker."

"Jenny survived a rape by the Cascade Killer, about six months ago," said Christine. "I'm going to check her pupils." She pried open the right eyelid and shone in a penlight. "The right pupil is fixed and dilated." Standing directly over Jenny's head, Christine looked into the eye. "Dr. Powers, what do you make of this?"

He leaned over. The center of the eye appeared to be a black void, except for an odd red glow coming from deep within. He stroked his mustache. "Some kind of red reflex? Room light reflecting off the retina? It gives me the creeps."

"Yes," she said, "undoubtedly it's a red reflex, but an unusual one." She checked the left eye. "Left pupil is also fixed."

"How long has she been pulseless?" he asked.

"Over thirty minutes," a paramedic in the corner shouted.

"I'm going to call it, unless anybody has an objection," Paul said. Nobody spoke. He thought it ironic Jenny had survived a brutal rape, only to take her own life. The physical and mental changes must have overwhelmed her. "Go ahead and stop the CPR," he told the burly nurse. Sweat ran off her face. "The girl's heart has been empty for half an hour. Cardiac compression doesn't work with an empty heart, there's nothing to pump." She stopped pumping, and the respiratory therapist disconnected the breathing bag. The room cleared quickly, he left with Christine and the burly nurse.

"What should I put on the death certificate?" asked the nurse, trying to catch her breath.

"Primary cause: suicide," said Paul. "Secondary: acute psychotic attack. And tertiary cause: post traumatic stress disorder."

"Good enough," said the nurse.

"The Cascade Killer reaches out from the grave to kill," he said. "But with Jenny's death, the saga ends."

"Not so," Christine said. "The Killer's on the news again. There have been four more murders."

"Impossible, I watched him die in the ICU."

"It's not the same man. They're calling the new murderer the City Park Killer. He's a copycat."

The nurse shook her head. "Doesn't surprise me. City's full of weird people." She walked away.

"Dr. Mason," said Wendy, the secretary. "I have a message for you." She handed Christine an envelope and returned to her station. "Dr. Mason" was typed on the envelope. Chris ripped the envelope open and pulled out a folded piece of paper. She unfolded it. Her eyes darted back and forth. The color drained from her face until only two spots of rose colored rouge remained.

"Bad news?" he asked.

"City's full of weird people," she said, handing him the paper, hand trembling.

He looked at the message. It was comprised of letters cut from a magazine and pasted on the page. He read: "You have ruined my life. Help me or you will pay with yours."

"Someone's idea of bad joke?" he asked, handing the paper back.

"I don't think so."

"You want to talk about it?"

"Meet me in the cafeteria in ten minutes."

He nodded. Christine hurried from the emergency room, and he wondered who would want to kill her. He remembered testifying to the medical review board about Rupp's drunken behavior, before he was expelled from the residency program. Rupp had to be responsible for the threats. But was he capable of murder?

Outside the emergency room, Paul collided with Marilyn Walker. She was dressed in the same black outfit he'd seen her wearing two months ago. Bill was nowhere in sight. Marilyn clung to his arms.

"Ms. Walker, I'm ..."

"Don't say it," she begged, "Don't say you're sorry."

She looked up at him. It was the first time he had seen her without tears in her eyes. "The evil died, it had to die," she said. "Jenny killed it. It was the only way. It's all over now."

She was delirious. He didn't know what to do. "Where's Bill?"

"Bill never understood."

"Never understood what?"

"Evil never rests."

Her eyes rolled back into her head, and she collapsed like a rag doll in his arms. He dragged her through the hallway to the emergency room entrance. The double doors opened.

"Jesus, what now?" said the burly nurse. She helped him drag the limp body into the emergency room. "Get me a cart," she shouted to the secretary.

The secretary jumped up and ran, returning with an empty gurney. The staff hoisted Marilyn onto the gurney, took her to the trauma room, and put her in the second slot. A curtain separated her from her dead daughter.

"That's her daughter," he said, pointing at the curtain. "The mother's name is Marilyn Walker. She's understandably distraught. I think she just passed out."

She started to move and moan.

"What would you like us to do with her?" asked the nurse.

"Have the chaplain see her first, then get a psychiatric consult."

The nurse nodded. "Anything else?"

"Yeah, get her out of this room."

He once again left the emergency room, and hurried to the cafeteria, reviewing the day's events. Jenny was dead on arrival, a suicide. Marilyn had gone berserk and passed out in his arms, and Christine was receiving death threats. What else could happen today?

Located on the ground floor, the cafeteria's dirty, off white walls gave way to a long stainless steel countertop. Several fat, mean looking cooks wearing white aprons stained with grease, scurried in and out of the kitchen, putting food away. Lunch had almost ended, so the selection was limited.

Christine waited in the center of the room, next to a hexagonal fish tank that stood on top of an oak pedestal. Steam rose from a cup on the table in front of her. She held it in both hands, drumming her fingers against the sides. The fish tank was the only pleasant feature of the room. As Paul approached, he realized the tank looked much cleaner than the cafeteria. "Hello, I was detained."

"What happened?"

"Jenny's mother passed out on me. I had to carry her into the ER."

"How is she?"

"She'll be OK. I'm going to get some coffee and something to eat. Can I get you a Danish or a hot dog?"

"I don't eat sausage or junk food," she said.

"You must be from Tibet, then."

She smiled. "How about wheat toast?"

"Yech."

He returned with coffee, a hot dog, and two pieces of wheat toast, and set the toast in front of her. Then he sat and emptied a packet of mustard onto the hot dog.

"It's Rupp, isn't it?"

She hunched over the table, inches from his face. He smelled the intoxicating rose scent of her perfume and studied the perfect curves of her lips. A blue fish swam along the front of the tank, periodically turning and puckering its lips.

"I don't know," Christine said quietly. "I can't be sure."

"This wasn't the first threat, was it?"

"No. Ever since I kicked Rupp out, I've been bombarded with threatening notes, letters, and phone calls. Whoever it is, he knows everything about me, but I have no idea what he wants."

He swallowed a bite and drank half the coffee in one gulp. An angel fish swam to the front of the tank and hovered.

"Have you told the police?"

"Yes. The calls are from a cellular phone that can't be traced. There's nothing they can do without proof."

"Is Rupp still around?"

"I haven't seen him. But the police say he's still in the area. They picked him up once for speeding, on a motorcycle. He was drunk. I'm afraid to go home at night."

"Do you think he's a killer?"

"I don't know."

He finished his hot dog and coffee, and wiped mustard from his mustache with a paper napkin. For the first time, he saw worry lines in Christine's forehead. A large catfish darted to the front of the tank, long whiskers trailing from its face. The startled angel fish swam away. The catfish attached to the glass by sucking with its mouth.

"You haven't touched your food."

"I'm sick of this cafeteria." she pushed the toast away and stared at her coffee.

He sat back in the black, plastic chair. "Would you like to get some real food?"

She looked up, eyes bright. "When?"

"Tonight? Dinner?"

Her perfect lips smiled. "Where?"

"You name the place."

"The Metropolitan Grill."

"The best. Let's do it."

She pulled a notepad from her pocket, wrote on one page, and then ripped it out. "That's my address and phone number. Pick me up at seven. I've got to go." She left the cafeteria.

He couldn't believe it. He had a date with Christine Mason. The day was full of surprises, and it wasn't over. He drained the remaining coffee too fast, the last drop carrying along with it a slurry of bitter grinds.

CHAPTER 12

CHRISTINE'S APARTMENT NESTLED in the heart of the University district, just off 43rd Street. It took Paul ten minutes to find a parking spot, and he had to walk several blocks back to her building. Instead of arriving early, he would now be late. So much for first impressions.

The streets bustled with young, eager college students walking, biking, and roller-blading. Numerous couples, infatuated with each other, wandered aimlessly. In the small cafes, bakeries, and coffee shops, students pondered homework while washing down vegetarian sandwiches with expresso.

The entire college scene had passed Paul by, devoured by his all consuming struggle to get into medical school. Walking through the University district reminded him college was supposed to be fun, and he felt regret.

He got his first close look at Christine's apartment building. Grey cement covered the four story modern structure, set back ten feet from the sidewalk. In groups of four, sliding windows trimmed in aluminum interrupted the bland cement, an architectural style he'd often referred to as Early American Box. From the looks of the building, he imagined it contained ten or fifteen apartments on each floor.

Opening a glass door, he stepped into an entryway. Built in mailboxes lined the walls on either side of the vestibule. A steel door faced him, with a sign that said: "SHUT TIGHTLY TO LOCK." Below each mailbox he discovered a white button, and he pressed Christine's. The door buzzed. He opened it and passed through, pulling the door shut behind him. An elevator took him to the third floor.

At a quarter past seven, he arrived, stopping in the hallway in front of Christine's door to straighten his tie. In one hand he held a gift, wrapped in black paper speckled with silver and tied with a white bow. Dinner at the Metropolitan Grill meant she preferred a formal first date. Protocol was high on her list of virtues.

He looked down at his suit. The floral arrangement of his silk necktie was laced with a flowing gold thread. The gray suit was more appropriate for a job interview than a first date.

After a final deep breath, he knocked on the apartment door. It swung open, and his jaw dropped. He couldn't believe his eyes. Christine stood in the doorway wearing a white bathrobe and a blue towel wrapped around her head. Water droplets beaded on her face, red from a recent scrubbing. Her feet were bare except for an old Band-Aid around her left big toe.

"Yes," she said, smiling. "It's the real me. I got back late."

"Maybe I should walk around the block or something."

"Don't be silly. Come on in. I'll hit the shower."

She disappeared into the bathroom. He entered the apartment and heard the shower running. The living room had a large couch in beige leather behind a heavy oak coffee table. Two matching end tables and a love seat completed the set. On the far end table stood a marble statue, with a three foot tall pair of slender arms and cupped hands that reached upwards. Paul liked the many green plants, and the highly polished hardwood floor looked clean enough to eat on.

On the wall behind the couch hung an oil reproduction of Renoir's "The Night Watch."

Along the wall facing the couch stood an open cabinet made of bleached oak, containing audio-video equipment and bookshelves. Surgery and neurosurgery textbooks made up the bulk of the collection. A TV and DVR occupied a position in the center of the cabinet alongside a stereo system containing a DVD player. On top of the DVD player was a copy of "Casablanca." Next to the stereo were six drawers of DVD's and CD's labeled A to Z.

He flipped through the first drawer and found all classical music. It made sense, Christine was the classical music type. Walking over to the bathroom door, he listened. The shower had stopped, so he knocked gently.

"Yes," said a muffled voice.

"Do you have any rock music? Or maybe an ipod?"

"Look under R."

He heard a giggle. Searching under R, he found Rachmaninoff, Symphony Number Two. He laughed and put on the CD. The orchestra softly entered the room. He sat on the couch, his nostrils flaring from the tangy smell of leather. A white and orange cat climbed onto his lap, meowing, and her rough tongue licked his hand.

"Hello, little girl. Where did you come from?" He ran his fingers through the soft fur.

A patch of black fur surrounded the cat's left eye and made her appear to be winking. She walked in circles on his lap, then curled up and fell asleep. He closed his eyes and dozed. During the soothing Rachmaninoff symphony, he heard a noise and opened his eyes.

Christine stood in the bathroom doorway, a cloud of water vapor escaping around her. A pink towel covered her head like a turban, her face fresh and moist. She tied the belt of her bathrobe tightly and walked to the living room.

"I see you've met Peaches."

"We've been sleeping together," he said, stroking the cat.

"Oh, really?" Christine walked to one of the end tables, to a telephone and answering machine. Pushing a button, she started the playback. "I'd like you to hear this."

"Hello, Chris," said a mechanical male voice. "I want my life back. Don't hold out on me, or I'll slit your pretty throat."

The machine beeped. "Six-forty-six-PM," it said.

"Just before I arrived," said Paul. "The caller's voice has been electronically altered."

"I know." Christine sighed. "He leaves me a message almost every day. The police say there's no way to reconstruct the voice."

"Are you scared?"

"Of course I'm scared. This isn't the City Park Killer, murdering at random. This is personal. It's like some great evil has invaded my life. And evil never rests."

"That's what Marilyn Walker said."

"Today?"

"Just before she collapsed in my arms."

Christine sat next to him, and he took a deep breath. Radiant heat spread throughout his body, carried by a clean scent better than any perfume.

"You're upset by Jenny's death, aren't you?" said Christine.

"She's like a ghost that keeps haunting me."

Christine shook her head. "I don't understand."

"I've seen pictures of Jenny from before the attack. She was beautiful. Reminded me of my younger sister, hopelessly withdrawn after living through a brutal rape."

"I'm sorry."

"Jenny's resuscitation and the Walkers' grief, reminded me of everything unjust, unkind, and evil in the world."

"But it didn't end there," she said. "You were involved in the police investigation. I remember Marilyn Walker chanting about the evil in Jenny. And you watched the Cascade Killer die in the ICU."

"Yes. And four months after the rape, Jenny returned for an abortion."

"An abortion?" Christine covered her mouth with both hands. "The Killer's baby?"

"Right." He nodded. "Jenny was psychotic. And her parents weren't much better."

"You gave the anesthetic?"

"Her father requested me. He wanted me to help her."

"How? With the anesthesia?"

"I don't know. His expectations were unreasonable." He shuddered. "The abortion turned my stomach. And ..." He stroked his mustache.

"And what?"

"Melvin showed up to collect the fetus."

"So?"

"So, the next day I watched you transplant fetal tissue into Joe Tyce's brain."

Christine took his hands. "I had no idea the transplant tissue came from Jenny Walker's fetus. Does it matter?"

"What if Marilyn Walker was right? What if there was evil in Jenny?"

"That's not very scientific," said Christine. "But Jenny did have the strangest look in her eyes."

"Yes. I saw it, too."

"What's the difference?" she said. "Jenny's dead."

"True. But what's become of Joe Tyce?"

Christine's eyes looked unfocused.

"What is it?" he said, shaking her gently back to reality.

"Joe Tyce never returned for his follow-up visit. He didn't have a telephone number, so I sent a letter. We don't have the resources to track down patients."

"And now," he added, "there's a copycat killer terrorizing the city."

"That's crazy. You don't think the transplant could have turned Joe Tyce into a killer? Do you?"

"I don't know if that's possible. But I'd sure like to find out. Who would I ask?"

"Professor Arens might know," she said. "He's read everything."

"I'll ask him, tomorrow. And I'll pay a visit to Joe, or his girlfriend. I'd like to get him back to you for a follow-up examination."

She held out her hand. "I'll help you with your ghost, if you help me with mine."

He shook her hand. "It's a deal. Let's start by lightening up." He gave her the gift.

"Thank you. You really shouldn't ..."

She tore off the wrapping paper, lifted the top off the box, and peered inside. She reached into the box, pulled out a sausage shaped object over half a foot long, and dangled it in front of his face.

"What is this?" She rolled her eyes.

He smiled. "That's the finest Italian salami Pike's Place Market has to offer. You'll love it."

"I'd rather die."

"I eat them all the time, and I'm not dead, yet."

She put the salami to her nose, sniffed and squinted. "I'll treasure it always." Holding the salami by one end, like a dead rat, she swung it away at arm's length and set it on the coffee table. "Why did you ever become an anesthesiologist?"

"Lucky, I guess. Dad was a pilot, anesthesia is similar. I take off, I cruise, and I land. But unlike dad, I have only one passenger and my feet stay on the ground. And why neurosurgery? You must be from a medical family."

"I am. Dad's a busy surgeon and I'm his only."

"So he pushed you to be the best, and here you are."

"It's getting late," she said. "I'd better get dressed."

He reached up and untucked one corner of her pink turban. The towel unraveled and fell into her lap, bringing with it a wave of silky, auburn hair that covered her face and stopped just below her shoulders. He smoothed the hair away from her face. She took his hand and pressed it against her warm cheek.

"Maybe dinner out is not the best plan," he said. "What would you say if I ordered a pizza."

She kissed his hand. "With lots of sausage?"

"Lots."

"I'd say you're corrupting me."

"I like that idea."

"And what would we do while we're waiting?"

"We could study anatomy," he said, tracing the edges of her lips, with his finger.

"I'm a neurosurgeon. I know my anatomy."

He slipped his hand beneath her robe and stroked her nipples. They were hard. "But I don't know your anatomy." His hand moved lower, following the curve of her abdomen, and coming to rest between her thighs. "And some structures are so far from the brain that you may need a refresher."

She put her arms around him and pulled him closer. They explored each other with pressed lips and groping tongues. The tempo of the symphony quickened. Peaches purred.

CHAPTER 13

PAUL AWOKE with Peaches' furry warmth against his bare back. As he rolled onto his stomach, she said, "Meow," raising one ear. Chris had left for work, and sunlight penetrated the window blinds, covering Peaches with a narrow beam. "Well, good morning girl. You found the sun." Paul arose and knelt on the edge of the bed, Peaches scurrying from the room. Parting the window blinds, he looked at the city. It was one of those rare late winter days in Seattle when the clouds briefly parted. To enjoy the sunshine, he'd have to hurry.

Calling in an old favor, he'd arranged for Dr. Beck, the other senior anesthesia resident, to work an extra shift. Paul dressed quickly, spurred on by the smell of hot coffee drifting in. He followed it to a fresh pot on the kitchen counter. On the glass cafe table, a plate with two uneaten pizza crusts sat next to a mug of cold coffee. In the refrigerator, he found the Italian salami, the grease stained pizza box, and a note: "Had pizza for breakfast. You've ruined me. Save the salami for me. Lov."

He ate a breakfast of coffee and microwaved pizza, thinking about Chris and their passionate lovemaking. Ten months had past since his break-up with Anne, and he continued to blame himself for the failure of their marriage. If he'd only spent more quality time with her, they'd still be together. Determined not to make the same mistake with Chris, he'd suggested last night that they schedule a fun week off together, and she'd agreed. But he wondered if he was ready to take on a new emotional commitment.

Chris had opened up to him and shared her fears. Her quiet nobility was totally different from Anne's uninhibited vigor. Behind Christine's conservative professional image, he'd discovered her vulnerability and her desire to explore life.

Peaches crunched noisily on dry cat food and lapped at a water dish. After leaping onto the table, she stayed until he finished breakfast. Then he walked from Christine's apartment toward the University campus, hoping to find Arens. According to Chris, Arens spent lots of time reading in the Stacks, the old library, on the top floor. After passing the Hub, the University center, Paul paused to watch benches and lawns full of lounging students, heads raised to the sky, worshipping the sun. He sighed and moved on.

He followed red brick walkways to the far end of the University, and the Stacks came into view. One of the oldest buildings on campus, the Stacks was also the most majestic. It's twin towers rose high above the main four floors. On each tower, elaborate Gothic columns, connected at the top by stone arches, supported the dome. The towers had been constructed in two sections, one stacked upon the other. A stone griffin perched on a pedestal jutted out from between the two sections of the East tower. The odd creature faced toward the center of the building.

The building walls consisted of large, tan colored stones, of varying sizes, intermixed with tiny, uniform bricks, like tiles. Lacy, stone ovals, and short posts, like arrows, surrounded elongated, stained glass windows. Cherubs and gargoyles hung from the walls, and ivy climbed up in thick, broken sheets, reaching into the towers.

A long row of wide stone steps led to square columns at the front of the building. Huge flying buttresses between the columns supported a high entryway. Under the arches stood tall doors made of dark wood and small, rectangular windows. Above the doors, a stained glass window depicted an open book with the words: "PER PORTAM AD VERITATEM." Although rusty on Latin, Paul loosely translated the phrase: "Through this door, the truth." The door opened as a student left the building. Paul slipped in before the door shut.

The elegant, hardwood floor resounded with his footsteps. Several portraits of benefactors to the library hung in the lobby, along with a brief directory, a floor plan, and a telephone. The building had an elevator, too, and he pressed the button to avoid climbing four floors. The old elevator creaked as the steel doors opened.

He stepped inside and the doors closed. The yellow Formica panelling was covered with graffiti and riddled with dark, pencil sized holes. At the foot of the walls, moldy, green carpet had peeled away from the floor. Overhead, two acoustical ceiling tiles were missing. Viewing the shaft as the car traveled upward, he saw modern steel supports and old wooden beams. The doors opened.

Except for his footsteps, the top floor of the Stacks was silent. A young student leaned out from behind a bookshelf, took one glance at Paul, and disappeared. Near the elevator door, a carved placard on an old wooden desk said "Circulation Desk." Journals cluttered the desk, covered by a thick layer of dust.

Books lined the walls, and freestanding bookshelves formed several narrow isles. Study carrels appeared like scattered notches carved into the musty bookshelves. Each carrel had a small wooden desk and three walls, like blinders on a horse, used to shut out the world.

The top floor, tiny and remote, was an ideal escape. Paul couldn't study in a place like this, because he felt too isolated. Arens, Paul realized, probably preferred to study in the Stacks for the same reason. One man's forboding isolation was another man's blissful solitude.

Large windows, ceiling to floor, consisted of multiple panes of stained glass. On one window, Paul recognized the giving of the ten commandments to Moses. A different biblical scene on each window glowed from the tiny bit of light filtering through the dark glass. Metal light fixtures hung in rows from a high ceiling and ended at the eight foot level, providing barely adequate illumination.

He rounded each corner, peeking into the study carrels. A startled student in one carrel acted as if the last sanctuary on earth had been invaded. "Sorry," Paul said, moving on. At the end of the last row of bookshelves, he peered over the back wall of a study carrel at a bald head bowed over a thick text. "Dr. Arens?"

The head rose slowly and the man sat back, his face more wrinkled than Paul remembered. A pair of black, half-lens glasses clung precariously to the tip of Arens' bulbous nose. A crooked index finger pushed the bridge of the glasses upward, making the blotchy nose look larger. "Yes, young man. What is it?"

Paul leaned over the wall of the study carrel. "I'm Dr. Paul Powers. I've heard you lecture, and we met a few months ago in the ICU."

Arens snorted. "What of it?"

"I've some questions on theoretical neurophysiology. I thought you might have answers."

"What kind of a doctor are you?"

"An anesthesiologist."

"On staff?"

"Resident."

Arens scratched his cheek with two fingers. "I see. I see." He pulled his chair out and stood, just a bit taller than the wall of the study carrel. After turning his chair around, he sat, waving at a nearby chair. "Grab a chair, my boy. Sit. And call me Professor from now on."

Paul walked around the study carrel, pulled up the chair and sat, facing Arens.

"Science," Arens said, in a melodious voice, "is like a door that opens to reveal yet another door." Paul nodded. "Neurophysiology, did you say? I ought to know something. I'm a physiologist as well as a surgeon. What's your question?"

"Is there any experimental evidence that behavioral changes can result from neural transplantation?"

Arens sat back and huffed. "Quite a question, son. Passing along learned responses by transplanting nerve tissue has been attempted with limited success in lower life forms. Flatworms, for example."

"How about humans?"

"Humans?" Arens mouth opened, but nothing more came out. He closed it and raised his thick, gray eyebrows.

"Yes, humans."

Arens shut his eyes for a few moments, as if consulting the heavens. "Neural transplantation in humans is very new. There's an experimental program underway at the University."

"I know," said Paul. "I'm involved in the program. That's why I'm here. One of the transplant patients is missing."

"And his behavior has been altered?"

"I don't know, but the tissue came from a fetus conceived during a violent rape by a serial killer."

"A Parkinson implant?"

"Yes. And there's a copycat killer loose in the city. In theory, could there be any connection?"

The black glasses slid slowly down Arens' nose. "The fetal tissue contains a murderer's genetic material. And predisposition to violence can be genetic, caused by unbalanced neurotransmission."

"In the brain?"

"Certainly, where else? The active fetal tissue implant could conceivably alter brain chemistry to make violent behavior more likely."

"Thank you, Professor. You've answered my question."

"Well, my boy. What now? The police?"

"Do you think they'd believe me?"

"Hardly. I wouldn't."

"I'm going to try locating the missing patient through his girlfriend."

"Be careful, son. If your theory is correct, you may be in danger."

"Thanks," said Paul, but he wouldn't let the potential danger keep him from following up on his hunch. If you needed surgery, then you had to take the anesthetic. To accomplish anything in life meant accepting risk.

"Let me know, son, if I can help you further."

"Thanks again, Professor."

Arens smiled. Shifting the chair around, he returned to his textbook, and Paul headed for the elevator. Helpful, well read, and brilliant, Professor Arens had time to listen. Chris was right. Arens represented the best example of what retirement could do for human nature.

The elevator crept to the lobby. Paul called the medical records department at the University. The clerk read Joe Tyce's admitting information from the hospital computer, and provided a local address for Bertha Miller, Joe Tyce's girlfriend. She lived in the Ballard area, and he would have to drive.

He left the Stacks, determined to enjoy the sunshine, but found pouring rain, instead. The lounging sunbathers had fled with the sun, and students ran along the walkways, covering their bowed heads with books. On a bench in front of the Stacks sat a man wearing an overcoat and dark glasses. He slept, head slumped to one side, rain pouring off his cowboy hat.

A low ceiling of clouds hung overhead, and Paul's wool suit soaked up the rain like a sponge. Burying his hands beneath his coat, in the pockets of his pants, he hunched over and ran out from beneath the shelter of the entryway. He followed the walkway to the right, around the Stacks, between the side wall of the building and a low hedge. He stopped, his path blocked by a huge man wearing a black motorcycle helmet and matching leathers. "Excuse me," Paul said, shivering.

A gloved hand swung upwards like a wooden club and connected with the left side of Paul's jaw. He fell to the pavement on his back, blind, rain beating on his face. A hand grabbed his belt, lifting him several feet in the air. "Hey, you there, leave him alone," shouted a voice he'd heard somewhere before.

Suspended in midair, gasping for breath, he finally fell, striking his head on the pavement. Still blind, he heard people running, and a motorcycle starting up and screeching away. Above, a blurry face came into focus, the man in the cowboy hat and dark glasses. "Are you all right?"

"Just dazed. How can I ever thank you?" The man turned. "Wait," said Paul. But the good Samaritan didn't wait for thanks. He left quickly, his long brown overcoat gliding away and fading into the rain like a ghost. Paul sat up, the back of his head throbbing. Pain radiated through his jaw, but he could still move it. Hadn't he met that man somewhere? He couldn't recall.

Cold rain fell in huge sheets and water ran down the front of his fully saturated wool suit. Should he call the police? Spending his precious day off in the police station didn't appeal to him. He doubted the mugger would be caught, anyway. Besides, he had to find Bertha, Joe's girlfriend. Shaking, he stood, his mind made up. He'd change clothes and visit Bertha. To be safe, he'd call the Task Force deputy, Jackey McCann, and ask her to meet him at Bertha's. Jackey knew him, he'd helped her before and she might take his transplant theory seriously.

Sitting alone on the sidewalk in the rain, he couldn't believe he'd been mugged. Seattle had always felt safe, especially in the daytime. He'd read about an increase in violent crimes in the city, but never imagined he'd be a victim. Perhaps he should consider carrying his pistol, which until now had only been used for target practice. He hoped it wouldn't come to that.

CHAPTER 14

AFTER A BRIEF PIT-STOP at his apartment, Paul headed out to find Bertha. His old Toyota pickup hummed down NW Market Street. His fresh, dry clothes raised his spirits. This time he intended to stay dry, so he'd put on a Gortex raincoat. The lump on his head still throbbed despite two Motrin, but his jaw felt better.

After an hour of hunting, he found Bertha's apartment. The address belonged to a four-flat badly in need of repair. At one time, it had probably been a fashionable single family home. Escalating Seattle real estate prices must have forced the owner to chop the building into four units. At the edges of a moss covered asphalt roof, water dripped from plugged rain gutters, fed by fine, unrelenting drizzle. Peels of dirty, yellow paint hung from narrow, wooden siding. Broken screens leaned against a cracked foundation. He hoped the original family had moved to a nicer place.

Jackey McCann had listened politely to the transplant theory and agreed to meet him at Bertha's. He'd been instructed by Jackey to sit in his truck until her arrival, so he parked the truck across the quiet street and waited. After half an hour, he felt restless and began to wonder if Jackey would ever show. He decided it couldn't hurt to take a walk and get a closer look at the outside of the building, so he left the truck and crossed the street.

Wide cement steps led to two doorways, side by side at the head of the stairs. He rechecked the address against a faded number painted in black on the siding of the house. There was still no sign of Jackey McCann, maybe she hadn't believed him. Climbing the steps, he scanned the four doorbells bordering the entrance. The tag below one doorbell read: "J. Tyce, B. Miller."

He rang. The left door opened, and Bertha's broad shoulders filled the doorway. She wore a terry cloth bathrobe and house slippers. Curlers protruded from beneath a plastic shower cap, and the shadow of a black mustache clung to her upper lip. "What do you want," she said, with a voice even deeper than he remembered. Her mustache twitched. "I'm not buyin'." She started to close the door.

"Wait. I'm Dr. Powers, anesthesiologist. Do you remember me?"

She looked him over, squinting. "You kiddin'? I sure do. I remember your bill. You're wastin' your time, I paid it." The door slammed shut.

"No, please," he shouted. "This has nothing to do with the bill. It's about Joe."

She opened the door. "Joe? I didn't know anesthetists made house calls."

"We don't, but this isn't about the anesthetic."

She pulled the top of her robe together and tightened the belt. "Yeah, all right, come in."

"Thanks."

The inside of her first floor apartment depressed him more than the exterior. A sagging couch and torn easy chair filled the tiny living room. In an attempt to add class, a Seattle art festival poster had been stapled to the wall next to gaping holes in the sheet rock. A boom box radio sat on the floor in the corner.

She led him into a greasy kitchen, dishes piled high in the sink. On the stove, a pot of coffee brewed, and it smelled strong. She opened the refrigerator, removed a coffee cake and set it on a small table. A big smile revealed a missing tooth. "Have a seat, doc," she said, gesturing to one of two chairs.

He wondered about Bertha's mental stability. A moment ago, she'd been hostile and slammed the door in his face. Now, she seemed overly friendly, serving him coffee and cake. Part of him wanted to get out of the dismal apartment immediately, but he'd come too far to leave without the information he needed.

After a brief search, and numerous rejects, Bertha located two clean mugs and filled them with coffee. More searching produced clean plates, forks, and a knife, and she gave them each a piece of cake. For a few minutes, they sat in silence enjoying the snack, it tasted surprisingly good.

"What's this about," she asked, "and why are you here."

"As I said, it's about Joe. He didn't show up for his follow-up visit. Dr. Mason and I have been worried about him."

"Don't bother. That's just Joe. As long as he's feelin' good, he won't go near a doctor."

"He improved after surgery?"

"Improved? Hell, it damn near cured him, but he's still a little shaky." Her cheek spasmed, and she massaged her face. He watched a trickle of fluid running down in front of her ear. Was it water or sweat? He couldn't tell.

"Are you all right?"

"Had a tooth pulled yesterday," she said. "Still hurts. I'll be OK."

"Dr. Mason would like to get Joe back for an examination."

"Yeah. I can't help you. He ain't here no more."

"Where can I find him?"

"Ha. Damned if I know. We had a fight and he took off. No tellin' if he's ever comin' back."

"Did he take all his things?"

"Rode his bike out, that's all he's got."

"A motorcycle?"

"No. A Harley." She rose from the table and went to the kitchen counter. From a drawer beneath the counter, she removed an envelope with the logo "Rapid Foto." After flipping through a stack of photographs, she pulled one out and looked it over, smiling. "Here," she said, handing it to him. "That's the bike."

Paul examined the photo. Red enamel flames flowed over the front fender of the motorcycle. Painted on the center of the V-shaped engine, on the round cover over the air cleaner, was the cross section of a tree depicting the many rings typical of massive, old growth, timber. Above the cut log, in a mural on the gas tank, a golden axe glistened, held by strong hands. "I've never seen another motorcycle like this," he said.

"You won't. It's a Heritage Softail. Custom." She pointed at the bike's seat. "All hand made."

Made of studded black leather, the banana shaped seat formed a mountain lion, his powerful haunches rising along the high seat back. Thick claws dug into the cover over the saddlebag, and front legs hugged the bike, in low profile, like a cat ready to pounce. On the top surface of the seat, in the lion's open mouth, fangs dripped studded drops of blood. Off the rear of the bike, the tail of a real mountain lion dangled. Paul thought about the attack this morning and the man in black leather. "You remember the plate?"

"The number? No."

"Does Joe have family?"

"We only have each other."

"Friends?"

"Just me."

"Any bars or other places he might hang out?"

She pounded her fist on the table, rattling the cups and splattering coffee. "Dammit, don't you think I checked. I tell you, he ain't there. He'll come home when he's good and ready."

Paul swallowed the remainder of his cake without chewing and washed it down with a gulp of coffee. "If you see him, please tell him it's important to return to Dr. Mason for an exam."

"Yeah."

He rose. "Thanks for the coffee and cake, it was just what I needed." She followed him and stood in the doorway as he started down the steps.

"Doc." He turned back. "I love him," she said, her eyes glowed red, full of tears. "If you see him, tell him to come back, damn him."

Angry, towering above him on the top step, she looked foreboding. He shuddered, wondering if Joe had won the last fight. "Yes, I'll tell him," said Paul. She closed and locked the door, leaving him on the steps, no closer to finding Joe Tyce.

At the base of the steps, Paul reviewed his options. He could call Jackey again and ask her to find out the license number of Joe's motorcycle. Even without the license number, the motorcycle was unique. Maybe the police could spot the bike and bring Joe in for questioning, if they believed the transplant theory enough to try. There was no law against missing a follow-up doctor's appointment.

Paul left Bertha's apartment and walked around the block to where he wouldn't be overheard. He tried to call Chris, to see if she would help him persuade Jackey to look for

Joe Tyce. First, he called her cell phone, then the operating room. Chris didn't answer her phone and she wasn't in surgery. Over and over, he paged her at the hospital. Finally, he called her apartment and the answering machine picked up, but he didn't leave a message. Instead, he hung up, crossed the street, and returned to his pickup truck. After fishing in his coat pocket for the keys, he reached for the lock.

Something big entered his peripheral vision from above, and he raised an arm to protect his head, still sore from hitting the pavement this morning. A huge figure leaped off the flatbed, knocking Paul to the ground, pinning him, two heavy thighs in blue jeans crushing his chest. He tried screaming, but too late. Thick hands closed around his throat, and no sound came out.

A stocking covered the mugger's head, making it look like a dark globe attached to the collar of a flannel shirt. Paul stabbed the side of the masked head with his keys, aiming for the indistinct outline of an ear. Roaring deeply like a wounded beast, the mugger grabbed Paul's wrist, slamming it against the pavement until the keys fell. Released from the choke hold, Paul sucked in the moist air. Over his head, an enormous knife descended, serrated edges dripping rain like saliva off the teeth of a mad dog. He held up his hands in a futile attempt to stop the blade. "Noooo."

Blood exploded onto his chest and the mugger pitched forward, knife clanking on the road. Paul caught the limp head, shoving it to one side. At the base of the skull, a gaping hole in the stocking oozed blood. With great effort, he rolled the heavy body off and then collapsed. Two tan hands caught him beneath the arms, preventing him from striking the pavement.

"Are you wounded?" Jackey McCann asked.

"No, nothing serious. But I didn't think you'd come, I didn't think you believed me."

"Your transplant theory is pretty far fetched, but I thought I'd check it out. Didn't you realize the danger?"

"Others warned me," he said, rubbing his throat and thinking of Arens. Sirens wailed in the distance. Everything hurt.

Jackey pulled off the mugger's bloody stocking mask. "Who is she?" said Jackey.

"God save us," Paul answered. "She's Bertha Miller, Joe Tyce's girlfriend."

"Your theory makes no sense. Joe Tyce got the transplant. How can his girlfriend be the Killer?"

"It makes perfect sense," Paul said, looking at his bloody hands, "if we're dealing with an infectious disease."

CHAPTER 15

PAUL REFUSED to go to the hospital for treatment, so Jackey took him directly to the police station for a statement. He recounted the story briefly, giving details of the attack, but leaving out his unsubstantiated transplant theory. The statement process tired him. He needed answers, not more questions. At least the police were now looking for Joe Tyce. For the second time in one day, he wondered if carrying his gun in the city might not be a good idea.

After the ordeal, he went home long enough to change clothes, and then returned to the Stacks. He found the top floor deserted, but noticed an old pay phone, a relic he'd missed before. Large and black, it had three silver openings for coins, and a white rotary dial. Lifting the receiver did not produce a dial tone, he was not surprised.

An old University faculty directory dangled against the wall on a chain near the phone. His luck held, and he found the number for Arens' answering service. Using his cell phone he called Arens. The service forwarded the call. Paul heard ringing, echoing like a bad connection, and he wondered where Arens might be. Arens finally picked up and he sounded very far away.

Paul tried to ask some genetic engineering questions, but Arens claimed it wasn't his area of expertise. He referred Paul to Mr. Wetlock, a graduate student who worked for Arens at the Research Center. After thanking Arens for the referral, Paul hung up the phone, pleased that the kind Professor had taken the time to help. Like the old journals in the Stacks, Arens had a wealth of knowledge.

University staff referred to the Research Center as the Hut. A short walk from University Hospital, the Hut rose skyward, square and white, a monument of poured concrete. Over the entrance, on the front of a massive cement awning, gold letters spelled out the name of the building. As Paul walked beneath the awning, a glass entry door slid open automatically.

Inside, a security guard looked up from behind a long, oak desk. Papers and brochures cluttered the desktop, surrounding a telephone and a computer. An abstract oil painting of a DNA molecule hung on the wall. In the picture, two corkscrew shaped strands of bubbles intertwined, forming the classic double helix.

"Who are you here for?" said the guard.

"Mr. Wetlock."

"Oh, him. Fella's always here. And who are you?"

"Dr. Paul Powers." From his coat pocket, he pulled his hospital security card and flashed it at the guard.

"OK, go on up, room 237."

The hallway on the second floor was sterile and white, broken at regular intervals by identical doors. He located door 237 and knocked softly. No one answered, so he tried again, harder this time, but with the same results. Disappointed at finding nobody in, he prepared to leave. The door opened.

Paul had never seen such a tired looking man as the one that stood in the doorway. Bags hung beneath his eyes, dark enough to have come from a bar fight. His frizzy, white hair desperately needed combing, and his wrinkled lab coat had certainly been slept in.

"Yes, yes, what is it? I haven't got all day."

"I'm looking for Mr. Wetlock."

"You've found him. Who sent you? What do you want?" He fidgeted from foot to foot and cracked his knuckles.

"Professor Arens sent me," said Paul, "He's been helping me with a, uh, project and he thought you might have some answers."

"The boss sent you, eh?" He rubbed his hands together. "Then come in, come in, I'll just be a minute." He flitted back into the lab.

Interconnected glassware and tubing, clamped to metal poles, covered a long laboratory workbench. At the back of the lab, ugly white machines covered the wall from top to bottom like a Laundromat. Paul recognized one of the machines as a gene sequencer and another as a 3-D printer. To Paul's right, against the side wall, a blackboard had been filled with equations. Nearby stood a low cot with dirty sheets. Opposite the cot, against the other wall, a coffee pot and several mugs sat on a small table littered with grounds.

Paul pulled up a chair at the coffee table, next to a garbage can overflowing with paper, mostly old donut wrappers. Wetlock leaned over the lab workbench, inspecting a flask with a bubbling blue fluid, adjusting the burner flame. He pulled a calculator from the pocket of his lab coat and punched the keys without mercy, scribbling the tally in a notebook and then chewing on his pen. Ten minutes passed.

"Mr. Wetlock?"

He jumped. "What? Oh, Dr.? Your name is?"

"Powers, Paul Powers."

"Yes, of course. Dr. Powers, you're so quiet, I forgot about you. Sorry." He set down the flask and joined Paul by the coffee table. "Would you like some coffee?" Paul nodded. Wetlock poured a cup of steaming coffee, handed it to Paul, and then filled another mug that bore the stains of long use and little cleaning.

Picking up a crumpled napkin, Wetlock unwrapped a chunk of donut, popped it into his mouth, and swallowed it like a pill. "Sorry, last one. Now, what can I help you with?"

"Genetic engineering."

"Excellent. My specialty. What's the question?"

"Bacteria and viruses have been used to alter genetic traits, to produce physical changes in plants and animals."

"Yes, and someday soon, in humans," said Wetlock. "So?"

"So, has anyone tried altering behavioral traits with a bacteria or a virus, and could such a process happen naturally?"

"Ah, a good question. But for the answer, we'll need to go to the animal lab." He pulled at the short curls on his head. "If I could only remember where I put my access card. Give me a minute, I'll find it."

Wetlock led Paul to an unmarked metal door on the fifth floor. A control station, like an ATM machine, protruded from the wall alongside the door. After looking both ways down the corridor, Wetlock inserted a plastic card and typed a code number into the control station. A few seconds later, the doorknob produced a dissonant buzz, and a screen on the control station flashed: "ACCESS GRANTED." With a turn of the doorknob, the two men entered.

A crowd of graduate students huddled around a microscope drinking champagne. "What's the party for?" said Paul, as a student handed him a glass. In the student's other hand a white rat struggled with its hind legs to kick a tiny, cone shaped, paper hat off its head.

"See for yourself. It worked," said the student.

Paul pushed his way to the microscope, and peered at the slide. A blood smear showed a preponderance of large, immature white blood cells, and a noticeable lack of red blood cells.

"That's a sick rat," said Paul. "I'd say its got leukemia, so what?"

The student spoke to the rat, "Did you hear that, Morris? What does he know? Imagine the abstract in *Cancer:* Common Levels of Electromagnetic Radiation, in the Presence of Enzyme Inducers, Produce a High Incidence of Leukemia in Sprague-Dawley Rats. Ah, wonderful."

Wetlock shrugged, "Another drunk bunch of research jockeys."

"Wetlock, you ass," said the student, "Go drink champagne and bask under high voltage lines. We don't care. Do we Morris?"

"This way, Dr. Powers." said Wetlock, his arm outstretched.

Climate controlled, glass enclosed kennels lined the perimeter of the lab. Stacks of cages rose against the wall, up to the ceiling, like boxes in a shoe store. Creatures of every size and description filled the boxes, but Paul could only name a few. He saw rats, mice, hamsters, dogs, and monkeys. The smell of urine and excrement nearly overwhelmed him. Another smell troubled him, too. It was thick and acidic, almost bitter. He'd smelt it before, but couldn't remember what it was or where he'd encountered it.

A criss-crossing array of black laboratory tables filled the enormous central area of the complex. The workbenches interconnected, making passage across the lab possible only at the extreme ends of the long room. "The arrangement of the lab bench makes it easier to deal with run-a-ways," Wetlock explained.

"Makes sense," said Paul. "But why the security door?"

"Ah, we can't have the animal rights people opening the kennels, oh no, or the press interviewing us for *60 minutes.*"

Paul strolled by the lab table, browsing through a shop of horrors. A disembodied cat head clamped in a vice had its eyes sewn open and electrodes protruded from its exposed brain. A pulsating light flickered on the cat's eyes, and the red hot stylus of a chart recorder clicked and whirred. A pregnant ewe, supported by a rack, had been slit open, exposing a living fetus within. A tangled mass of wires and tubes dangled from her gut, like the guide ropes of a helium balloon in a parade. The partially dissected remains of a squid quivered on the table. He suddenly recognized the troubling smell. It was the stench of death.

"Here's what you came to see," said Wetlock, as he led Paul into a monkey kennel. "Where did I put those keys?" He searched his pockets. "Ah, here we are." A glass door opened into an outer workstation containing a file cabinet, and a desktop computer. A glass wall separated the workstation from a small laboratory containing monkey cages and other equipment. A red sign on the door of the inner lab warned "SECRETION PRECAUTIONS REQUIRED."

"Dr. Powers, I'd like you to meet Poco." Wetlock pointed to a large monkey in a small cage. Poco walked on his knuckles, pacing, his long arms dragging. "Here, put these on." Wetlock handed Paul protective gear: a white jump suit with a hood, gloves, and a bulky filtered mask that protected his eyes and mouth. "There's a microphone in the mask so I can hear you," said Wetlock, clipping a small microphone to his lab coat.

With the gear on, Paul entered the inner lab and approached the cage. Breathing through the mask required extra effort. He guessed Poco stood about four feet tall and weighed at least 110 pounds. The monkey went wild, jumping and hooting. Wetlock's voice came from a speaker on the wall. "Bow your head," said Wetlock. "Show him you're submissive."

Paul bowed and the monkey quieted. After a few moments of silence, Paul raised his head. Upright, the monkey held on to the bars at the front of the cage like a human in prison. His small nostrils flared, and the eyes in his sunken face glowed an eerie red. Saliva fouled his greasy brown beard. He reached through the bars, fingers trembling, and then he spit, hitting the clear plastic faceplate on Paul's mask. "Shit! Nice monkey!" said Paul, backing away, out of reach of the next volley. "Did you teach him that?"

"No, I didn't. And he's not a monkey, he's a chimpanzee, and he's been mean for as long as we've had him. Very short tempered." At the front of the cage, Poco swayed from side to side, grunting and panting.

"I hope you're not doing AIDS research."

"In fact, that's exactly what I'm doing," Wetlock said. "Chimpanzees are ideal for AIDS research because they can carry the AIDS virus, but don't get the disease. I'm working on a research grant from the National Institute of Health, investigating drug resistant viruses."

"Drug resistant viruses?" Paul echoed.

"Yes, and I'm using the AIDS virus as my model."

"Why AIDS?"

Wetlock smiled. "The money. There's a separate allotment for AIDS research, and I wanted a piece of it. Besides, few viruses have been as well studied as the AIDS virus."

"Are there any drug resistant AIDS viruses?" Paul asked.

"Yes, but very little is known about drug resistant viruses. We're in the same situation with viruses as we were fifty years ago, with bacteria. Do you understand?"

Paul nodded. "You're referring to the overuse of early antibiotics against bacteria. The drugs worked like magic, until, of course, drug resistant bacteria began to emerge. Now, we keep needing better antibiotics."

"Precisely," Wetlock agreed. "The strongest bacteria learned new skills to survive, such as producing enzymes to break down penicillin."

"Darwin was right," said Paul.

"Yes," said Wetlock, "but Darwin studied natural selection. I'm afraid we live in a very unnatural world. Our efforts to control nature with technology actually propel evolution forward."

"I understand. The principal of survival of the fittest is blind. It doesn't care whether the environmental pressures are natural, or man made."

"Correct! As resistant viruses appear, we'll have to develop better antiviral drugs. My goal is to develop drug resistant viruses in an animal model."

Paul felt sweaty in the jumpsuit. "You're trying to speed up evolution in the lab, to create drug resistant viruses and determine what new antiviral drugs will be needed."

"Exactly."

"But where does genetic engineering come in? That's my interest."

"Hang on, I'm getting to that," said Wetlock, "First, you needed to understand the theory behind my work. Now, let me tell you what happened. As you know, the drug AZT is used for both treatment and prevention of AIDS. I infected a chimp with AIDS, and then treated it with low levels of AZT, to encourage resistant forms of the AIDS virus to emerge."

Wetlock walked to a computer sitting on a small desk and turned the monitor so it faced through the window to the inner lab. Removing a CD from a plastic disc bank, he checked the label. A few switches brought the personal computer to life. The disc drive eagerly ate the CD with a satisfied sounding munch. "Are you familiar with infrared spectroscopy?"

"Not much," Paul admitted. "Just enough to know that every substance will absorb infrared light in a unique fashion."

"That's enough," said Wetlock, "Recently, the light microscope has been combined with infrared spectroscopy to produce a new device: the Fourier Transform Infrared microspectrometer, or FTIR microspectrometer. For the first time, we can look at specific areas of a cell, and identify minute differences in molecular structure."

"Such as?"

"The crystalline structures of viruses and the organic chemical byproducts of cellular metabolism, for example." Wetlock's fingers danced gracefully on the computer keyboard, lighting up the monitor screen with a blue background. The left and lower borders of the screen displayed the "L" shaped axis of a graph, in yellow. An irregular white line ran across the screen, creating numerous narrow downward spikes, like icicles hanging from a roof. "This is an FTIR microspectrogram," said Wetlock. "It shows the profile of a cell membrane in a chimp with AIDS."

Wetlock tapped the keyboard, gently. The first white line disappeared and another line swept across the screen. "The next record is from the same chimp, after three months of low level AZT treatment. Notice the downward spike here, at a wavenumber of 2600. It was not present before."

"What's that from?" Paul pointed at the screen.

"I think it's a cell marker for a new virus, a protein based calling card. The new virus is resistant to even high doses of AZT."

"What both you and Darwin predicted," said Paul.

"Exactly," Wetlock agreed. "But the surprise came when I attempted to transmit the new virus. I put a healthy chimp on high levels of AZT, and then injected him with a tiny amount of serum from the original chimp."

"What happened?"

"The new virus transmitted easily, but the AIDS virus did not."

"In other words," Paul summarized, "the new virus is more infectious."

"Yes, that's the gist."

"But what does the new virus do?"

"I'm getting to that." Wetlock worked his fingers on the keyboard. Again, the white line vanished, and another line swept across the screen. "This is a cell membrane in the brain of the newly infected chimp."

"The spike is tremendous." said Paul. "The new virus must like nerve tissue."

"Precisely, it's a neurotropic virus." He pointed to the next cage. "I have one more chimp for you to meet.

"Not this again, I hate sputum."

"Go say hello to Loverboy."

Loverboy? Paul was amused. How bad could he be? Smaller than Poco, Loverboy strutted around the cage upright, grunting. He looked almost human, except for his peculiar eyes. Dark and sunken, they glowed red, like two burning coals. As Paul approached, the chimp jumped and swung from a trapeze, hissing. Landing at the front of the cage, he scooped up feces from the floor and flung them, screeching. Paul managed to dodge the flying feces. "I suppose he was also born mean?"

"He was not," said Wetlock, pulling a wallet out of his back pocket. "Come out of the lab."

Paul gladly left the inner lab, shedding the hot jumpsuit, mask, and gloves in marked receptacles by the door. He washed his hands and filled his lungs with cool air. Unrestricted breathing felt good. Wetlock pulled a picture from his wallet and handed it to Paul. In the photo, a chimpanzee nestled contentedly in Wetlock's arms. The caption said "To Dad, From Loverboy."

"That picture's a joke from the other grad students," Wetlock explained. "I named him Loverboy, because when I picked him up, he cuddled and fell asleep."

"That's got to be a different chimp," Paul argued, "or else he's tranquilized. I've seen chimps pose for those kind of pictures at county fairs."

"No, not so," said Wetlock. "It's the same chimp, and he wasn't drugged. Loverboy received the infected serum, and within twenty-four hours he had fevers and shaking chills. I hydrated him with intravenous fluids, certain he would die, but he survived and acquired Poco's bad temper."

"You think Poco's personality transferred along with the virus?"

"Exactly."

"How's that possible?"

"Viruses are like pirate ships in the night, they commandeer the cellular machinery of the host, and turn it to their own use. They insert new DNA and take over the cells of the host."

Paul stroked his mustache. "So the new virus copied a critical strand of Poco's DNA and then infected Loverboy, inserting the new DNA."

"Correct. The more DNA a virus controls, the more likely it will survive. The new virus is smarter. Remember the bacteria that learned to defeat penicillin by manufacturing a new enzyme?"

"I remember," said Paul. He took a last look at the picture of Loverboy and gave it back. Then he watched Loverboy's swaggering walk. "Could an intelligent virus learn not to kill the body it inhabits, to live symbiotically?"

"Why not? It doesn't make evolutionary sense to kill your host."

Paul swiveled the computer monitor and traced the graph. "And your new virus loves nerve cells. In humans, this type of virus could effect the functioning of the brain. Behavior. Personality."

"Yes, doctor, anything and everything we are. A virus could learn to control the human mind."

"So, it's possible," said Paul "to transfer behavioral traits by an infection."

"Yes, I believe so," Wetlock agreed. "Research is underway in several centers to develop viruses capable of redesigning human DNA. Some limited medical applications have already been approved."

"Wait a minute, Wetlock, the aim of human genetic engineering is to cure disease by altering physical traits, not behavior."

"Ah. Quite true. But scientists don't have a monopoly on creating new viruses. Natural selection may cause viruses to evolve that can alter human behavior."

"It may have already happened."

"You've seen a case?"

Paul shuddered. "Perhaps."

"Extraordinary." Wetlock ran his fingers several times through his frizzy, white hair. "If you're right, then the next phase of viral evolution has already begun and we're not ready for it. I'd like to help. Who's the patient, where is he? I could run some tests."

Paul sat in front of the computer and stared at the screen until his eyes no longer focused.

He tried to digest the new information. "The patient's in the morgue," he said. Wetlock terminated the computer program, and the screen went blank. Paul thought he'd better talk to Chris right away. "Wetlock, I've got to make a phone call."

"Go ahead," Wetlock replied. "I'd like to hear this, too."

Paul called Chris and explained Joe Tyce's illness. "An infectious disease," said Chris, "like AIDS? That turns you into a murderer? Is that possible?"

"From what I've seen in the animal lab, I believe so."

"You're saying I transplanted contaminated fetal tissue into Joe's brain?"

"Yes. We must find Joe Tyce before he spreads the virus. At least McCann took care of Bertha."

"Paul, haven't you heard? Bertha is about to become a multiple organ donor."

"What? But I thought she was dead!"

"Of course she's dead. Certified brain dead, by me. They're waiting for the heart team from Stanford. The harvest should start around midnight."

"Who gave permission?"

"Bertha did. She signed the forms when Joe Tyce went to surgery."

"I'll call Jack McCann and tell her to stop the transplants," said Paul, "with a court order, if necessary. And I'll contact the Center for Disease Control. They may be able to prevent an epidemic."

"One of my medical school classmates works in Atlanta for the CDC," said Chris. "He was also a close friend."

"Then call him."

"But Paul. An epidemic of serial killers? No one will believe you without proof. What are you going to do?"

He massaged his head. "I don't know, but I'll think of something. Meet me in the OR, at midnight." He hung up, staring at the telephone.

"Imagine," said Wetlock. "A plague of violence. Fantastic, if it's true."

Paul stroked his moustache. "Wetlock, what would you need to test someone for a new virus?"

"I'd need a tissue sample."

"How long would the test take?"

"Anywhere from 12 to 48 hours. And it's far from perfect. I might not find the virus you're looking for, even if it's there."

"I understand the limitations. How large a sample do you need?"

Wetlock held out the pinkie of his right hand at eye level. "Can you get me a piece of tissue about the size of my little finger?" he asked.

"I'll get you a finger," said Paul, "even if I have to steal it."

CHAPTER 16

THE LATE EVENING surgical rush had ended by the time Paul arrived at the hospital. The doctor's locker room bore the ravages of a busy day, littered with abandoned scrub clothes and half-filled Styrofoam cups of cold coffee. Bloody footprints criss-crossed the floor, like in some kind of demonic dance studio. He changed quickly and entered the operating area.

The LCD board listed Bertha Miller for multiple organ donation, with harvesting of her heart, kidneys, liver, pancreas, corneas, skin, and bones. A nurse approached the computer and deleted the "skin and bones." Chris walked into the operating area through the double doors. In spite of her crisp makeup and immaculate clothes, he noted worry lines in her forehead. "Paul, what are you doing in scrubs?"

"Shhh." He put a finger to his lips and motioned her away from the control desk. "I'm going to do whatever it takes to prevent the harvest."

"But."

"Don't try to stop me. Did you make the call to Atlanta?"

"Yes. My friend says the CDC gets all sorts of false alarms and crank calls. He needs proof before he can even discuss it."

"Great."

"What about Jack McCann?"

"We spoke," said Paul, "but she didn't seem convinced."

A phone rang. "Dr. Powers, there's a Jack McCann on the phone for you," said a nurse at the control desk. Paul walked back to the desk and took the phone.

"Paul Powers."

"I'm sorry, Powers. Your theory didn't impress the judge, you're gonna need proof. Organs are in short supply and trauma victims are an important source. No one's willing to give me a court order to stop the transplants. But the skin and bone bank depends on the coroner, and the coroner owes me a few favors."

He held the mouthpiece close to his face and spoke softly. "Then it was you who stopped the skin and bone harvest?"

"Yes, it seems there's more than enough skin and bones to go around."

"Thanks," said Paul, "but there must be a way to stop the organ transplants."

"Sure, call me if you find it. You got my number."

"Wait. Don't you believe me?" The nurse at the control station glared.

"I'm no doctor," said Jackey. "I don't know what to believe. I've done what I can."

He hung up the phone. "Trouble?" said Chris.

"Yeah. No court order."

"Can I help?"

He led Chris away from the control desk. "Yes, I need to know where the organs are going and who the recipients are. You can find out from the transplant coordinator, Dr. Melvin."

"That goofball pathologist? What makes you think he'll give me the information?"

Paul smiled. "Use your charms."

"What am I supposed to do?" said Chris, frowning. "Seduce him?"

"Yeah. Take him out on a date, if necessary."

"That's a laugh. I'll bet Melvin never had a date."

"Then it's about time," said Paul. "I've got to see Bertha to get my proof. I'll text you later."

Chris shook her head and the worry lines increased. "I can't believe this is happening." She took his hand and squeezed it tightly. "Be careful, Paul. Those donor organs are important to a lot of people. Powerful people."

He nodded. "I'll be careful." She let go and he watched her leave. Then he returned to the control desk. "When's Bertha Miller coming?" he asked the nurse.

"The donor? Already in OR three," she said.

Paul ran into the operating room. Bertha Miller lay on the table, the ventilator of the anesthesia machine pumping oxygen in and out of her lungs. Her heart beat within her open chest, illuminated by overhead spotlights. It looked like a glistening pearl in the mouth of a giant clam. Dr. Benga and Dr. Norton tidied up around the heart with an electrical cautery, a blue plastic stick with a red hot tip. Puffs of acrid smoke rose from the open chest each time the cautery tip touched the oozy red tissue. The heart folded and rolled, stamping out a primitive beat.

At the head of the table sat Dr. Beck, his face gaunt and his eyes droopy. "I'll relieve you," said Paul.

"Thank God you're here," said Beck. "I've been at it since last night. Did you finish what you needed to do?"

"Not entirely. I might need more coverage, soon."

"Then I'd better get some sleep."

Paul put his hand on Beck's shoulder. "Good idea, and thanks." Beck rose slowly from the low stool, unfolding his tall, scrawny body. He sighed, rubbed his lower back, and left.

Paul took his place behind the ether screen, the blue drape at the head of the table. Circulating nurses often walked behind the drape, and the surgeons looked over the top. He couldn't cut a tissue sample from Bertha in the operating room without being seen, but he might be able to stop the transplants.

No one watched him close enough to tell which drugs he injected. Most drug filled syringes looked exactly alike, so he could secretly give anything to Bertha. The drug could be detected later by sophisticated tests, but he doubted anyone would bother to test a dead organ donor.

Reaching behind to the anesthesia cart, a silver chest of drawers filled with drugs, he took out a bottle of Beta-blocker. In small doses, Beta-blocker slowed the activity of the heart. He pocketed the bottle.

Bertha's heart looked strong and healthy, snapping rhythmically in her open chest. He found it hard to accept that she was dead. He wondered if a law existed making it illegal to kill a dead person. Probably, no one had ever asked the question. He didn't even want to think about the moral issues.

A nurse opened the door and stuck her head in the room. "They're here," she said.

Paul heard wooden Birkenstock shoes clicking against the hard floor. A few moments later, a tall man entered the room. Water ran from his outstretched hands, down his forearms, and dripped off his elbows. Black plastic glasses hung over the top edge of his mask, and an extra paper shield partially covered a bushy, black beard. In a deliberate, almost frantic dance, he dried his hands and plunged his arms into a paper gown. He held out the gown's belt to no one in particular. A nurse held the belt while the man spun in a complete circle, wrapping the belt around his waist and tying it.

The two surgical residents parted as the new man stepped up to the operating table. "How was the trip from Stanford?" asked Norton.

"Let's get started," said the new surgeon. His heals clicked to attention. "It looks like a healthy specimen." He looked at Paul. "Give me fluids, lots of fluids."

Paul nodded. Four fluid bags hung from the ceiling. He opened their valves until the fluids flowed freely through plastic tubes into the patient.

"We'll cross-clamp on my signal," said the visiting surgeon. "Ready with the cardioplegia?"

"Ready," said Benga, preparing to infuse the heart with ice cold preservative solution.

A nurse stood by the wall, checking a container, plastic wrapping, and a cooler. The celebrity surgeon passed white cloth ribbon around the thick blood vessels leading in and out of the heart. The heart didn't know it would be ripped out from its moorings, packed in ice, and flown 900 miles across the country. But the surgeon knew. He lived for this.

Behind him, a special table had been prepared. Draped with a green cloth, the table featured a huge silver basin filled with ice water. Two nurses stood on either side of the table, their arms folded like chefs waiting to carve a roast fresh from the oven.

Paul watched the new surgeon's eyes as his crow's feet turned upward. Beneath his mask, he appeared to be smiling as he prepared to separate the heart from Bertha's circulation. Paul made his final decision. He reached into his pocket for the bottle of Beta-blocker. As he had so many times, he assembled a needle and syringe and drew up the medication. Only this time he drew up the entire contents of the bottle, a lethal dose. He injected it into the intravenous tubing, wondering if he was now a murderer.

The heartbeat slowed to a stop, the hollow chambers swelling like a child's balloon. The surgeon's eyes bulged, all traces of the smile vanished. "What the hell's happening?" He looked at Paul. "What are you doing?"

"Just giving fluids, sir, like you asked." Paul shook.

"The ventricle's failed completely. The heart's worthless."

"I'm sorry, Doctor," said Benga, "You saw how good the heart looked. It must've had a hidden defect."

"Apparently. A waste of my time. I'd better get back." He left the table and ripped off his operating gown, throwing it in the trash. Shaking his head and grumbling, he bolted from the room, the rapid clicking of his shoes faded.

"Don't feel sorry for him," said Benga. "He'll probably get home before us."

Paul turned off the ventilator on the anesthesia machine. He knew someone would die without Bertha's heart. In that sense, he'd become a murderer. Did he have just cause? Maybe, but he still lacked proof that the organs posed a serious threat. One way or another, he'd get the proof. Unfortunately, poisoning the heart might not stop the surgeons from harvesting the remaining organs. That was Benga's decision.

Norton flushed the kidneys with a cold preservative solution used for organ transport. "I've already started to prepare the kidneys," he said. "But should we take them?"

"Depends what killed her," said Benga. "Looks like she died of heart failure, so the other organs should be fine." He picked up a scalpel.

"I don't agree," said Paul. Every head in the room turned.

"Why not?" asked Benga.

Why not? Paul swallowed. "Because recent studies show that sudden heart failure in organ donors is usually the result of overwhelming infection, making the organs totally unsuitable for transplantation."

Benga put his scalpel down. "Infection? You're reading too much again, Pauley. So what causes the infection?"

Paul felt like he'd walked into a minefield. "Failure of the immune system."

"I've never heard of anything like that," said Benga, "but I may be a little behind on my reading."

"Maybe Paul's right," said Norton, "We don't want to ship infected organs."

Benga stepped away from the operating table, placed his bloody hands together, and bowed his head like he was praying. Then he looked up. "No," he said, "I don't care what the literature says. I know what I saw. Let's proceed."

Paul sighed. He'd lost the battle to stop the harvest of the remaining organs. Now he needed a moment alone with Bertha to get a tissue sample for Wetlock's test. If he could prove the presence of a harmful virus, then he might still prevent the organs from being transplanted.

The kidneys, fresh from the body, looked like crescent shaped purple-brown sacks about six inches long. After wrapping in several plastic bags, the surgeons sealed each kidney in a separate plastic jar. A nurse put the jars on a wheeled cart full of ice.

Bertha's huge liver wiggled like a dark jellyfish in Dr. Norton's hands. Triple wrapped and sealed in a plastic mixing bowl, the liver also went on ice. Similarly, Bertha's worm-like pancreas joined her liver on the ice. Finished harvesting the internal organs, the surgeons quickly sewed Bertha's chest and abdomen together.

An ophthalmologist arrived to remove Bertha's eyes. The disembodied eyes stared at Paul from a tray at the head of the table, giving him a creepy feeling. He felt better after the ophthalmologist wrapped the eyes and put them on ice.

The harvest ended and the room cleared except for one nurse. The six plastic containers on ice looked like frozen leftovers. Dr. Melvin, the pathologist, arrived to retrieve the iced organs. He held each jar up to the light and grinned. In their plastic jars, the kidneys looked indistinct, like dark, tubular blobs. Melvin pushed the ice cart out of the room, leaving a trail of fallen ice cubes.

The remaining nurse started preparing the body for transport to the morgue. She never left Paul alone with Bertha in the operating room, so he never got a tissue sample. He decided to wait until Bertha got to the morgue. Then he'd sneak in and get the sample. Hopefully, at this time of night, nobody would see him. The morgue was not a popular place, especially in the middle of the night.

CHAPTER 17

RICHARD SCHLESINGER DESCENDED into the New York City subway station at 4:00 AM, just in time to see the doors of the A train chomp closed. The graffiti-covered cars fled from the filthy station like waste flowing through a sewer. At least he'd escaped from the brown snow and bitter cold of the city streets to the relative warmth of the underground. At this hour, it would be a long wait for the next train, but he had plenty of company. The usual assortment of derelicts and drunks loitered in the station, and the homeless slept along the walls, covered with rags or cardboard.

Monday, Wednesday, and Friday, for the last three years, Richard rode the early A train to stay alive. Today, he arrived at the treatment center at 5:00 AM. From a reclining chair, he watched his entire blood supply drain from his body. The sterile smell, the bleached white walls, and the background hum of the machines made him feel like a monstrous creature, stripped of all individual identity. The dialysis machine kept him alive, but he hated it.

Three years ago, his ruptured appendix had nearly killed him. A rampant abdominal infection had followed, necessitating the use of a potent antibiotic, gentamycin. The drug had eliminated his infection, but destroyed his kidneys. Thirty-two years old, he felt like an addict, dependent on a fix from a machine.

Since the loss of his kidneys, he'd never felt healthy. Steadily accumulating toxic waste within made his skin yellow, his body unclean. At every meal he consumed handfuls of medication. Scars criss-crossed his bruised arms, a grim reminder of the huge needles he had to endure three times a week. And how many operations had he undergone on his arms? Nine? Ten? He'd lost count. During each surgery, an artery had been connected directly to a vein, to expand it for easier access. Only organ transplantation could provide a fully functional natural kidney that would allow him to lead a normal life.

Why did he have to suffer? What had he done to deserve this kind of life? Still, he considered it lucky to be teaching history at Brooklyn Tech, the best high school in New

York City, with good attendance and little gang warfare. Everyone at Tech knew he went for dialysis, and his wait for a kidney transplant had prompted the students to distribute organ donor cards.

A pen sized pager in his shirt pocket sat a silent vigil. Along with thousands of others, he'd put his name on a list and prayed daily for a compatible donor. At least he had a chance to free himself from the dialysis ball and chain. The dream of a kidney transplant helped him to go on living.

CHAPTER 18

CHRIS FOUND DR. MELVIN standing alone in the deserted hospital laboratory, surrounded by styrofoam coolers and cardboard boxes. He was packaging the harvested organs for shipment. Idle electronic devices lined the cluttered, black countertops. The white floor glared in the brilliance of too much overhead fluorescence, and the air smelt antiseptic. She envisioned the lab at the height of the workday, a different world, technicians scrambling, phones ringing. But in the dead calm of early morning, with only disembodied organs for company, Melvin looked lonely, like a lost child.

Beneath his lab coat, an untucked white shirt bore the stains of either his dinner, or secretions from one of today's specimens. Absorbed in his work, he ignored her presence until she moved close enough to see a bare roll of fat hanging over his belt. Then, he swung around, apparently startled.

"Oh, Dr. Mason. Can I help you find something?" he asked, awkwardly tucking in his shirt.

"I came to check on some routine lab work," she answered in a deep, slow voice, running her fingers under the lapels of his lab coat. Beneath her fingertips, she felt his heart pounding. "That's the problem with our work," she said, "everything is so routine. All the long hours and the hard work. I get so bored, and lonely."

He jumped away, bumping a chair over and catching it before it hit the floor. "Oh God, excuse me a moment," said Melvin. He opened the lab refrigerator. From among the specimens, he pulled out a can of ginger ale. Popping the top, he chugged it down. "Ahh, want one?" Chris shook her head and followed him to the lab computer. "Let me pull up the results for you," he offered, sitting down at the computer station.

"Thank you," beamed Chris, leaning over his right shoulder. "We've known each other for over five years. Did you realize that?"

He breathed loudly. "Patient name?" he asked, avoiding her face.

"Uh, Tibeau. Gregory Tibeau." She reached around both sides of his fat neck. "I can spell it for you," she whispered, and then typed the name, slowly, one finger at a time. "That's a French name," she said. "Kind of sexy, isn't it?"

He nodded, face red. "What test do you need?"

"How about electrolytes?"

His thick fingers pounded the keyboard, but the first try produced an error message. "Oops, clumsy of me, just a second." He tried again, successfully. "There, I'll make a printout." He entered the appropriate commands and a printer across the room sprang to life."

"To get a printout," she asked, reaching over him, "do I just click here?" The printer chattered again.

"You just did it again," he laughed nervously.

She massaged his tense shoulders. "I'm really interested in your organs," she teased.

His shoulders relaxed. "God, I love it when you talk dirty," he said. "Anything you want to know, just ask."

"How do you keep it straight? I mean, all that cross-match data."

"Ha! No problem, actually, NUOS, the Network for United Organ Sharing, does all the work. All I have to do is feed data to their website, and pull the finished product off the computer."

"Fascinating. Show me how it works."

He smiled, fingers pounding the keyboard.

"Their website is now connecting to the NUOS computer in Richmond, Virginia."

She watched as text appeared on the screen: "Network for United Organ Sharing-Please enter user code." He did. "Welcome to NUOS-Enter command or request menu."

"What do you want to know?"

"Who are the recipients of these organs?"

"Simple." He entered the appropriate commands.

After a moment of hesitation, text continued scrolling across the computer screen: "NUOS liver match results-Based on WAHB donor-ID-CDR138-Status 1-Zone B-size match-ABO compatible-Recipient Name-Ethering, C-Age 35-Phoenix-AZHS-(602) 555-3960-NUOS kidney match results-Based on WAHB donor- ..."

"Can you print this, too?"

"Sure, I'll make a copy."

The printer awoke, again. Several new pages rolled off, stacking on top of Christine's lab reports. "Do you want anything else? I've got to get back to work."

"How soon will the organs be shipped?"

"Soon. On the 5:30 AM Airwest flight to Phoenix." Melvin reached into a styrofoam cooler and pulled out a plastic jar. "Except for this kidney, a perfect, six antigen match headed for New York City on the next available flight, after it gets to Sea-Tac. If there's anything else you need, it'll have to wait. The airport courier is on the way and I've got to finish packing." The printer stopped. "That's it," he said, logging off the computer and then returning to the organ cart.

Chris took the lab results and transplant data pages from the printer. "Thanks for being so helpful," she cooed, "I had no idea you knew so much about transplants."

"I'm transplant coordinator for the University," he reminded her, sealing the liver container in a plastic bag.

"Yes, of course. I never realized what a big responsibility it is."

From a cabinet beneath the lab table, he pulled a flat cardboard box and began assembling it. Unfolded, the box measured two to three feet on all sides. He struggled to tape the bottom.

"I'd like to know more," said Chris, "We should get together."

Half the tape stuck to itself and half to the box. Pulling the tape off ripped the cardboard down to the corrugations. He punched out the bottom and threw it on the floor. "Shit. Sorry." His mouth opened, but nothing came out. He looked ready to drool. "Are you talking about a date?"

A date with Melvin? She couldn't believe it either. "Yes, a date. How about dinner? Three nights from now, at the Cactus by Lake Union."

"God yes," he said, his eyes glazed over.

"Well, bye now," Chris said. "I'll see you soon."

She left the lab and called Paul's cell phone. "Where are you?"

"Alone, in the surgery lounge. Chris, what did you find out?"

"Almost all the organs are leaving on the 5:30 AM Airwest flight to Phoenix."

"Good work. But what's not going to Phoenix?"

"One kidney. It's a six-antigen match."

"Six-antigen match?" said Paul, "What's that?"

"A perfectly compatible kidney for a recipient in New York City."

"Like winning the Lottery. What else did Melvin say?"

"He's looking forward to our date."

"I'm sorry."

"It's all right. He must know a lot about transplantation protocol, testing, and legal issues. At worst, I'll get indigestion."

"Listen. I'm waiting for Bertha to be tucked into the morgue for the night. Then I'm going to get a tissue sample for testing. You got the names of the recipients?"

"Yes, all of them."

"Good, hang on to the list. I'm going to follow the organs to Phoenix."

"Paul!"

"I've got to stop the transplants."

"How?"

"I don't know. But you'll have to stop the New York kidney transplant."

"Now you've gone too far, Paul. I'm not chasing a kidney to New York."

"You don't believe me, do you? You don't trust me."

"That's not fair, of course I trust you. But like everyone else, I'd prefer proof."

"I'll get proof. But meanwhile, an epidemic may get out of control."

"I want to help you, Paul. But there are proper channels. I can't interfere with legitimate organ transplants."

"You're worried about your career, aren't you?"

"Of course I'm worried," said Chris. "But for the both of us. You could be chasing a fantasy."

"I need you Chris, more than I've ever needed anyone. I'm not asking you to believe in a fantasy, I'm asking you to believe in me. I'll call you from Phoenix."

After a long silence, Chris said, "I must be crazy, but I'll do what I can. I'll try to stop the New York kidney transplant, somehow."

"Thanks. We're both off next week. Together, we'll convince someone in the transplant network of the potential danger."

"Let's hope so," said Chris. "But stopping transplants is not how I'd hoped to spend our vacation."

<u>CHAPTER 19</u>

PAUL DESCENDED several staircases in the hospital, and wound through the dim passageways to the morgue. As a matter of tradition, the hospital didn't clearly mark the way. Special carts that looked empty carried dead bodies to the morgue concealed underneath the gurney surface by a hanging sheet. It was a reasonable deception, hiding death to promote hope.

At the door connecting the hospital to the morgue, Paul hesitated. He'd promised Chris to be careful, and he'd have a hard time explaining his presence here in the early morning. Trying the door, he found it locked, and suspected it might also be alarmed at this hour. Announcing himself by ringing the night bell didn't seem like a good idea.

Through a small, vertical glass window in the wooden outer door, he peeked into an empty reception area. Pressing his face against the door to the left side of the window enabled him to see to the right through another window into the main offices of the morgue.

In the front of the brightly lit office, a night investigator in a tweed sport coat and white shirt sat at a desk, facing the window. Unscrewing the top of a thermos, he poured out what looked like orange juice and slurped it down. Flipping through a stack of papers, he scribbled a few notes, put down the pencil, and shifted his wide body in the chair. Pleats of loose, dark flesh hung like curtains under his eyes, dissolving into red, overstuffed cheeks. After reaching below the table with his right hand, he held up a flat, curved flask, unscrewed the top, and emptied a clear liquid into the thermos. The flask disappeared beneath the table, and then he poured himself another cup of juice.

Paul moved away from the door, wondering how he could enter the morgue unseen. He needed to get the tissue sample right away. He had a plane to catch. Without the sample, what chance would he have to prove his theory? If he could only get the investigator to leave the morgue for a few minutes. But how?

Walking back toward the operating room, Paul searched for a telephone. He dialed the

Dependable Ambulance company and claimed to be Dr. Melvin, the head pathologist at the University. He said they had an emergency and needed help. "There've been a number of deaths tonight," he explained, "and we're way over capacity in the morgue. We're trying to transfer a few out to funeral homes."

"Are you kidding? At this hour?"

"I know it's a bit irregular," said Paul, "but I've made the arrangements. All we need is transport. Can you help us?"

"Why not?"

"Good. Just send an ambulance to the morgue entrance. Ring the bell when you arrive, we'll be ready."

Outside the hospital, Paul walked up the long driveway that ran along the west side of the building to the morgue entrance. The driveway ended in a tight U-turn and two steel garage doors that led to a loading dock for removing the dead. A maintenance truck sat outside the loading dock. The truck was parked in the east corner created by the sharp turn in the driveway. He crouched down behind the truck in drizzle and darkness to wait for the ambulance.

Half an hour later, the ambulance backed up to the garage door on the west end, furthest from his hiding place. He froze, afraid the slightest noise or movement might give him away.

The driver climbed out of the cab and opened the rear doors of the van. Then he rang the bell and waited. Nothing happened. He rang again, but still no one answered.

Paul wondered if the investigator he'd seen earlier inside the morgue had gone home. If so, no one would be there to open the door. Minutes passed. The driver rang again, waited another minute, and then closed the doors to the van. A security guard appeared around the corner of the building with a radio in his hand. "It's an ambulance," he said into the radio. "Go ahead and open the door."

The huge metal garage door on the east end, closest to Paul, came alive, screeching as it rolled upward. In the open doorway, the investigator appeared on the loading dock and walked out of the morgue. "Thanks for coming," he said to the guard. "I had no idea who was ringing the bell, and I'm here all alone."

"That's my job," said the guard.

The driver folded his arms. "What's going on? The dispatcher told me to pick up a corpse."

"I don't care what he told you," said the investigator. "I'm the only one here, and I know nothing about it."

The three men walked around to the driver's side of the ambulance, out of Paul's view. But he heard the beginning of a heated argument over who told what, when, and to whom. Sodium vapor lamps outside the hospital cast a soft golden glow, and long shadows from the three men crossed on the driveway like swords.

This is it, Paul thought. He didn't have much time. Darting from behind the maintenance truck, heart pounding, he slipped though the open garage door onto the loading dock and into the morgue. On his left was a huge freezer door. He pulled on the latch, and after several loud clicks, the door swung open, and he ducked inside the freezer. The massive door swung shut behind him with a deafening snap.

Icy cold air bit through his rain soaked hospital cover coat, and he could see his breath. The walk-in freezer was 25 feet long on each side, with a dozen stainless steel carts lining the walls to his left and in front. On the right of the freezer was a separate storage area, caged, locked, and currently empty. On the far edge of the right wall, another door led to the morgue. He guessed it must lead to the autopsy room.

White sheets covered the motionless silhouettes of the dead. Most of the carts were occupied. Clean sheets covered the few empty carts that stood ready to receive more bodies. He shivered and tried to catch his breath. Then it struck him, each covered cadaver looked alike. Which cart held the remains of Bertha?

He lifted the sheets up one at a time. The first cart contained the ghastly gray corpse of a very old woman. The second, a young man covered with bruises. A third body had decomposed beyond recognition. He removed the sheet from one more. The eyelids sank deep into their sockets, into a head with no eyes. A plastic breathing tube protruded from blue lips, below a thin moustache. He'd found Bertha.

He pulled a pair of gloves from his coat pocket, put them on, and lifted a lifeless hand. But he'd forgotten to bring a knife. After searching the room for a cutting tool, he exited the freezer through the second door. It made as much noise as the first one. As he suspected, he now stood in the autopsy room.

It was a huge room with multiple stainless steel countertops and sinks. Each counter had raised sides, and good drainage. The floor sloped to a drain in the center, so the entire room could be hosed down for cleaning. A scalpel handle lay on the first counter, but the handle had no blade. It would have to suffice, he was running out of time. He grabbed the scalpel handle and reentered the freezer.

The dull, metal spike on the end of the scalpel handle had been designed to hold a blade in place, not to cut flesh. He jammed the spike into the knuckle of Bertha's small finger using the steel cart as a backstop. A twisting motion drove the spike further, and with a gristly crunch the tip emerged from the other side of the finger. He wound the scalpel handle in a complete circle around the finger several times until the last sinews of the finger broke.

After covering Bertha, he pulled his gloves off, turning them inside out, over the severed finger. On the sheet, he wiped off the scalpel handle. Then he placed the finger and gloves, and the scalpel handle, in the pocket of his coat.

The freezer door clicked several times, someone was opening the door from the loading dock. Paul couldn't get back to the other door in time, so he looked for a place to hide. Frantic, he pulled down one of the sheets on an empty cart, jumped on top, lay down, and threw the sheet over his head.

CHAPTER 20

CHRIS SURPRISED DR. MELVIN by returning to the hospital laboratory.

"Did you forget something?" he asked, with a warm smile.

"I remembered one more thing," said Chris. "Do you have the time to check a serum protein electrophoresis? I ordered it yesterday." Chris smiled.

"Well, actually, that is I ... Oh, for God's sake, why not. I've got everything packed to go, except for the New York kidney. Then I have to make out the labels, and do the paperwork. No problem. What's the patient's name?"

"Farmer, Margaret."

"OK, I'll get the results. It'll just take me two minutes."

Melvin left the main lab, and headed for the protein analysis section.

Chris gazed at the organs waiting for transport. She reached into the pocket of her white coat, scanning the laboratory to be sure she was alone.

<u>CHAPTER 21</u>

PAUL HEARD the freezer door into the morgue creak loudly as it opened. "Dum-de-dum-dum, hello boys," said a man as he strolled through the morgue. The door snapped shut. "Did you know someone wanted to take you out dancing tonight? Ha."

Paul recognized the voice, it was the investigator. The palms of Paul's hands stuck to the cold, steel surface of the cart. Shivering made it hard for him to keep still. He could hide for a while beneath the thin sheet, but if he didn't leave the freezer soon, hypothermia would kill him.

In his pocket, he had incriminating evidence. He couldn't imagine explaining to the authorities that he'd been stealing body parts. He heard a sheet rustle on the next cart, and felt the warmth of the investigator standing nearby.

"Let's see," said the man. "What have we here? Hmm. Gunshot wound to the brain." He had uncovered Bertha. "Wow. Nice shot." Papers rustled. "Multiple organ donor, I see. That's odd. No mention of a severed finger." Paul's teeth chattered.

"Whoa! What's that?" said the investigator, bumping the cart. "For a moment I thought you tried to talk behind my back. Ha. Too many late nights." More papers crunched. "Hmm. You're not on my list. Who are you anyway?"

Above Paul's head, a warm hand grabbed the sheet and lifted it off, slowly. To keep from chattering, he clenched his teeth. Closing his eyes, he held still as an ice cube.

"No wonder you're not on my list. You look like a very recent addition."

Paul popped his eyes open, bared his teeth, and growled, watching as the investigator's cheeks turned white. The man's eyes bulged, the bags beneath them seeming to disappear. "Blood! Blood! I need blood!" Paul shouted, sitting up on the cart, reaching for the man's throat.

After momentary paralysis, the investigator's clipboard clattered to the floor. Tripping over his own feet, he turned and ran from the freezer into the autopsy room, screaming, never looking back.

Paul jumped off the cart and bolted out the other freezer door onto the loading dock. He found the control for the electric garage door, opened it, and ran nonstop from the morgue to the Hut to look for Mr. Wetlock.

CHAPTER 22

IN THE PATHOLOGY LAB, Chris waited for Melvin to return. He walked in, waving a sheet of paper. "I've got the results you wanted."

"Thanks," said Chris.

A uniformed man with a large wheeled cart entered the lab.

"Gibraltar Couriers," he said, checking a clipboard. "You Dr. Melvin?"

"That's me, but I'm not quite ready yet. It'll be just a minute."

He hurriedly packed the last box and affixed orange florescent labels to the six boxes. The labels said, "KEEP IN UPRIGHT POSITION-ORGAN/TISSUE FOR TRANSPLANT-NUOS -HANDLE WITH CARE."

"Sign here," the courier requested, pushing a clipboard full of duplicate forms in front of Dr. Melvin. On each box, the courier affixed a round silver sticker embossed with the winged shoes of the messenger god Mercury. Melvin took his receipts, and then helped the courier load the boxes onto his cart.

The liver box, two and a half feet long, two feet high, and two feet wide went on the cart first. On top of the liver, he put two smaller boxes, containing the kidneys. On top of the kidneys, he set the three smallest boxes containing the eyes and the pancreas.

"That should do it. I can take it from here," said the courier, leaving Melvin and Chris alone again.

"I don't know why," said Melvin, "but God I'm glad to be rid of these particular organs."

"We've both been up all night," said Chris.

"Yes. Multiple organ donation is an exhausting circus. I'm ready to go home. But tell me, three nights from now, what time should I pick you up?"

"Seven's OK," said Chris. She wrote on the edge of the lab report, tore the piece off, and smiled as she handed it to Melvin. "Here's my address, see you then." She wondered how much trouble she'd gotten in today.

CHAPTER 23

INSIDE THE HUT, Paul Powers pounded on the door of Arens' lab for several minutes. Mr. Wetlock finally appeared, hair disheveled, rubbing his eyes.

"Dr. Powers. What happened? You're out of breath."

"Never mind me. I've got a tissue sample. Can you run the tests?"

"A tissue sample?" Wetlock asked. "From a patient you suspect has been genetically altered?"

"Yes, of course."

"Can it wait until morning?"

"Do I look like it can wait until morning?"

"OK, OK, just give me a few minutes to make some coffee," Wetlock pleaded. "Come on in."

"Why don't you get started on the tests," Paul insisted, handing Wetlock the finger and the gloves. "I'll make coffee for the two of us."

Wetlock held the ball of gloves up to the light. Paul could just make out the finger within.

"How did you get this?" said Wetlock. "I thought you were joking about stealing a finger."

"This isn't a joke. It's an attempt to stop a deadly epidemic while we still can. I need the test results. And one more thing, can I use your 3-D printer while I'm here?"

"OK," said Wetlock, "Make the coffee, and make it strong."

Wetlock ran off to start processing the finger, and Paul brewed a pot of strong coffee. It was going to be a long night, and an early plane ride in the morning. He booted up one of Wetlock's computers and searched the internet for a file he'd read about in a background article on medical uses of 3-D printers. But the file he needed wasn't medical. He found it and paid for the download.

It was relatively simple to open the 3-D printing file and start the printer. Small, white, plastic parts of various shapes fell into the receiving tray of the printer one by one. A few hours passed before the last piece of the puzzle had came off the 3-D printer. Paul assembled the parts in order to inspect the finished product. It was small, sleek, and looked fully functional.

Wetlock entered the room. "I've started the DNA analysis, but it could take days. You can go, and I'll call you when I'm done." Wetlock looked at Paul's 3-D creation. "What on earth do you need that for?"

"I have to stop some organ transplants," said Paul. "And I'm preparing for the worst."

CHAPTER 24

AFTER DIALYSIS, Richard Schlesinger walked six blocks from the treatment center to Brooklyn Tech. Snow flurries sparkled in the predawn haze, falling under his upturned collar, creeping up his neck, making him shiver. He barely arrived in time for his first class, exhausted already because his day had started six hours ago. His thirty-four tenth grade students fell into three categories: falling asleep, waking up, and asleep.

"I hope you all read your assignment last night in Modern History," he said, raising his voice above the ever present background conversations. "We'd like to believe Lincoln put an end to slavery for purely moral reasons," he almost shouted. "However, as last night's chapter explains, Lincoln, like all American presidents, had practical political reasons for bringing slavery to an end."

His pocket pager chirped. After a moment of silence, the students cheered.

CHAPTER 25

CHRIS RAN into the intensive care unit, into an alcove filled with white, blue, and green coats. Some kind of crisis was underway, and she'd been summoned by Dr. Swan, the junior neurosurgery resident. He stood by the bedside, his white eyebrows squeezed together like ditto marks.

On the bed, an elderly black man shook violently. Thick veins on his arms strained like taut ropes, and sustained spasms yanked on the leather restraints. A nurse squeezed a breathing bag, pumping oxygen into the man's barrel shaped chest.

"Meet DJ Jackson," said Swan. "DJ was admitted to ICU for lung cancer with secondary pneumonia. The seizures are new, and I can't get them under control."

"Has the patient received Valium?" Chris asked.

"Right. Thirty milligrams."

"Let me have another syringe," Chris said calmly, trying to soothe the anxious crowd. Her calmness came mostly from extreme exhaustion, rather than clinical acumen. A path cleared for her to the patient's bedside, and Swan put a syringe in her hand.

"Check off another ten milligram syringe of Valium," said a nurse. A ward secretary grabbed an oversized pen dangling from her pink necklace. After searching a clipboard for the appropriate spot, she made a notation.

Chris injected half the contents of the syringe into DJ's intravenous tubing. "That's five more milligrams of Valium," she said.

The seizures stopped. The nervous mob waited patiently, to see if the seizures might return.

"That ought to do it," said Chris. "Schedule a brain scan in the morning: Rule out metastatic tumor."

The group dispersed until only Dr. Swan remained at the bedside with Chris. He bore the look of a hurt puppy that had upset it's master. Chris knew that look all too well.

"You did all the right things," Chris said. "Sometimes, it takes a little bit more. There's no magic to it."

"Sorry I had to call you," he said, frowning. "Barring something outrageous, I'll keep it quiet for you until Delianis takes over."

"I'd appreciate that," Christine admitted. "I'm exhausted, and could use the rest."

Swan's jaw dropped. "Right. Enjoy your week off."

"Thanks," said Chris. "I'll certainly try."

The cool predawn sidewalks around the hospital were deserted as Chris walked to her car thinking only of sleep. She made it a habit never to count her waking hours, but she felt like her last rest had been in a prior lifetime. A short walk through the parking lot, and she'd be on her way home, to the soft bed waiting in her apartment.

If only Paul could be there waiting, but he was on the way to Phoenix. She hoped he'd be successful in stopping the transplants, without getting himself into trouble. Bucking the medical establishment could have adverse repercussions on his future career. Most residents wouldn't dare oppose the status quo. Paul had the guts to stand by his convictions, and she respected him for it.

A dark figure appeared in Christine's path and she stepped out of the way. Gloved hands grasped her neck in a viselike grip, and she couldn't breathe. In the early morning shadows, a huge, black leather creature stood at arm's length. It had no face. Instead, a motorcycle helmet perched itself on top of a thick neck. Broad muscular shoulders spread out sideways below the neck.

Christine's pain faded instantly, replaced by a strange sensation, not being able to inhale or exhale. She felt like her body had been split into two pieces, and the bottom portion pleaded for air from above the obstruction. But air wouldn't come, and fear of death wrung all other thoughts from her mind. She tried to fight, to think of a way to escape.

The tall boots planted firmly before her had two massive, kneeless legs joined in a sharp black crease. She swung her right shoe into the crease, penetrating the softened leather into the flesh beyond.

The assailant moaned and his grip loosened for an instant. She sucked in a fresh breath, like breathing through a straw. Grasping at the top pocket of her long white coat, she pulled out a plastic pen. Thrust into an eye or an ear, a pen could be an effective weapon. Then she realized that the man's helmet fully protected his eyes and ears, and the pen clattered to the sidewalk.

The man bent his elbows, drawing her closer, digging his thumbs deeper into the soft flesh of her neck. His breath traveled up her nostrils, laden with alcohol and the stench of rotting food. She wondered how much worse the smell would be if she could breathe.

Reaching her right hand into the side pocket of her coat, she felt her wallet and makeup, useless against this vicious beast. The night darkened. She needed more air, more time. To scream. Something. A cold glass cylinder met her searching fingers. The Valium syringe! She'd forgotten to return it.

Clutching the syringe, she worked her thumbnail under the rubber cap. Flipping the cap off, she freed the long needle. She knew an injection of five milligrams of Valium into a huge madman would normally have no effect. But with her free hand, she reached behind the murderer's neck. Probing beneath the rear lip of his helmet, the first two fingers of her left hand straddled the bony base of his skull. In one smooth movement, she thrust the needle of the syringe between the fingers of her left hand. She held the syringe like a dagger, pushing the barrel until his skin stopped it. Then her thumb pushed the plunger, injecting five milligrams of Valium into his spinal fluid, deep within his brain.

As she withdrew the empty syringe, he shuddered and let go. Stiffening, he arched backwards, and fell. As he landed, he looked like a stone bridge with only his helmet and boots touching the pavement. But then he convulsed, flipping onto his left side, coming to rest curled in the fetal position. A pool of urine formed beneath his buttocks.

The world vanished for a few moments, as Chris stooped over the limp body, gasping for breath. Night reappeared and she trembled. The cold, brick walls of the hospital hung over her head. Was he alone? She imagined worse dangers lurking in the darkness. Running from the fallen man and the terror of the night, every shadow turned her head, every sound made her stumble. She thought of one thing, getting home.

Fear followed her to the parking lot and into her car. She locked the doors and stifled her tears, turning the urge to cry into hatred for the man. For a lifetime, she'd lost herself in her work, denying her loneliness, striving for perfection. But he'd forced her to loose control, to face her vulnerability, to become like everyone else.

The scenery on the ride home was a blur, the once familiar streets foreign. She drove absently, automatically, from the memory of hundreds of identical commutes. The threats to her life had come daily over the past few weeks. Perhaps Rupp had finally cracked under the strain of a ruined career and a drug problem. But was it Rupp who had attacked her? And had she killed him?

She parked the car and ran up the stairs to the door of her apartment. Fumbling with the key, her breath as short as during the assault, the fatigue of countless hours on call merged with exhaustion from the fight.

Inside, after turning on every light, she needed a moment of peace before calling the police. Collapsing on the bed, head buried in a pillow, she closed her eyes, trembling. She wanted Paul to put his arms around her and whisper something lovely.

Peaches jumped onto the bed and growled. The image of a black monster rising from a pool of slime flashed before Christine's inner eye, like an old B-grade science fiction movie, in black and white. The monster bellowed in pain and disappeared, sucked back into the slime. She forced her eyelids open, and the light comforted her. Drawing the soft kitten close, she caressed it and listened to the unusual silence of the night.

__CHAPTER 26__

PAYING THE TAXI DRIVER, Paul added a generous tip for rushing to Sea-Tac airport. Wishing he'd been able to pack leisurely, he tried to plan, to think. Time had permitted only a brief shower and a change of clothes at his apartment. Now, with less than an hour left until the flight to Phoenix, he clutched his carry-on bag and worried about the contents. Inside, he'd packed a change of underwear, a toothbrush, toothpaste, some useful drugs, his laptop, and the disassembled pieces of a 38 caliber pistol.

The pistol was all plastic, except for the two rounds he'd hidden among the coins and metal containing toiletries in order to conceal them from x-ray screening. He'd constructed the pistol using Wetlock's state of the art 3-D printer, from a blueprint file purchased online. The rounds came from his own 38 semi-auto.

He wanted the gun to be in his pocket when he touched down in Phoenix. Two muggings in one day had given him plenty of reason to be paranoid. He tried to dismiss the attacks as purely bad luck, but a crazy thought kept surfacing. Maybe someone doesn't want the transplants to be stopped. Hadn't Arens warned of danger even before the search for Joe Tyce? And Paul still heard Christine's voice, "Be careful, those organs are important to a lot of powerful people."

Destroying Bertha's heart had dashed someone's hope for a new life. The intended heart recipient might never get another chance. No matter what, the shortage of transplantable hearts meant that Paul had killed someone. At least one name would be removed from a long list of desperate people waiting for organs. One more would die for lack of a heart, murdered by a most circuitous route, but murdered nonetheless. That the dead patient remained anonymous didn't count. The lives of organ recipients depended on prompt delivery of the organs.

The airport pulsed, wide awake, welcoming early morning travelers with taped announcements instructing them where not to park. A policeman waved his ticket book threateningly at vehicles that hesitated too long. The travelers answered with car horns, long good-byes, and diesel fumes. Buses, cars, and taxis fought for space at the long curb. Tourists in leisure clothes stood out among business executives.

Paul exhaled, watching the steam as the warm vapor clashed with the cold air. Pulling his Gortex coat closed in front, he vowed to follow the infected organs to the hospital in Phoenix, if necessary, to prevent the transplants. The potential horror of an epidemic of crazed murderers prevented any other course of action. The nationwide transplantation network, set into motion, had gathered overwhelming momentum. Somehow, he needed to find the brakes.

The last few days merged into one frantic blur, worse than the longest night on call. A liberal distribution of bruises and aches reminded him of the beatings he'd taken. At least the residency program wouldn't miss him, thanks to Dr. Beck and a week of scheduled vacation. Paul resigned himself to living at the hospital for several weeks to pay Beck back. Some vacation.

Paul's belly growled. He couldn't remember his last meal, and his last good night's sleep was like a distant dream. Part of the residency curriculum included enduring long sleepless hours, and he had a talent for it. Years of practice had enhanced his natural ability to stay alert a little longer, to think clearer, to work another hour, to push the limit. The plane ride promised food and a few hours sleep. He looked forward to the respite.

Inside the airport, the vaulted steel and glass ceiling amplified and blended hundreds of conversations into one roll of continuous thunder. Above the wall of airline ticket counters hung view screens with flight information. On Airwest airlines' departure screen, he found the 5:30 AM flight to Phoenix. It was on time.

He got in line at an Airwest airlines ticket kiosk. In front of him, a man printed out a boarding pass. Next to the man was a six foot long plastic packing tube and a wooden board with four wheels that looked like a giant skateboard. Paul recognized the contraption. It was a landsurfer. He'd tried one at Manzanita Beach last summer, an experience much like windsurfing, but without the water. His sailboard had been one of the only possessions he'd managed to salvage from his broken marriage. He wished he could be on his sailboard right now, skimming along the Columbia River, the wind at his back. He thought about the freshwater spray and the power of the bulging sail. "Are you using this station?" said a woman behind him.

The image of the river faded. "Yeah, sorry," said Paul. He stepped up to the kiosk, swiped his credit card, and retrieved the ticket he'd reserved. It was a first class ticket to Phoenix. Unfortunately, the only seat left on the plane when he bought the ticket was in first class. But he had no choice. He had to be on this flight, even if it took him forever to pay off his credit card. The machine spit out his boarding pass and Paul sighed. He'd rather use the money to do something special with Chris next week, not to chase disembodied organs across the country.

Paul checked the LCD monitors above him again. Flight 436 was still on time. He had his seat assignment, one carry on bag, and less than forty minutes until takeoff.

He reached the airport security checkpoint entrance, sweating profusely, heart pounding. After a TSA agent checked his ID and boarding pass, he followed the crowd through a twisting maze to the screening area. Two security stations sat side by side, one idle. A short line formed in front of the station in use. He joined the line, looking side to side, trying to avoid the gaze of the TSA agents. What if his nervousness raised suspicions? Didn't they have special training, profiles of dangerous people? They can't read minds.

But a lump in his throat made breathing difficult.

A female TSA agent, in a white shirt and blue pants, monitored the screen above the x-ray conveyor belt. She yawned. Behind the metal detector, another uniformed agent remained in constant motion. She darted between the metal detector and a full body scanner, peeking through the rectangular portals and waving a silver wand, a miniature version of the big metal detector. On the other side of the metal detector, on a table, were several bins for holding coins and other metal objects that might trigger the alarm.

An overweight policeman sat behind a podium, beyond the security checkpoint, near a table used for opening suspicious bags. A large automatic pistol clung conspicuously to his side. A sign hung overhead: "All Jokes Will Be Taken Seriously."

"Step through."

The man ahead of Paul walked calmly through the open gateway, and the metal detector remained silent.

"Put the bag on the conveyor belt," said the attendant, running around to the side of the x-ray machine.

Step through, step through," she said, motioning with the wand and frowning.

As Paul walked through the metal detector, the alarm sounded and his heart skipped a beat.

"Empty your pockets, please."

His heart raced as he dug deeply into the pockets of his jeans, and discovered a handful of loose change.

"Put it in the bin on the table. Step back and come through again."

He did, and the metal detector remained silent. Then Paul saw the TSA agent on the gate side of the x-ray booth holding up his carry on bag. "Is this your bag?" said the agent. Paul couldn't breathe. He nodded his head, and watched in horror as the agent started searching his bag. She would find the gun and the bullets for sure, Paul thought, and he would land in jail. Then he'd never be able to stop the transplants, or practice medicine again.

She held up one of the white plastic gun components and looked it over. Paul felt like he'd swallowed a lead weight. To Paul's surprise, the agent tossed the plastic piece back into the bag, and zipped it shut. She handed the bag back to Paul. He took a deep breath.

Paul remembered debating his father for hours about the surest way, theoretically, to smuggle a gun on board a commercial jet, never imagining a reason to actually do it. A pilot for over twenty years, his father had noted many loopholes in airline security.

Paul checked his watch. The flight left in ten minutes. After running through the concourse, he arrived out of breath at the gate with a minute to spare. No one except the gate agent waited by the entrance to the jetway.

"Just made it," said the gate agent, as she scanned Paul's boarding pass. "Hurry. We're about to close the doors."

Paul stepped up to a tall flight attendant with heavy makeup and blond hair. She checked his boarding pass.

"You must be a busy man, first class and last on board."

Paul smiled, "True. I'm a doctor, and my schedule is tight."

"Glad you made it, doctor. Will that bag go under your seat, overhead, or would you like to put it up front in the closet? We've got plenty of room up front."

"It'll fit under my seat," he said, "I'd like to keep it with me."

Her huge crimson lips smiled from ear-to-ear. "That's fine. Take your seat. And welcome aboard."

Several hours passed uncomfortably and the much anticipated sleep never came. He watched the blond flight attendant as she prepared drinks for the flight crew, a steady stream of water and coffee for the pilot and copilot. The only time the cockpit door would be unlocked was to admit the flight attendant or if one of the pilots needed a bathroom break.

Seated next to him was a matronly woman, rotund and covered with gaudy costume jewelry. She never made any conversation, but she smiled at him when he looked her way.

Trembling, he thought of the gun being discovered, even though it was in pieces and well hidden under his seat. A child somewhere behind screamed, grating on his already frayed nerves. He tried to read the Seattle Times, but couldn't concentrate, so he stared out the window at the ever changing tops of clouds. He wondered what he could do in Phoenix to prevent the transplants.

The overhead speakers crackled. "Captain Ridgeway here again. We'll be crossing into Utah soon and flying south, west of Salt Lake City. We've got strong winds in our favor, and should arrive in Pheonix a few minutes ahead of schedule."

The scene through the Plexiglas window, the tops of clouds, looked like a vast Arctic snow field. Paul felt chilled, like before coming down with the flu, and even his coat didn't help. Poking with his fork at scrambled eggs on a plate in front of him, he tried unsuccessfully to coax an appetite. In small sips he managed to finish a cup of coffee.

After the flight attendant spirited away his tray, he folded the table up into the back of the seat in front and locked it. The flight gave him time to think up a plan. He decided to call Wetlock from Pheonix, to see if he had proof yet that the organs carried a deadly virus. Then someone at the hospital in Phoenix might listen to him. But what if Wetlock couldn't give him proof? What then? No one, not even Chris, believed as strongly as he did that the transplants must be stopped.

A terrifying thought seized him. He was on his own. Totally alone. He felt the terrible burden of being the only person capable of stopping a worldwide epidemic of psychotic killers. The AIDS virus originated long before anyone knew of the potential for human suffering. No one had an opportunity to stop the AIDS epidemic. But now he had a chance to stop a new epidemic, and a moral obligation to try. But at what cost? How could he weigh the personal consequences of taking aggressive action against the potential for mass devastation?

The passengers didn't know about the dangerous cargo in the hold, below. What if no one in Phoenix believed him? How would he stop the transplants? If he could only buy time to prevent the organs from reaching their final destination. Time for what? Maybe to convince Christine's friend at the CDC of the danger? Or perhaps to publicize Wetlock's results? Once the organs reached Phoenix, they'd travel by special courier to the hospital. How could he possibly intervene?

The speaker crackled again. The Captain had been on the intercom every few minutes, narrating the entire flight. "Captain Ridgeway again. We'll be flying over the Great Salt Desert in about 20 minutes, and the Bonneville Salt Flats, home of the famous Bonneville Speedway. There's not a cloud in the sky over the desert today. You should be able to get a spectacular view of the Salt Flats soon, flat as a runway."

The Captain's last words flashed like neon in Paul's mind. Flat as a runway. He shook his head, trying to rid it of another crazy thought, but the idea grew. Today was the day for crazy thoughts. He needed a solution to a deadly problem, and he'd found it. Hijack the plane.

He thought about the consequences. *I'm a doctor, for Christ's sake.* But what about an epidemic of madmen leaving a trail of human destruction? Could he stand by and allow a million more Jenny Walkers, like his own sister, withdrawn, afraid, or an entire world paralyzed with fear?

The madness he'd seen in Jenny's eyes still lived in the cargo hold, ironically, a hitchhiker, courtesy of a mindless technology. He thought about the unspeakable evil, hurtling toward Phoenix at over five-hundred miles per hour.

He stroked his mustache and made up his mind. The epidemic must be stopped, here, now. He'd worry about the consequences later. He knew that hijacking could bring the death penalty in spite of his honorable intentions. All airplane hijackers probably thought they had a sacred cause. In any case, he'd be guaranteed to have his say with the federal authorities and the media.

He needed to act fast, but time passed slowly in a surreal way. The woman in the seat next to him got up for a bathroom break. He quickly assembled and loaded the 3-D gun inside his carry on bag. From his bag, out of a kit containing medications, he removed a small bottle of ipecac. A small amount of ipecac would cause extreme nausea and vomiting almost immediately. Paul had entertained the wild thought of using ipecac to disable one of the transplant surgeons. That was a tame thought compared to what he was planning now. He zipped the carry on bag shut, and stashed it beneath the seat in front.

Paul's opportunity came a few minutes later, when he saw the blond flight attendant in the galley preparing two more cups of coffee for the pilots. Paul got up, pretending to head for the occupied bathroom. He waited outside the bathroom door, next to the galley. An obvious open compartment at far edge of the galley was full of magazines. "Do you happen to have any magazines I could read?" Paul asked the flight attendant.

"Sure do," she said, and she walked to the edge of the galley to retrieve the magazines.

That was all the time Paul needed. While she was looking through the magazines at the far end of the galley, Paul dumped a generous dose of ipecac into one of the cups of coffee. The flight attendant handed him a copy of "Business Week" and "Inc."

"Thank you," said Paul. The bathroom was still occupied, and Paul took the magazines back to his seat. He unfolded the Seattle Times on his lap as the old woman next to him returned to her seat. Under cover of the newspaper, Paul unzipped his carry on bag and grabbed the gun, flipping it into the paper in one quick motion. Folding the paper in half concealed the gun from view. The woman next to him never noticed anything. Paul saw the flight attendant enter the cockpit with the two cups of coffee, and come out with an empty tray.

A few minutes later, the galley phone started flashing like a strobe light. The flight attendant picked up and listened. Color drained from her face, in spite of her heavy makeup. "Right away!" she said, and then hung up the phone. She walked right up to Paul. "Can I speak to you for a moment, by the galley?"

Paul nodded and headed for the front of the aircraft with the Seattle Times covering the gun, each step heavier than the last, concentrating on slowing down his breathing. It felt like last summer, when he'd stood on the bridge at Goldbar, ankles strapped to a bungee cord, trying to convince himself to take the plunge. But bungee jumping had a relatively predictable outcome, and it was legal.

Toting a gun down the aisle of a commercial jet made bungee jumping seem easy by comparison. The closer he got to the front, the more he pushed himself. Stay alert, he told himself. Keep going, think clearly, push the limit.

At the front of the aircraft, in the galley, the flight attendant spoke in a hushed voice, "The copilot has suddenly taken ill. I want to avoid making a general anouncement for a doctor. I don't want a scene that might panic the passengers. Can you please take a look at him?"

"Sure thing," said Paul, grasping the gun tightly inside the folded newspaper, with a sweaty hand. The plastic 3-D gun held two rounds, but he didn't intend to shoot anyone. He needed the gun to provide a convincing threat. It certainly scared him.

The passengers in first class looked very drunk and didn't seem to care as Paul and the flight attendant approached the locked door of the cockpit. The flight attendant phoned into the cockpit, and a few moments later, the door opened. The flight attendant entered first, then Paul entered in silence. A wall of high technology electronics engulfed them. The monitoring gauges and controls reminded him of his anesthesia equipment, but on a grander scale. A wrap-around windshield created the impression of skimming effortlessly through a blue sky. The flight attendant shut and locked the cockpit door.

The copilot in the right hand seat dry retched violently into an airsickness bag, his face ashen. There was vomit on the floor, likely from when the ipecac had first hit. It was sheer luck that the copilot, and not the pilot, drank the tainted coffee.

"You're going to be OK," said Paul. "It will pass in an hour or so."

"How can you be so sure?" said the flight attendant.

"Because I'm the one who made him sick." He uncovered the pistol, immediately gaining the undivided attention of the pilot, copilot, and the flight attendant. They said nothing, awaiting his next move. Had they been trained to simply submit? He knew the crew had been trained to deal with emergencies like these, his father had told him about the training. Ultimately, the Captain would call the shots. So, as the prolonged silence continued, Paul studied the Captain.

Returning Paul's scrutiny, Captain Ridgeway appeared calm. Ruggedly handsome, his short silver hair parted in the middle above a pair of dark eyebrows, slightly frosted, like black ice. Wrinkles radiated from his eyes like the runway layout at an international airport. An angular jaw pressed his thin lips together in an unwavering line.

Looking more outraged than upset, his face tightened. "What is it you want?"

"I want you to land on the Salt Flats," said Paul.

"That's impossible," the Captain protested. "There's not enough room to land on the desert. I need at least a seven thousand foot strip."

"You're going to land on the Salt Flats. You can find 10,000 feet down there if you need it."

"But the ground's too soft."

"Don't bullshit me. The ground's as hard as cement. My father's a pilot. He once told me landing on the Salt Flats would be safe and easy."

The Captain exchanged glances with the retching copilot, who looked as young as Paul, and probably just as scared. "OK, I'll put it down on the Flats. Then what?"

"Then? That's all you need to know for now."

Paul caught the Captain's arm as he reached for the radio headset. "No communications."

"I've got to tell them something. Salt Lake will pick up our course change. If I don't respond, they'll have the whole air force out looking for us."

Paul's grip tensed on the gun, now slippery with sweat, his hand trembling. Unclenching his hand steadied the gun. "That's not true, and you know it. When they realize something's gone wrong, they'll track us on radar until we set down. And they'll still have to locate us on the ground."

"I suppose you're right." Arm released, the Captain's hand came to rest on the central console, his middle finger brushing a small knob.

Paul reached down and flipped a toggle switch on the console. "And no transponder distress code, either." Thankfully, his father had discussed flight operations, including many of the airline security precautions. But how many might come as a surprise? And what other tricks did Captain Ridgeway know?

A loud alarm horn sounded in the cockpit. The Captain snapped to attention, checking the controls.

"What's wrong?" asked Paul.

"We've got a problem with the fuel feed," said the copilot.

Sweat ran from Paul's forehead. The gauges on the wall stared back at him, like a hundred unfriendly eyes. He felt claustrophobic. Suddenly, the cockpit was too small, the air stagnant, and his heart fluttered. "What is this? What's going on?"

"I've got to bring the plane down at Salt Lake," insisted the Captain, reaching for the radio headset. "I'm going to call for emergency clearance."

"No!" Paul shouted, checking the controls. Between the pilot and the copilot, the large handles controlling the engine throttles angled backward. He realized the copilot must have secretly eased the throttles back. "It's the stall warning, right? Yes, it must be. Bring the throttles up. Now."

The Captain shook his head, but eased the throttles forward, and the alarm horn quit. He looked down the barrel of Paul's gun.

"Please, no more false alarms," said Paul.

"Look," said the Captain, "Sharon is my A-line, my senior. She's got to get back into the cabin, or the other attendants will know something's wrong."

Paul noticed blue mascara running above Sharon's eyes. She bit her lip and smeared her bright red lipstick.

"OK," he said. "Go back to the cabin. Act like nothing happened. Another member of my team is in the cabin, and he'll be watching you. Don't discuss the situation with anyone. Don't try to pass a message or make a phone call."

"Do exactly as he says," ordered the Captain. "Don't talk to anyone, understood?"

"I understand," she said, straightening the back of her hair. "I can handle it."

Paul opened the cockpit door. Sharon took a deep breath and entered the cabin with a big red smile for the first class passengers. He locked the door behind her.

"What do you think the surface is like?" the copilot asked.

"Hard packed, likely," said the Captain. "It can probably hold our footprint." He turned to Paul. "May I inform the crew? The passengers need preparation for emergency landing."

"Go ahead. Just don't tell them it's a hijack."

The Captain sighed, pausing for a moment before activating the intercom. "Attention. This is the Captain. We have a mechanical problem that will require us to land immediately. The landing area is a smooth, unpaved desert strip. Aside from a few bumps and a lot of dust, we should have little difficulty. As a precaution, flight crew will instruct all passengers on emergency landing procedures."

A loud murmur in the cabin grew to a deafening roar. Paul heard crying, along with every manner of Western and Eastern prayer. The jet shuddered as the Captain lowered the landing gear. He made a first pass over the landing strip, and then circled back for his final approach. The ground looked whitish-brown, unobstructed, a flat bed of sand for as far as the eye could see.

"It's been a long time since I've landed without instrument guidance and without the tower," said the Captain, beginning the final approach. "Jettison the excess fuel," he ordered. The copilot complied.

The ground zoomed up to meet the aircraft, approaching faster than during any landing Paul had watched through a side window. *Easy, Dad said.* The landing strip looked clean, but what if the desert contained a hidden hazard: a fence, a pothole, a telephone cable? What if the surface contained a soft area, and the heavy jet sunk? Too much could go wrong.

Landing reminded Paul of anesthetic emergence, bringing the patient out of the anesthetic at the end of surgery. So many things can go wrong, but the anesthesiologist, like the pilot, has the training to compensate. Most often, emergence happened according to strict guidelines that worked under normal circumstances. Sophisticated machines and electronics guide the process. But machines can not be trusted, for they fail occasionally. And waking up a sick patient, like landing on the desert, requires a craftsman with a healthy blend of art and science. Hundreds of split second judgments must be made the old fashioned way, by the human brain.

"Pull up! Pull up!" shouted a mechanical voice.

"Shut the damn thing off," said the Captain.

As the ground drew closer, the passengers quieted. With the surface close enough to touch, the engines screamed. The two rear wheels struck first and bounced back into the air. Down they went again, jarring the plane, bumping uneasily along the earth. The cockpit vibrated violently, and Paul held on tight to the back of the Captain's chair. Sand swirled against the windshield. The tires screeched, and the roaring wind fought the plane's forward momentum. A loud bell clanged.

"Fire on number one," shouted the copilot.

The Captain reached up and pulled a red, T shaped handle. "Number one out." More bells filled the cockpit. "Hellfire! Must be the sand. Shut everything down at the end of the roll."

After a long, unsteady roll, the jet came to a complete stop and the copilot pulled the second fire handle. "Engines down," he said. Cheers rang out from the passengers, sand settled on the windshield.

Paul couldn't believe he'd actually taken over a jet and forced it down in the desert. He felt light, warm. A definite high. Now he understood the corrupting lure of pure power.

"What now?" asked the Captain.

Basking in his ill-gotten glory, he'd almost forgotten his quest. "I want the organs."

"What?" The Captain squinted.

"The live organs. What cargo hold are they in?"

"That's a strange request from a terrorist."

"I'm an anesthesiologist, not a terrorist," said Paul.

"Anesthesiologist?" The Captain's mouth opened again, but nothing more came out.

"I don't have time to explain. I want the live organs, I'm sure you've read the manifest. Where are they?"

"First cargo compartment. Up front, starboard," answered the Captain. "I can open that one for you." He toggled a switch in the cockpit. The plane shuddered, a mechanical whirring and groaning came from below.

Paul slipped the gun into the pocket of his coat. "I want the both of you to evacuate out the forward door."

The Captain looked at the ashen face of his dry retching copilot. "All right," he said. "You heard the doctor. Let's do what he says." Taking the lead, the Captain entered the cabin, and the passengers all tried to talk at once. He held up his hands for silence. The plane quieted, a baby's cry the only sound. "It's all right," said the Captain. "Just remain calm and in your seats. Buses will be here, soon. We're going outside to inspect the exterior of the aircraft."

The Captain opened the forward door and activated the escape slide. With a loud pop, it unfolded like some kind of strange, yellow flower blooming instantly in a time lapse video. A cold breeze swept away the stale cabin air. The copilot left the plane first, followed by the Captain.

Standing in the exit doorway, with his gun concealed in his pocket, Paul looked down at the two men outside. "Move away from the slide," he shouted. And they did. He jumped onto the slide, landing on his feet at the bottom, the gun still in his hand.

The morning sun rose in the east. A strong wind whipped across the Flats from the northeast, blasting him in the face with cold and sand. Wind made the air feel colder than Seattle, but he thought the actual temperature must be warmer. As far as he could tell, the plane sat alone in the desert. But he assumed the area would soon be crawling with police. "Open the hold and remove the live organs."

On the right side of the plane, the forward cargo door had been opened, exposing the interior of the plane. The jet looked like a giant silver lizard with a slab of meat cut out of its belly. After reaching up along the floor of the hold, the Captain pulled out a flexible, mesh ladder. He climbed into the compartment, and started handing out the oversized cargo, which had been loaded in last, including the landsurfer and the plastic packing tube, several bicycles in cardboard boxes, and some musical instruments. The copilot received the cargo, setting it aside on the desert floor.

At last, a box appeared with an orange florescent label beneath a sticker depicting a pair of silver winged shoes. Judging by the size of the first box, it had to be the liver. Four other boxes followed in rapid succession, and then the Captain climbed down from the compartment. "That's it, they're all here," he said, wiping his hands together.

"Open them," said Paul. "Spill them on the ground."

The crew tore the cardboard lids off the boxes, opened the styrofoam coolers, and removed the triple wrapped plastic containers. One at a time, the Captain opened and dumped the plastic containers. Out plopped the liver from its wide plastic tub like wet mud from a child's pail. On the sand, the kidney quivered like a brown water balloon, and the pancreas dried out instantly like a sunbathing snake. The eyes bounced and rolled across the ground, coming to rest like two exhausted fish out of water. One of the winged shoe stickers tumbled along the sand.

"All right, its done," said the Captain. "Now what?" He stood stiffly, arms folded, waiting for an answer.

Paul didn't have one. Destroying the organs had been his goal. He still needed proof from Wetlock, and to stop the kidney now on its way to New York, a perfect kidney, a six antigen match. Chris had promised to try stopping the lone kidney, but had she? Soon the police would arrive, and he'd rather not be here when they did. He'd have a lot of explaining to do. If he could only escape, finish his task, and face the authorities later. He couldn't get into any more trouble if he left right now. They could only hang him once.

The Salt Flats looked endless. The wind blew sand into his face. There it was, right in front of his eyes, the way out. "Move away, all of you."

The crew members backed away, moving toward the plane. For the first time since the beginning of the hijack, Paul released his grip on the gun, leaving it in his pocket. Then he picked up the long packing tube that had been thrown from the cargo hold. Screwing off the top, he spilled out the contents, a sail and its main components, and began to assemble them.

At the Columbia River Gorge he'd made a game out of rushing to rig his sailboard, so he wouldn't miss a minute of fun. This time it wasn't a game, and it wasn't fun, either. But it took only a few minutes to rig the sail, hook the mast foot into the board, and catch the northeast wind. As the landsurfer shot across the Flats, he looked back in time to see the Captain scratching his head.

CHAPTER 27

THE WIND BLEW FIERCELY across Paul's back, filling the white sail of the landsurfer, propelling the giant skateboard due south. Thankfully, he had the morning sun in the east to orient him. Struggling to hold the boom out over the port side, the sail bulged with a steady northeast wind. He could hold this broad reach for a long time, if the gnawing cold didn't zap his strength. But could he last long enough to cross the Flats?

Speed counted now, more than ever. And he had speed, perhaps thirty miles per hour or more. The wheel bearings screamed, drowned out by the rushing wind. If he fell off the narrow board at this speed, he'd never have to answer to the police, or anyone else. The landsurfer took the speed well, it had been designed for high speed. Heavy, rubber treaded steel wheels glided over the bumpy earth.

Traveling across the barren Flats driven by the wind, he imagined himself an explorer on an alien planet. The ground flying by beneath gave him hope, made him feel free. Hiding behind the sail and navigating through the clear window provided some protection from the apparent wind. Sunshine warmed him slightly, and every fiber of his body pulsed with exhilaration.

He tried to judge how long he'd been landsailing by gauging the growing ache in his forearms, and the increasing numbness from the cold. Except for rolling mountains on the distant horizon, the Salt Flats continued, vast and featureless. Again, he imagined himself sailboarding on the Columbia River, tossed by the waves, battered by the wind, happy.

As long as the ride lasted, he expected his glee to continue. But the ride couldn't last, because the tall, white sail rose up like a signal flag, easy to spot on the flat desert. How long would it take for the police to find him? And where did he hope to go?

A noise cut through the wind, a mechanical noise. Above him, a helicopter shadowed his movements. It followed him for a minute, and then veered away in the direction of the airplane. He assumed the safety of the passengers came first, but expected the helicopter, or someone else, to return soon.

Then he noticed an interstate highway. It had to be Interstate Highway 80. The landsurfer rapidly approached a rest stop. He sailed into it, met by the astonished and curious glares of tourists and truckers. More than anything, he wished he could disappear. The last thing he needed was notoriety.

Scrambling off the board, he disappeared into the men's room. At least he'd escaped the scrutiny of the crowd. When he came out a few minutes later, the curious crowd had dispersed.

At the water fountain, he drank deeply, not knowing when his next chance might come. The water tasted metallic. Leaning against the wall of the rest room building, he tried to look nonchalant. It was just another day out landsailing on the Flats. Didn't everyone? On the ground, the sail luffed in the breeze, the board at rest.

Venturing into the parking lot, he walked among the trailers, trucks, and cars. One driver left his car and stretched, another driver raised his hood to check the oil, and two children played tag on the sidewalk. A beat up pickup truck, loaded with empty burlap sacks, pulled in and rolled to a stop. Two men dressed in Cowboy boots and leathers left the truck, headed for the bathroom.

Paul leaned against the back of the pickup. When no one appeared to be watching, he climbed over the tailgate and buried himself beneath the burlap. The flatbed smelled of mildew and manure. A few minutes later, the truck doors slammed and the engine started. He heard a police siren, and it kept getting louder. The truck rolled slowly through the parking lot, stopping abruptly as the siren passed by. He huddled motionless underneath the burlap, hardly breathing. But the truck started moving again and accelerated onto the highway as the siren faded.

The burlap kept him warm and a clump of it served as a crude pillow. Exhausted, unable to sleep, he tried to rest as the truck rumbled down the interstate. It stopped only for gas, bathroom breaks, and fast food, and none of it for him. Hungry and thirsty, he didn't dare leave the truck, not even to relieve himself.

They kept heading west. From time to time he peeked over the tailgate, reading a sign on the opposite side of the road. Night fell and the driving marathon continued. He guessed the men were going to stop in Reno, eight to ten hours from the Utah border. No matter what their final destination, he planned to get out of the truck in Reno.

As he had predicted, they left the interstate highway and entered downtown Reno. From beneath the burlap he watched thousands of lights turn the night into an unnatural day. People milled through the streets from casino to casino. For those too drunk to find the casinos, slot machines in the doorways faced the streets. He ducked back into hiding, hoping for the truck to stop soon.

It did. After the drivers left, he slipped out from beneath the burlap and climbed out of the flatbed. He needed to know the fate of the kidney headed to New York. He didn't dare turn on his cell phone, figuring the call would be traced. So he found a pay phone and called Chris, but she didn't answer her cell phone. Without giving his name, he called the operating room, but she wasn't in surgery, either. Then he dialed her apartment and the phone rang and rang. He thought it was strange, because her answering machine should pick up.

He wondered why she'd turn off the machine, since she should be expecting his call. Maybe she'd gotten tired of the telephone threats, or perhaps something bad had happened. He'd been mugged twice in Seattle while hunting for Joe Tyce. Now he'd involved Chris in the investigation and in his quest to stop the transplants. If she'd gotten into trouble, it was his fault and he might be the only one who could help her.

He finally hung up, thinking it best to get back to Seattle as soon as possible and find Chris. Then he could get the test results from Wetlock and consider turning himself over to the authorities.

For now, he'd have to feed himself, find a way out of town, and avoid anyone trying to find him. It made sense for the police to watch the airports. Every airline security agent probably had his description by now. Travel by bus was the only alternative. He had plenty of cash. With a little luck, no one would be watching the bus stations. Connecting through to Seattle might take days, but at least he could sleep.

The smell of food filled the street, but eating had to wait. Getting back to Seattle took precedence. To get to the bus station fast, he hailed a taxi. The fat, round face of the driver looked at Paul through the rearview mirror. On the radio, a commercial ended and the news began: "Our top story at this hour. Police are still looking for the man who forced Airwest airlines flight 436 down on the Bonneville Salt Flats today, sailed away on a landsurfer, and disappeared."

As the newscaster continued, Paul closed his eyes and sank into the seat. Then came his name and description. Authorities are looking for a white male, five-foot nine, one hundred fifty pounds, sandy brown hair and mustache." Other news said his picture was already on TV. He figured they must have raided his apartment.

He opened his eyes, turning away each time the driver looked in the rearview mirror. When they reached the bus station, Paul paid the fair and avoided eye contact with the driver.

Inside the station, he treated every face with avoidance and suspicion. At the ticket booth, his luck held. A bus to Sacramento left in twenty minutes. From there, he could catch a midnight bus up interstate five to Seattle. After all the stops, he'd arrive in Seattle at 6:00 PM tomorrow night.

But he needed food, enough to last the entire trip. Leaving the bus, even for a minute, would increase the risk of being identified. One wall near the ticket booth was lined with vending machines. He removed his coat, tied the sleeves together, and filled the makeshift bag with enough pop, cookies, candy bars, and chips to last for 24 hours.

From another machine he bought a cheap pair of sunglasses and a traveler's shaving kit, complete with a disposable razor and a miniature can of shaving cream. Ducking into the rest room, he shaved off his mustache and then stroked the bare skin above his upper lip. After putting on the sunglasses, he examined his new face in the mirror. At least now he didn't match the police description so exactly. With a few minutes to spare, he ran for the bus.

Onboard, he sat far in the back, stashing his food by his side on an empty seat. Now he could rest. Until 6:00 PM tomorrow, he had nothing to do but eat and sleep. Leaning the seat back, eyes closed, he sighed, and despite his gnawing hunger, fell soundly asleep.

CHAPTER 28

IN THE PRESURGICAL SUITE at New York University, Richard Schlesinger daydreamed, looking at the ceiling, ignoring for the moment the cold, hard gurney beneath his back. He smiled, for all his prayers had been answered. No longer did he fear living forever like a freak of nature. A normal life awaited him. He imagined a week in the countryside, hiking through fields of wildflowers, a thousand miles from the nearest dialysis machine.

A nurse appeared at the door. "I just got the news. The helicopter landed. It'll take a while for them to get crosstown. I'm going to take you into the operating room now. Dr. Goodall will OK the kidney before they put you to sleep."

"Can I see it?" Richard asked.

"Of course," she replied, and began pushing the gurney out of the room, into the hallway, and toward the operating room.

He thought about the amazing computer network that had located the perfect kidney for him, a six antigen match, in Seattle of all places. How remarkable to choose him above all others, simply because of his compatible genetics, and rush the kidney three-thousand miles across the continent. He realized there must be people waiting for a kidney in Seattle, too. He felt blessed.

Inside the operating room, two surgical residents stood ready, dressed in full sterile attire, talking shop. As the nurse rolled Richard into the room, he got the impression that participating in a kidney transplant must be a coveted educational experience. A teacher as well as a patient, he didn't mind the residents. The young doctors needed experience to become specialists like his attending surgeon, Dr. Goodall. Richard had great respect for Goodall, for both his competence and his upbeat bedside manner.

After Richard had finally warmed up the gurney, the nurse moved him onto the ice cold operating table. Dr. Goodall entered, a mask partially concealing his round face, his bright eyes and rosy cheeks betraying a smile. In his hand, he carried a jar wrapped in several clear plastic bags. "Hey, hey. Rich. She's here at last," said Goodall, holding up the jar. "A fine specimen, I'm sure. Take a look."

Through the layers of plastic, Richard could barely discern the dark, cylindrical outline of his new kidney. He took deep breath and felt his heart beating in his throat. At last, it was real. If the final inspection showed the kidney to be in good condition, then the operation could begin.

Goodall removed the outer packaging and handed the inner package to one of the residents. After untying the two remaining clear bags, the resident removed the jar. He unscrewed the cap and opened the wide mouthed plastic jar.

"Well," said Goodall, "how's it look?"

The two residents peered into the jar, and then at each other. "I think you'd better see for yourself, sir," said one resident, reaching into the jar with a blunt, scissor-like clamp. He removed the kidney, dripping wet, and held it in the air.

Goodall tore his mask from his head. "Is this someone's idea of a bad joke?"

"What is it?" said Richard, sitting up on the operating table, his old fears returning. "What's wrong with the kidney?"

Goodall snatched the kidney and shook it in the air, sending the metal clamp flying across the room. "What's wrong? I'll tell you what's wrong. It's a goddamn salami! That's what's wrong."

CHAPTER 29

AN HOUR LATE pulling into Seattle, Paul couldn't wait to get off the bus. Out of fear of detection, he'd hardly moved for 24 hours, except to change buses. Luckily, no one had recognized or tried to stop him. The diet of pure junk food took a heavy toll, his gut rumbling. He'd slept a little, recovering from complete exhaustion, but still dazed and tired.

Disembarking after 7:00 PM, he flagged down a taxi and headed for Christine's apartment. His sunglasses made night in the city disturbingly dark, but he felt too afraid to remove the disguise. Chris and Wetlock were the only people who might be able to help him. But Chris might need help, too. Paul wondered if Rupp or the man threatening Chris had finally acted on his violent threats.

After the taxi dropped Paul off, he stood in the vestibule of Christine's apartment building, in front of the locked door. About to buzz her apartment, he noticed the steel door was ajar. So he opened it and climbed the stairs. Standing in front of Christine's door, about to knock, he hesitated. Something didn't feel right. For a moment he stood there, transported back to the night of his first date with Chris, waiting by the door, wondering why he felt so afraid.

Testing the door, he found it unlocked, and realized Chris would never leave it open. After removing his sunglasses, he put them in his coat pocket and retrieved the gun. Taking a deep breath, holding the gun raised in both hands, he kicked the door open.

The living room had been ransacked. Papers, books, tapes, CDs, and DVDs littered the floor. The marble statue had fallen, leaving a pile of fractured arms, hands, and fingers, like a puzzle. The leather couch had no pillows, and the oak coffee table lay on its side on top of a crushed Renoir. Someone had smashed the answering machine. He wondered what they'd been looking for.

"Chris, are you here?" he said, entering the room, cautiously, the gun leading the way. He found no sign of her as he made his way to the kitchen. It looked like the living room, a total mess. Every cupboard had been emptied. Broken glasses and dishes crunched beneath his feet. He noticed Peaches' water and food dishes, unbroken, empty, and figured Chris must not have been in the apartment for at least a day.

"Peaches? Here girl. Peaches?" The cat didn't come. He wondered if she was still in the apartment. If so, she'd be hungry. In the rubble, he found a box of cat food. After pouring it into Peaches' bowl, he filled the other bowl with water, and waited.

"Meow. Meow."

Peaches appeared from behind the refrigerator, dirty and disheveled. She hesitated and cocked her head sideways at him. Then she sprinted to her bowls and began to lap up the water.

Next, he checked the bathroom. The contents of the medicine chest were strewn around the room and multicolored towels covered the floor. The shower curtain and rod lay broken in the tub.

Lastly, he checked the bedroom. Sheets and blankets, stripped from the bed, blocked the doorway. The mattress and box springs stood upright against the far wall, crushing the window blinds. Clothes from the drawers formed piles everywhere. All the hangers in the closet had been ripped from the pole.

Although worried where Chris might be, he felt relieved he hadn't found her dead or injured. Putting the gun away, he used the bedroom phone to call the hospital and page her. He hadn't turned his cell phone back on since getting on the plane, for fear of being tracked. Chris didn't answer her cell phone or a page at the hospital, and he wasn't surprised. Nowhere in the apartment had he found any signs of forced entry. Someone had entered the apartment without breaking in. Chris must have let them in. That meant it had to be someone she knew, and it also meant she'd been here. Whether or not they'd found what they were looking for, they'd probably kidnapped Chris.

Asking the police for help was not an option. Somehow, he had to find Chris, himself. For several minutes, he stood in the bedroom, wondering where to start. Then he noticed something strange on the floor in front of the upright mattress: a dozen long stem, red roses. He stooped to pick them up.

Someone jumped on his back, sending him crashing to the floor on his knees. Fists pounded his head, pushing his face into a pile of clothes. Reaching up blindly behind his head, using his shoulder for leverage, he grabbed the assailant's coat and heaved him forward, flipping him onto his back.

Now kneeling over the man's upside down head, Paul clasped his hands together and batted the face once on each side, like a volleyball. He raised his arms to deliver another blow.

"Enough! OK! Stop!" said the man, trying to guard his head.

Paul lowered his arms, turning the face around in his mind, the dumpy body, the fat fingers. "Jeromy Melvin?"

"Yes, yes. It's me. Oh God. Powers, right? I didn't mean ..."

"What the hell are you doing here?"

"Chris and I, we had plans for tonight, a date. I got here and found this mess. Oh God. I heard you come in. Got scared. Hid behind the mattress. Oh God," he gasped.

Paul knew the part about the date must be true, and the roses confirmed the story. "Take it easy, get up," he said, helping Melvin into a chair. "Wait here a second," he ordered, leaving the room. Searching the kitchen, he found an unbroken glass, rinsed it and filled it with cold water. Returning to the bedroom, he forced Melvin to drink. "Go ahead, it'll calm you down."

Melvin gulped down the cool water, choking and coughing. He closed his eyes and slowed his breathing, handing the glass back. "Thanks, I feel better already. What in God's name is going on here?"

"I was hoping you could tell me," said Paul, rubbing his battered head. "All I know is some of the transplant organs you processed may be infected with a virus that makes people violent."

"A disease?"

"Yes, potentially an epidemic."

"So that's why Christine wanted all the transplant recipient data."

Then it struck Paul. "I forgot about the information you gave Chris. That might be what the burglars were looking for."

"What?"

"Chris and I have been trying to halt the transplants, to convince someone of the danger, someone with the authority to intervene."

Blood trickled from Melvin's nose, dripping onto the bedroom carpet. "That may explain the call I got this morning from the Transplant Coordinator at New York University. I sent them a donor kidney and somebody stole it. God. Can you believe it?"

Melvin had to be telling the truth. Chris must have stolen the kidney, and Paul had pushed her to do it. He'd gotten her into serious trouble.

"I had to tell Arens," said Melvin, "and he's furious."

"Arens? I consulted him several times for advice," said Paul. "But what has he got to do with the transplants?"

Melvin's right eye had swollen shut. His left eye squinted. "Arens runs the program."

"What?"

"Arens runs the transplant program: compatibility testing, specimen preservation, storage facilities, transport protocols, surgical equipment, medications, electrolyte solutions, the works."

"The fetal tissue transplants, too?"

"Yes, everything."

"Since when?"

"Since the National Organ Transplant Act in 1984."

"I'm not familiar with it," said Paul. "Tell me about it."

"Before 1984, the nationwide transplantation network consisted of loosely affiliated, competing organizations, most of them bankrupt from lack of public and private funding. The Organ Transplant Act set up a computerized network to efficiently and equitably coordinate organ transplants. Arens heads the regional authority and also sits on several committees at the national level. Years ago, he rescued the local organizations with Alumni cash, and continues to solicit huge contributions for the transplant program."

"It sounds like a one man monopoly." Paul shook his head. "I can't believe Arens hasn't been hit with an anti-trust suit."

"You don't understand," said Melvin. "The whole organization is non-profit, Arens has a thankless job, and both the University and the government love what he's doing. But I can't understand, he's so meticulous, if you told him about the infection ..."

"I didn't exactly tell him," said Paul, "but I told him enough to figure it out. You mean, he has the authority to stop the transplant program?"

Melvin nodded. "No doubt. If Arens said shut it down, they'd shut it down. I wonder why he didn't?"

"That would ruin his perfect reputation," said Paul. "Arens has the confidence of the medical community. A mishap in the transplant program would shatter that confidence."

"God yes," said Melvin. "An embarrassment like that would make it hard to solicit Alumni cash."

Paul stroked his upper lip, surprised for an instant to find his mustache missing. "That doesn't seem like enough incentive to kidnap a neurosurgeon."

"Christine? Kidnapped? My God. By whom?"

"I don't know, but maybe Arens knows. He seems like the place to start."

"Is there anything I can do to help?"

Paul thought for a moment. "Hmm, yes, there is. Go home and don't talk to anyone. But if you don't hear from me by 8:00 AM tomorrow, call the Sheriff, ask for Jack McCann, tell her everything you know, OK?"

"I understand, I'll do it."

"You won't have to," Jackey said from the doorway. Darkly tanned, dressed in civilian clothes, both hands held her gun outstretched. The fringe on her brown, leather coat dangled from her arms. "Hands on your heads, fingers locked together." Melvin complied. "Hands on your head, Powers, then get down on your knees."

"Jack, I ..."

"Do it! Now, dammit!"

He did. She circled behind him, grabbed his fingers and squeezed them together, painfully, with one amazingly powerful hand. He felt cold steel cuffs close around his wrists and heard them clicking tighter until they pinched his skin. "Where's the gun?"

"Jack ..."

"The gun."

"Right pocket."

She reached into Paul's coat from behind and removed the gun. "What the hell kinda gun is this?"

"3-D printed, home made," said Paul.

Then she walked back into his view. "Who's this guy?" she asked, gesturing toward Melvin.

"Jeromy Melvin, a pathologist. He's got nothing to do with the hijack, he came to see Chris. He's harmless."

"Hijack?" said Melvin. "Oh God. Can I leave, now?"

"Do you have ID?" asked Jackey. Melvin reached down. "Very slowly," she said, pointing her gun at him. He pulled his wallet from his back pocket and handed it to her. She backed away, checked the driver's license, and then returned the wallet. "Looks all right. Do you need an ambulance?"

"I can make it home," he said, rising unsteadily, wiping the blood off his face with his sleeve. "No permanent damage, I think."

"All right, you can go, but I want you to keep your appointment with the Sheriff tomorrow, like you promised Dr. Powers."

"I'll call at 8:00 AM."

"Good."

Melvin left the apartment, and Jackey put her gun away. "Have a seat, Dr. Powers. Did you know the whole FBI is out looking for you, it's remarkable you got this far."

"Dr. Mason's been kidnapped."

"We'll turn that over to the FBI, too."

"But she may not have the time."

"You pulled quite a stunt, but I knew where to find you. Did you also turn over this place?"

"Of course not. Someone doesn't want to admit that the transplants may be deadly, that they may all have to be stopped. Someone's willing burglarize, kidnap, even kill to keep the secret."

"But you destroyed the organs, isn't that the end of it?"

He stood up, pleading with his shackled hands. "Don't you understand? It's not over, yet." He paced, kicking at a pile of clothes. "The City Park Killer, you still after him?"

"Yes."

"I thought so. How many new victims?"

Jackey rested her right hand on her hip, close to her gun. "Two or three a week. The city's in a panic."

"Now think about it. Joe Tyce is still out there. He could be the Killer, or maybe the Killer's more than one person."

"You mean, doc, maybe your hypothetical epidemic has already started to spread? And we're seeing only the tail end?"

"It's possible. I've traced the madness from Earl Dobbs forward, but maybe it didn't start there."

"Then where did it start?"

"When Dobbs died, you mentioned his wife's death drove him berserk."

"Apparently, but ..."

"She died young. Do you know what killed her?"

"The police report said she died after a long illness. I don't know the details."

"Maybe there's a way we can find out. I need to make a phone call."

"You'll get one phone call at the station. I'm going to take you in." She reached for his arm.

"No, you're not," he said, backing away. "It isn't going to make any difference if you drag me in now, or a few hours from now. You've got a killer on your hands, I've got a missing neurosurgeon, and neither one's likely to be found soon by the Task Force or the FBI. I know if we find Chris, we'll find your killer, too. We've got to do this ourselves, and we've got to do it now." Paul held up his cuffed wrists. "Unlock the cuffs, let me make the call."

Jackey stared at the handcuffs. "Dammit. I shouldn't do this. It's definitely not by the book." She took the keys from her belt and unlocked the cuffs. "Don't make an ass out of me." She put the cuffs away.

Paul rubbed his wrists and headed for the telephone. "You made the right choice. Give me a couple of hours. If we haven't found Chris by then, I'm all yours."

She walked in his path, her wide, muscular body eclipsing him, her eyes glaring down. "You're mine, anyway," she said.

He swallowed, sidestepped, picked up the telephone and dialed.

"University Hospital," said the operator.

"Medical records, please." Seconds passed.

"Medical records, can I help you?"

"Yes, this is doctor, uh, Melvin, I want some old information on an ex-patient of mine."

"I can check the computer, patient's name?"

He froze. *Name*? "Just a second, I wrote it down." Cupping his hand over the microphone, he waved Jackey closer. "Dobbs' wife, what was her name?"

She closed her eyes, he waited. "Trudy, Trudy Dobbs."

He uncovered the microphone. "Trudy Dobbs," he said, gambling that she'd been hospitalized at the University. A minute passed.

"Dr. Melvin, is Trudy Dobbs deceased? Gee, she was young."

"Yeah, that's the one." The gamble paid off.

"I have a lot of old admission dates, the last one several years ago, long hospitalizations, many outpatient visits."

"Can you pull the chart from her last inpatient visit?"

"There are no electronic records, she must have been a patient here before we went digital. It might be on microfilm. Give me a few minutes to go in the back and look. Do you want me to call you back?"

"No, I'll hold." He waited over ten minutes, wondering if he'd been disconnected.

"What's going on?" asked Jackey.

"They're looking," he said, tapping on the handset. "Come on already, come on."

"Hello, Dr. Melvin, you still there?"

"I'm here."

"Sorry it took so long. The chart's all on microfilm, but it's peculiar."

"What's peculiar?"

"I can't find it anywhere. It's got to be here, somewhere. It must be misfiled. If it shows up, I'll put it in your mailbox. Can I get you anything else?"

He massaged his temples, trying to relieve a whopper of a headache. "Yes, how about the death certificate? Do you have a copy of it?"

"We should have. Death certificates are filed separately. I'm going to put you on hold, again."

"OK."

Jackey folded her arms. He guessed her patience must be wearing thin. If his hunch didn't yield anything new, she might change her mind and take him right to jail. He waited.

"Hello, Dr. Melvin?"

"Yeah, I'm here."

"I found the death certificate. Let's see, born in Whitechapel, England. Died in Seattle, Washington. You want the time of death?"

"No, the cause." Paul wasn't interested in Trudy's birthplace. He'd heard of Whitechapel, but couldn't recall why.

"Let's see," said the records clerk. "Primary cause: suicide."

A chill ran down his spine. "Do they list any secondary causes?"

"Uh, huh. Secondary cause: acute psychotic attack. And tertiary cause: post traumatic stress disorder. That's all."

He shivered and hung up the phone, speechless.

"Well," said Jackey, "what killed Trudy Dobbs?" The silence continued. "Answer me, Powers, or I'll take you in right now."

He forced out the words. "She died of the same thing that killed Jenny Walker, suicide. She had the virus, I'm sure of it. Trudy and Jenny killed themselves to stop the violence growing in their minds."

"But how did Trudy get infected?"

"I don't know," he said. "But Professor Arens might know. He runs the entire transplant program. I'm certain he must have known about the virus."

"You mean he could've stopped the transplants?"

"Yeah."

"So why didn't he?"

"I don't know. We'll have to question him."

"Arens?" Jackey shook her head. "I've dealt with that old fossil. You won't get any useful information out of him."

She was right. Arens hadn't been completely honest in the past. If he had anything to hide, questioning him wouldn't uncover it.

"You're right," said Paul. "We'd be wasting our time with Arens. But there's someone else who might be helpful, and he's got test results on the virus waiting for me. Jack, I think it's time I introduced you to Mr. Wetlock."

They left Christine's apartment in Jackey's patrol car and drove to the Hut in the pouring rain. At Arens' lab, Wetlock answered the door, scowling, his blue lab coat stained with coffee. "What do you want, now?" he said. "I'm very busy here."

"I've come for the test results," said Paul. "Are they ready?"

"They're inconclusive. Now leave me alone." He started to shut the door, but Paul put his foot in the doorway.

"I've got a few more questions for you," said Paul. "May we come in?"

"Another time, maybe," said Wetlock. "Not today."

"Yes, today," Paul insisted, forcing the door open.

Wetlock threw up his hands. "Oh, whatever. Suit yourself."

He returned to the workbench and bent over a microscope, revealing a bald spot in the center of his curly, white hair. Peering into the microscope with one eye, he examined a slide, ignoring Paul and Jackey as they entered the lab.

Paul walked alongside the workbench, admiring the complex experiment. On the twenty foot long tabletop, odd shaped glassware hung on numerous beaker stands, metal poles with a cast iron base. Tubing, made of rubber and glass, connected the various kinds of glassware. Multicolored liquids dripped their way through the maize of tubing, stopping only long enough to boil above the open flames of several Bunsen burners. "Wetlock," he said, "do you do genetic crossmatching here for the organ transplants?"

Wetlock cocked his free eye toward Paul. "No, that's all done in the University hospital pathology laboratory." He selected one of the many pencils from his upper coat pocket, and proceeded to write notes on a clipboard.

"Does Arens keep tissue samples in the hospital lab for other purposes?"

Wetlock pointed the pencil at Paul. "Look, Powers. That place is crawling with federal inspectors. Arens would need to justify every stored item. Why would he use their storage facilities, when there are no research facilities there?"

"Yeah, you're probably right," Paul admitted. "But is there any other place Arens might store tissue samples for research?"

Wetlock got even paler, the pencil snapped in two, he slammed the clipboard on the table. "Why don't you ask Arens yourself? I don't know anything else. Leave me alone."

"What's with you?" Paul asked. "You used to be friendly. Did Arens tell you not to cooperate with me?"

Wetlock's face flushed, he wobbled, grabbing the workbench for support. "I think you ought to leave, now. I don't have to answer any more questions."

Jackey leaned against the far wall in silence, her arms folded. Paul knew Wetlock was hiding something, but extracting more information from him would be difficult. Strolling alongside the lab bench, Paul picked up an empty beaker stand and unscrewed the long metal rod from the base.

Wetlock snapped to attention. "What are you doing with that? Leave that alone." He trembled, Jackey moved forward.

Paul slapped the metal rod against his left hand. "Wetlock, you're lying, you're very nervous, and you're making me nervous, too." He walked toward Wetlock. "When I get nervous, do you know what happens?" Wetlock backed away from Paul and the workbench. "I have accidents." He swung the rod once across the workbench, reducing a five foot long section of glassware to rubble with a deafening roar.

"Oh, how clumsy of me." Paul smiled.

"You fool!" Wetlock shouted. "That's six months work!"

"What, that?" Paul passed the rod over the rubble, and on the return sweep smashed another foot long section of glassware, closer to Wetlock.

"Stop it! I'll call the police!" said Wetlock, his hair standing straight.

"I am the police," Jackey said, now at Paul's side.

Wetlock staggered to the small table in the back of the lab and collapsed in a chair.

Shaking, he unsuccessfully tried to pour himself a cup of coffee. Elbows on the table, he buried his head in his hands.

Paul put the rod down on the table, and poured a cup of coffee for Wetlock and himself. Jackey shook her head. Across the table from Wetlock, Paul pulled out a chair, reversed and straddled it, supporting his arms on the backrest.

A long silence followed while Wetlock sipped at the coffee. Then he raised his head. "Arens instructed me not to give out any information," he began. "He said others might use the information to compete for grant money. He reminded me of the controversies surrounding organ transplantation, and the terrible repercussions of adverse publicity."

"Wetlock, something odd is happening, and its already having terrible repercussions. I'll do my best to keep you out of it," said Paul. "But you've got to tell me everything you know."

Wetlock drank the coffee, no longer trembling. "You're right, I have noticed some odd things."

Paul leaned closer. "Like what?"

"Like the routine budget requests and inventory lists I submit each year. A few years ago, Arens put in a request for a new protein sequencer."

"A what?" asked Jackey.

Paul, with his hand, chopped in the air at an imaginary object. "A relatively large machine used to break up proteins," he said, "and sort out the parts."

"Correct," said Wetlock, "Our protein sequencer, although rather archaic, still functioned. We put it up for sale. Arens told me it would go to some university in South America, Brazil, I think."

"Is that unusual?" Paul asked.

"No. The sale of used scientific equipment is an important source of income for the University. They keep a full time secretary in accounting to handle all the transactions. Early on, I learned to be very friendly to the secretary, in order to find out what used scientific equipment might be available for interdepartmental trading."

"So what's unusual?"

"Hang on, I'm getting to that. The secretary never handled the transaction for the old protein sequencer, it didn't appear on her list."

"Who submitted the list?"

"Arens."

"Did you mention this to him?" Paul asked.

"Exactly," said Wetlock. "Arens claimed he'd arranged the sale in private, personally. That ended our discussion."

Paul drank his coffee. One missing piece of equipment from a University research lab didn't mean a thing. "Did you lose track of anything else?"

"Nothing major, like the sequencer," said Wetlock. "But, I've lost track of many smaller items. A Petri dish, a test tube, an Erlenmeyer flask, and so on. The losses seemed random, at first. But later, I recognized a definite pattern."

Wetlock slouched in his chair like a marionette with severed strings, his head bowed. Minutes passed, Paul played with the rod on the table, then crushed his Styrofoam cup and tossed it into an overflowing garbage can.

Jackey shook her head. "You want to fill me in?"

"Yeah," said Paul. "I think Mr. Wetlock's trying to tell us Professor Arens is siphoning off supplies to equip another laboratory."

"A secret lab?" asked Jackey.

Wetlock raised his head. "Precisely."

Paul rolled the metal rod on the table. "But if this hypothetical secret lab exists, where is it?"

Wetlock sat upright. "If I had to find it, I'd look in the Stacks."

"The Stacks?" said Jackey.

"The old University library," said Paul.

"Three years ago," Wetlock explained, "the University wanted to tear the Stacks down and put up a modern building in it's place. Arens started a "Save the Stacks" campaign. His passionate speeches about history, tradition, and symbolism enlisted many of the University's most prominent and generous Alumni. But saving the Stacks from the University didn't end the campaign. Arens fought until Congress granted the Stacks "National Historic Landmark" status. No one can destroy the building, now."

"Yes," said Paul, pounding his fist on the table. "The Stacks. That's got to be it. Arens spends hours there, and the building's been remodeled many times. He knows the old place better than anyone alive." Paul jumped up, away from the table.

"Wait. There's one more thing," said Wetlock. "The test was positive. The tissue you gave me is infected with a mutant form of the AIDS virus, similar to the one I discovered in the animal lab. But this virus is different, it's not detectible by standard tests. And judging by it's structure, I don't think it would cause AIDS. In fact, I'm not sure what it does."

"I knew it," Paul said, shaking his fist. "Come on, Jack. We're going to the library." Nearly out the door, he turned back, surveying the tremendous pile of broken glassware, multicolored liquids, and other debris lying on the lab floor. "Oh, and Wetlock, sorry about the mess."

CHAPTER 30

THE SKY EXPLODED with torrents of rain and thunder, drowning the evening din of the inner city. Paul marveled at the ferocity of the lightening, an unusual sight in the Pacific Northwest. Backlit by lightening, the silhouette of the Stacks looked foreboding. Above the dim lights of the University campus, the ivy covered twin towers of the Stacks rose threateningly into the dark sky, appearing and disappearing magically with each burst of light from the heavens.

From high above the entryway to the Stacks, the sculptured cherubs and gargoyles glared down, and on the tower to Paul's right, the wet eyes of the stone griffin flashed, reflecting the electric sky. Running for cover, Paul reached the protected stone canopy over the entrance, shivering. He stood in front of the heavy, wooden doors, frozen by the aura of the old building.

Thunder resounded like sadistic laughter, fading into the unrelenting chuckle of rain pounding the pavement. The Latin inscription over the doorway became a dare, rather than a promise: "PER PORTAM AD VERITATEM."

Several students exited the building. Doomed to be drenched, they walked, probably realizing the futility of running from a fate they couldn't control. Then a man left the building, running. He wore a cowboy hat, dark glasses, and a long overcoat. Paul spun around, his coat dripping cold water. The man in the cowboy hat disappeared into the dark haze.

Jackey appeared at Paul's side. "Are you planning to go inside, Powers?"

She broke his immobilizing trance, and he pointed at where the stranger vanished. "That guy chased a mugger away from me, near the Stacks, a few days ago."

"Only caught a glimpse," said Jackey. "Now that you mention it, he looked familiar to me, too. Can't place him. Forget it. Let's go." She opened the door. "You first."

The vast, empty lobby of the Stacks resounded with their footsteps as they walked toward the elevator. The steel doors of the ancient elevator scissored open, and they entered the dilapidated car. A trail of water followed them, adding to the musty scent of the small compartment. After the door closed, the elevator waited.

"What floor?" asked Jackey.

"Four. Arens always studies there. It's as good a place as any to start."

Paul pushed the button. A sudden tug shook the car, and the two passengers drifted upwards.

"Maybe the good Dr. Arens will take us on a tour," said Jackey, smiling.

"I'm hoping he'll lead us to Chris," said Paul. "It's my fault she's in this mess. I've got to find her."

"You love her, don't you?"

"Yeah, I do."

Moaning and groaning, the elevator climbed slowly. Parts of the elevator shaft revealed numerous remodels of the Stacks. Old hardwood timbers merged with modern four by six studs. Rusted bolts and metal plates crisscrossed huge wooden beams.

"This whole elevator shaft is like a geological core sample of the building," said Paul. "We could trace the construction history by reading the shaft."

Jackey nodded. "A patchwork, held together with spit, a real antique."

The elevator stopped abruptly, and the door creaked open. Paul stepped out, tripping, falling to the floor. The lower lip of the elevator hadn't quite made it to the fourth floor. Jackey stepped up, onto the fourth floor, and grabbed Paul by the arm.

"You all right?" She helped him up.

"Yeah, no damage done." He tried unsuccessfully to brush the dust off his soaking wet clothes.

"That elevator's a landmark by itself," said Jackey.

"True," he agreed.

They stood at the threshold of the room as the elevator door sealed behind them with a disturbing clank. The floor looked deserted, and a quick walk around confirmed the impression.

"No one in any of the study carrels," Paul reported. "I didn't see anyone among the bookshelves."

"We're alone," said Jackey. "Top floor of the Stacks must be unpopular."

"Yeah. It contains the most obscure scientific journals and books." Paul shivered. "I couldn't study here, this place gives me the creeps."

"Me, too. Perfect place to hide the entrance to a lab."

The overhead fluorescent lighting failed, and battery powered emergency lights on the walls activated simultaneously, plunging the room into relative darkness. Long, dim shadows stretched across the room.

"Damn. Just what we need," said Jackey. "A power failure."

"Once we get used to the dark, the emergency lights will be enough," said Paul. "I'm just glad we didn't get stuck in the elevator."

They waited for a minute, their eyes adjusting to the low lighting conditions. On one wall of the room, through five large double-hung windows, lightening pulsed, the room flickered wildly. Thunder rattled the windowpanes. A fierce wind howled and whistled.

"Come on, Jack, let's find the door.

Three doors led in or out of the fourth floor: the elevator door and two metal doors at the stairwell exits. A brief look around the main staircase, located next to the elevator, revealed extensive wear. Paul realized students must use this staircase daily, to avoid the old elevator. A thorough search uncovered nothing.

At the far end of the floor, a second staircase provided an alternate emergency exit. But instead of a doorknob, a red alarm box protruded from the middle of the door. Across the door, connected to the box, a metal lever bar carried a warning, in red:

"EMERGENCY EXIT ONLY-ALARM WILL SOUND."

Meeting back at the elevator, Jackey shared her disappointment. "Maybe we're on a wild goose chase," she said. "Should we search another floor?"

"No, let's not give up, yet," Paul pleaded . "It feels too right." He pointed to the rotary pay telephone. "I called Arens from my cell near that old phone, and the call was forwarded. I remember wondering where Arens took the call. I heard an echo, he sounded far away. But I don't think he was far away. I think he was here. There's an entrance somewhere on this floor. I can feel it. But where?"

"Powers, think like a detective. When I wanted to catch the Cascade Killer, I learned as much about the man as I could. You know Arens better than me. Try to understand his thinking. You've got to think like him if you want to find the lab."

"If it exists," said Paul.

"But you're convinced it exists."

"I see your point. My intuition is only as good as my conviction. If I believe, and I understand the Professor, then I'll find the lab."

"I'll make a detective out of you, yet."

"I called Arens from here," Paul said, thinking out loud, walking slowly among the bookshelves. Following behind, Jackey kept silent. Paul continued. "I asked Arens for information, and he sent me to Wetlock. But, Wetlock wouldn't talk to us, at least, not willingly. And now, we're back in the Stacks, a full circle. All this to find a door. Jack, is this getting us anywhere?"

Jackey followed in silence, like a shadow.

Paul sighed. "OK, I know. Think like the Professor. But, I really don't know him, do I? He's a scientist." Paul pulled a scientific journal off a bookshelf and flipped through the technical articles. "We talked about science, mostly. Finding the answers. But every new answer creates a new question. That's the fundamental problem with the scientific method. The more we seek ultimate truth, the further we travel from it." He replaced the journal on the shelf. "That's it!" he said.

"What's it?"

"The scientific method. That's how Arens thinks. Hypothesis, theory, test, conclusion. We're looking for a hypothetical door, and we theorize that a search will help us find it."

"You lost me."

"Don't you see? Searching for the door leads us farther away from it. But there can only be one truth, one door. What was it the Professor told me? Yeah. He said science is a door that opens to reveal another door."

Running to the far end of the floor, into the metal bar on the emergency exit, Paul crashed the door open into the stairwell. A piercing shriek leaped from the alarm box. The staircase looked unused, made of polished hardwoods. Jackey searched the stairwell, while Paul held the door open.

"Damn. Nothing here," she shouted, over the screaming alarm.

"I was wrong," Paul yelled, gazing at his reflection in the floor.

"It's OK," said Jackey. "Let's get the hell out of here, before someone comes. Go down." She turned him by the shoulders and coaxed him down the stairs. "This is a local alarm, it may not be answered for awhile. The thick wooden walls will muffle it."

He ran down the staircase, Jackey following. The stairwell door closed automatically. After one last look back, he stopped. "Jack. Turn around, look at this."

In the wall that had been hidden behind the open emergency door, he could barely discern the outline of a large wooden door, frameless, and without visible hinges. Matching vertical grains of hardwood in the wall camouflaged the leading edge of the door. The trailing edge of the wooden door became the corner of the stairwell wall. The top of the wooden door touched the low ceiling, and the base ended at the floor. Together, the four seams of the wooden door blended into the wall, nearly vanishing. Only a small keyhole betrayed the door's presence.

Jackey ran her fingers along the leading edge of the door. "It must be over a hundred years old," she said, "and God only knows how thick."

"Can we open it?"

"We can try," she answered, bracing her left shoulder against the hidden door.

Paul braced his right shoulder against the door, looking Jackey in the eye. The two began counting together.

"ONE, TWO, THREE!"

Sweat beaded up on their red faces, but the door didn't budge.

"Stop, stop," said Jackey. "It's not gonna work."

Paul stopped, gasping for breath. The air in the stairwell felt hot, stale. "This door could've been nailed shut a hundred years ago, for all we know," he said.

Jackey scrutinized the door. "We've got to defeat the lock," she said, kneeling onto one knee. After peering into the keyhole, she put one ear against it. Plugging the other ear to muffle the alarm, she rapped her knuckles on the door. "Sounds kinda hollow, I'll bet this old lock mechanism takes up most of the thickness of the door." She pulled out her Beretta, flipping off the safety. "Get back in the library."

Both of them returned to the relative sanctuary of the library. Jackey's forearm and face peeked around the stairwell door. After taking careful aim, squinting in the dim light, she withdrew her face from the stairwell. Firing blind, she pumped six rounds into the wooden door.

Reentering the stairwell, the duo surveyed the damaged wooden door. The acrid smell of spent gunpowder filled the confined space. All six bullets had passed through the thin layer of wood covering the old lock mechanism. Wood splinters littered the floor at the foot of the old door.

"Bullseye. Great job," said Paul.

"Let's try forcing it, again."

Back to back, shoulder to shoulder, the countdown began.

"ONE, TWO, THREE!"

Paul detected a slight vibration of the door through his shoulder. "Again," he said, pausing to renew the air in his lungs.

The duo surged against the weakened door until something popped within the lock mechanism, and the door wiggled slightly. They continued the pounding, the old wood groaning under the stress. The groaning turned into a wrenching wail, as the wood around the lock tore apart. Each thrust coaxed a little more movement from the door, but it continued to resist. They continued the pounding.

Instantly, all resistance vanished and the huge door flew open, nearly weightless on it's hinges. Springs, metal screws and other pieces of the broken lock flew in every direction. Catapulted into the room, Jackey and Paul recovered their footing and stood in silent disbelief.

A huge chamber unfolded before the two startled intruders. They had entered another section of the fourth floor, below the east tower of the Stacks. Emergency lights lined the stone walls at infrequent intervals, providing dim illumination. Eight large laboratory workbenches formed two rows in the center of the room, with four workbenches in each row. Cluttering the surface of the benches were glassware, tubing, and mechanical appliances. Bunsen burners blazed brightly under bubbling glass balls of colored liquids, and steam rose from numerous vents.

Large machines lined the walls on either side of the room. On one side, a circular metal staircase spiraled upward, to a second level. It consisted of a narrow, circular, stone balcony covered with bookshelves, filing cabinets, and office furniture. An iron railing ran the length of the balcony. A personal computer station stood next to an old fashioned roll top desk.

Part of the balcony contained a bed, and chest of drawers. In another section stood a refrigerator, and a small table with a box of cereal on top, and one chair at the side. As it crossed the balcony, the circular staircase became an iron ladder, soaring upwards, disappearing into the absolute darkness above the second level.

"Incredible," Paul yelled, still competing with the stairwell alarm.

"I wonder if anybody's home," said Jackey, scanning the room.

"We never considered knocking," said Paul. "This must be where the Professor took my phone call. No wonder it echoed."

The room abruptly flooded with light from long florescent fixtures suspended above the workbenches and under the balcony, and the second level also lit up. The fixtures had been invisible previously, in the dim light. The emergency lights turned off simultaneously.

"The power must be back in the Stacks," said Paul. He could see the room more clearly, now. A periodic table of the elements adorned the walls of the main floor, next to a pictorial depiction of man's evolution. High above, in the bedroom area of the balcony, hung an enormous black and white photograph of Albert Einstein. He smiled a mixture of madness and genius, his unkempt white hair disappearing beyond the borders of the picture.

A poster above the roll top desk depicted a map of the United States, with two hands clasping over it. A boldface caption on the top edge of the poster read, "GIVE THE MOST PRECIOUS GIFT OF ALL, GIVE LIFE." Printed across the bottom of the poster was a single familiar word: "NUOS." Over the small kitchen table hung a three foot long mobile, a molecular model of DNA. It spun slowly.

"Let's see what kind of research they do here," said Jackey. "You check the equipment. You're the scientist, maybe you can make sense of it."

Paul inspected the workbenches, with particular attention to the simmering liquids.

"What are they?" asked Jackey.

"Stills, being used to manufacture chemical reagents."

"For what purpose?"

"I can't tell, they could be useful in many types of experiments. I saw some filing cabinets upstairs. Let's check the files."

"OK. I'll wait down here."

Paul climbed up the circular staircase to the balcony, the rickety iron steps shaking. At the top, a wall filled with books and journals caught his eye. Several monographs stood out, and he silently skimmed through the titles: "Genetic Engineering in the Twenty-First Century, Viral Vehicles for Human Gene Insertion, Rejection of Transplanted Organs: Genetic Mechanisms, Genetic Control of Cellular Aging, Unique Properties of Fetal Tissue."

He found five vertical file cabinets on the balcony, each containing five drawers. So, he began to run through the files blindly, with no clear idea of what he was looking for. The files detailed over ten years of experimentation, mostly the testing of various genetic theories. He discovered evidence of diverse experiments, covering every conceivable aspect of biogenetics. Study of organ transplantation rejection was a recurrent theme.

Finally opening the twenty-fifth file drawer, he flipped through rapidly. Stopping abruptly, he backtracked, removed a folder and opened it. He pulled a page out of the folder, and put the folder away. "Jack, I've got something," he said, slamming the file drawer shut. She didn't seem to hear him over the persistent din of the emergency door alarm. After running down the stairs, he handed Jackey the paper. "Take a look," he said. It's a copy of an operative report for Trudy Dobbs. A kidney transplant. We've been chasing the tail end of an epidemic."

She read the sheet. "Damn. You're right. We may already be too late. But what does it all mean?" She handed him back the paper.

"I don't know yet," he said, folding the paper and putting it in his shirt pocket. "Let's look around the lab some more."

Walking by small machines on the workbench, he recognized a centrifuge, for the separation of substances according to mass; a microtome, to slice tissue samples for microscopic slides; and a microscope with slide preparation equipment.

Investigating the large machinery on either side of the room, he found the missing protein sequencer, of which Wetlock had spoken. There was also an autoclave, for the sterilization of surgical instruments. Next to the autoclave, an incubation cabinet filled with Petri dishes grew cultures of unknown origin. Against one wall stood a small portable isolation laboratory, for the study of hazardous substances, in this case, biological substances, Paul suspected. He shuddered at the sight of four climate controlled live animal cages, all empty.

At the rear of the lab, he found half of the back wall concealed by a curtain. Along the other half of the wall, he saw an all too familiar sight, a surgical scrub sink. Next to the scrub sink stood an ice machine, and two large freezers. The freezers looked like standard meat lockers: short, long, rectangular. They opened from above.

He reached for one of the freezer handles, trembling. Holding his breath, he opened the chest. Icy mist rose from the chamber. Through the clearing mist, he saw plastic bags, their contents frozen, each bag carefully numbered. "Jack, look at this," he said, above the unrelenting clang of the stairwell alarm.

Jack leaned over the freezer, gritting her teeth. "Yech. What the hell are they?"

"Solid organs. Frozen for future research, I suspect."

"Deep freeze, huh?"

"That's the idea. It looks like we found Arens' tissue storage facility. We also found a sophisticated biogenetics laboratory."

"Unbelievable," she said, looking away from the freezer.

He let the freezer lid slam shut. "But what's behind the curtain?" he asked.

"You tell me, Powers."

He drew the curtain aside, revealing a door, and three hospital gurneys: two empty, and one with the motionless body of Christine Mason. He held his breath. For a moment, he thought he'd lost her forever. Then he examined her, checking the pulse in her neck and lifting her eyelids.

"Is she?"

"She's alive, but heavily drugged. Possibly a massive dose of barbiturates, or something like that. Her color is good. I think she'll be all right." He sighed with relief. He couldn't bear to lose her now. If she didn't recover, part of him would die, too.

"What's in the other freezer?" asked Jackey.

"Let's go see," he said.

They hovered over the second freezer as he opened the lid. Inside, the chamber was cool, filled with organs like the first freezer, but the organs weren't frozen.

"It's the fresh food section," she said.

He pulled out one rather odd looking plastic bag, about the size of a loaf of bread, and held the bag up to the light. Both Paul and Jackey stared, as he turned the package in a circle. It held a perfect, little human.

"Number 233," said Paul. "I wish I knew what the number meant."

Transfixed by the odd package, they stood in silence, except for the rushing of the wind and rain outside. It took a moment for Paul to realize the staircase alarm had stopped.

"That, Doctor Powers, is Jenny's baby."

Together, Paul and Jackey whirled around. Arens stood in the doorway, his long overcoat dripping wet, holding a derby hat with both hands. Dark circles outlined his eyes, and fluorescent light beamed off his bald head.

Paul put the fetus back into the refrigerator, and closed the heavy lid. "You've been using the Parkinsonism brain transplant research as an excuse to legally obtain fetal tissue," said Paul.

"Very astute, son. I was right to be worried about you. Don't bother to introduce yourself, mam. We've already met."

"An impressive lab," said Jackey. "What kind of research do you do here?"

Arens grinned. Entering the room, he shut the huge wooden door. The pupils of his eyes looked like tiny dots in a sea of white, as he walked toward the rear of the lab.

"In this laboratory, I attempt to redefine the limits of life. I study the genetic basis of cell growth, development, and control. More importantly, I apply these findings to the clinical situation."

"Why the fetal tissue?" said Paul.

"Ah. Fetal tissue is the ultimate stem cell, and can be rapidly grown into any type of cell, making it invaluable for my research. I'm particularly fascinated by the almost one-hundred percent success rate of fetal tissue transplants. You see, I want to completely eliminate the rejection of transplanted organs, by attacking the real problem. All prior attempts to stop organ rejection have relied on external means, such as drugs. I want to alter the organs themselves, to render them one-hundred percent compatible."

"Imagine the potential," said Arens. "Any organ could be transplanted into anyone, with a one-hundred percent success rate. The recipients wouldn't need any of the horrible immunosuppressant drugs used today."

Paul frowned. "I see. No Institutional Review Board or Human Experimentation Committee required. Your research can progress rapidly, because you ignore all the safeguards. Why the rush?"

Arens walked toward Paul slowly. "Boy, I'm seventy-one years old. I don't have all the time in the world. Do you know what happens when a full University Professor reaches age sixty? They retire him, and make him a Professor Emeritus."

The lines on Arens' forehead turned into deep crevasses, his eyes sunk into darkened sockets. Bulging veins on his neck trembled. "Do you know what Professor Emeritus means? Let the younger faculty do the research. Let the new ones get the grants. Give the new fellows a break."

Arens puffed his cheeks, his face grew fiery red. "Oh, there's the honorary lecture, of course. The great honorary lecture. Let the man speak for an hour. Look at him. He used to be a great man, in his day. Resurrect him in a bad situation to handle the press, because the old man generates sympathy. Bring him out during Alumni fund raisers, squeeze every last dollar out of him. That's all he's good for."

"As a Professor Emeritus, I haven't been able to get a grant for anything more than the support of one graduate student. I think they gave it to me out of pity."

"But you built all this," said Paul.

"What you see here is made possible by contributions from wealthy Alumni, nationwide. Alumni always remember and support great minds. They realize their hope for the future rests in supporting their contemporaries."

"Did you say: their hope for the future?" asked Paul. "Is the ultimate purpose of your research to benefit the aged group financing these experiments? Do you intend to obtain donor organs, somehow make them perfectly compatible, and then provide them to a select group of dying individuals?"

Arens stood about fifteen feet from Paul and Jackey. Wind roared around the outer walls of the tower. "Yes, my boy," said Arens, "in the short run, I hope to provide a supply of fully compatible organs to those who support my research. However, prolonging life is a temporary goal. I assure you, my final goal is far more noble."

"What is your final goal?" asked Paul.

The Professor grinned, reflected light from his teeth merging with the gleam in his eyes. "Immortality," he said.

"I got it," said Jackey. "You're a nut."

"Young lady, I'm far from crazy. I've discovered how to program viruses to reconstruct the DNA of living human cells. It's only a matter of time before I'll be able to repair and regenerate damaged human cells."

"I get it," said Jackey, "the virus acts like a repairman."

"Yes, young lady, that's the idea. I'll soon master control of the DNA sequences that regulate the aging process. I'll eliminate the time limit on human life."

"How convenient," said Paul. "You could create a master race of immortal beings and control the technology. Then the elite get to decide who lives and who dies. You'd be like a Greek god. How close are you to your goal?"

"Very close. So far I've used this new genetic engineering to make transplanted organs one-hundred percent compatible."

"How's that possible?" asked Paul.

"Basically, son, I add a genetically engineered virus to an organ, prior to transplant. I add the virus to the cold preservative solutions I supply to the operating room. The virus remains dormant in the cold packed organ. The moment the organ is transplanted, the virus infects the recipient. During the initial infection, the virus incorporates the DNA information that determines each cell's unique membrane structure. Finally, the virus attacks the transplanted organ, inserting the new DNA. The result is a donor organ whose cells have been genetically altered to look identical, on the surface, to those of the recipient."

Jackey's right hand moved to her hip. "Powers, what's he talking about?"

"The Professor infects the person needing a transplant with a virus. Then the virus changes the fingerprint of the transplanted organ, using the person's own DNA."

"Damn, you mean the Professor's been infecting people with a deadly virus he created?"

"It wasn't intentional," said Arens. "I designed the virus to be harmless."

"That's why we have safeguards and committees to oversee and control genetic research," said Paul. "But you couldn't wait for any safeguards."

"I'm an old man. My research has progressed a hundred times faster than it could have under the noose of some bureaucratic committee."

Paul's head pounded as he tried to fully understand. "So, Professor, tell me what went wrong. Why did Trudy Dobbs, the wife of the Cascade Killer, commit suicide after she received a kidney transplant?"

"You've been in my files, young man. Trudy Dobbs was the mistake. I was looking for a short cut. At the time, none of my experimental viral models were ready. Wetlock chanced upon a mutant version of the AIDS virus that could do the job of transferring DNA. Wetlock's virus was easy to produce. I tested a modified version of Wetlock's virus on Trudy Dobbs."

"That virus should have been safe, I tell you. I altered the virus to make it minimally infectious. I partially inactivated the polymerase, the enzyme that allows the virus to reproduce. The donor kidney given to Trudy Dobbs contained massive amounts of a very weak virus. The virus should've been able to infect only Trudy Dobbs."

"I made a mistake. Something went wrong. The virus became very infectious. It must have repaired the inactivated polymerase and altered a portion of Trudy Dobbs' DNA, inserting a mutant strand of DNA that causes psychosis and violent behavior. I have no idea where that mutant strand of DNA came from. But the violent behavior rapidly became addictive. Just like with narcotic addiction, the violence caused abnormal activation of the endorphin-enkephalin control system. The DNA sequence containing the violent behavioral traits passed to everyone infected with the virus."

Jackey held up her hands. "Wait. Are you saying the virus causes a physical addiction to violence, like a drug?"

Paul interrupted. "Yeah, that's exactly what he's saying. The Professor's reckless experimentation caused an entire epidemic of addiction to violence. Trudy Dobbs, Earl Dobbs, Jenny Walker, Jenny's baby, Joe Tyce, and Bertha, all addicted. Earl Dobbs died withdrawing from the addiction. Trudy Dobbs and Jenny Walker cured their addiction to violence and their psychosis by killing themselves. And Joe Tyce is still unaccounted for."

"I'm sorry for the error," said Arens, But the epidemic is now under control."

"Bullshit, you're sorry," Jackey said. "Tell me, did you know about the infected organs on the plane?" Arens didn't answer. "Your silence counts as a yes," Jackey continued. "You knew the organs were dangerous, but you didn't care."

"You'd rather keep your research going than prevent an epidemic," said Paul. "And you almost killed Chris. I think it's time to stop you, before anyone else gets hurt."

From behind the hat in Arens hands, he pulled an ancient revolver. "Remove your gun slowly, young lady, with your left hand." She did. "Place it on the floor and kick it away." The gun went sliding across the wooden floor. "Very good."

"Do you really think you can get away with killing a physician and a sheriff's deputy?" said Paul.

"Why not, child?" Arens replied. "This room is virtually soundproof with the two doors closed. I can repair the inner door easily, and my little lab will remain a secret. The two freezers will do nicely for what's left of your bodies. It's usually such trouble to obtain extra donor organs for my own uses. However, I should be able to salvage some of yours. Maybe some part of your genetic material will someday join me on the journey toward immortality."

"A disgusting thought," said Jackey.

The door to the laboratory swung open, and in walked Joe Tyce, carrying a large cardboard box. "Where should I put this, Professor?" he said. He didn't seem to notice Arens was holding two people at gunpoint.

"Set it down anywhere, Joe," shouted Arens, "and come meet our guests." Arens lowered his voice, "When I discovered the aberrant virus, I took Joe Tyce into my care."

"To study him?" asked Paul.

"Of course not," said Arens. "I did it to help him."

Paul was impressed by how powerful Joe Tyce looked. His solid arms, attached to a set of broad shoulders, contained enough muscle for several men. Below his shoulders, a rock hard chest protruded from beneath a black T-shirt emblazoned with the logo "EAT MY DUST." Blue jeans packed with powerful thighs carried the upper body forward.

Impressive as Joe's body was, it couldn't conceal his vacuous mind. A stubby brown crew cut adorned his head. He spoke in a monotone, and his prominent, red eyes looked unfocused. "I still have the headache, Professor. And I don't see so good."

"I'll get you some more medicine in a few minutes, Joe," answered Arens, "but first, I need your help with these intruders."

"Should I kill them?" Joe asked.

"Don't bother." Arens sneered. "I'll take care of that."

"Will you be able to live through all eternity as a murderer?" said Paul.

"Son, I've too much at stake here to allow you to spoil it. I've already made the decision to kill, if need be, for a greater good. Society condones such killing. How else do you explain capital punishment, or war, or ..."

"Or killing a young, female, neurosurgeon?" said Paul. "Is that when you made the decision to kill?"

"When you started asking questions, child, I had Joe rough you up. I hoped you would abandon your quest for the truth. I was wrong. Then Dr. Mason joined the investigation, so I tried to kill her.

"Unfortunately, young man, Joe failed to murder Christine. Since that night, Joe hasn't been the same. I think his brain is suffering from an increase in pressure. I can't run him through the University CT scanner, for obvious reasons. I may have to operate on Joe, myself, to relieve the pressure."

"How nice," Jackey added. "Your own private hit man."

"Until I find a cure, Joe needs a certain amount of controlled violence. He's addicted to it. If I'd left him on the street, many more people would have been hurt."

Paul shook his head. "Professor, I don't understand why you kidnapped Chris, after first trying to kill her."

"I can explain," Jackey volunteered. "After Christine survived the murder attempt, the Professor found out about the hijack. He searched Christine's apartment to recover the transplant data, and kidnapped her to attract attention from the FBI."

"I see," said Paul. "The FBI would connect the dots. I'd be the prime suspect in Christine's kidnapping, and probably get blamed for the violent threats she's been receiving. With Wetlock silenced, and Chris out of the way, no one would believe my virus theory. I'd be branded a lunatic and locked up forever."

"You're very good detectives," said Arens. "The fates have treated me with kindness. I now have under my control the only three people who know I created a deadly virus."

"Are you going to kill us all, Professor," asked Paul, "just to cover your mistake?"

"Please understand, I have no other choice. My research must continue."

Arens handed his revolver to Joe Tyce. "Hold this Joe, and if they move, kill them." Joe took the revolver obediently, and glared at the two prisoners through glazed eyes. Arens left the room through a door at the back of the lab.

"Give me the gun, Joe," said Jackey. "You don't want to kill us."

Joe didn't even seem to hear. He stood motionless with the revolver ready. It was Paul's turn to try, "Joe, put down the gun. We won't hurt you." Again, Joe remained steadfast.

Arens reentered the room, carrying two syringes filled with liquid. Uncapping the needles, he handed the syringes to Joe Tyce, in exchange for the revolver. "Give them the shots, Joe."

Paul and Jackey stood helplessly, as Joe approached, a loaded syringe in each hand. He injected the contents of one syringe into Jackey's upper right arm, through her coat sleeve. She didn't flinch. A second later, the other syringe lanced through Paul's coat, into his left arm. He felt stinging as the bolus of medication spread within his muscle.

A warm glow grew within Paul's chest, until he could feel his heart racing. His head throbbed with every heartbeat, the room filling with music. He heard hard rock music, but then he recognized the piece. It was Rachmaninoff, Symphony Number Two, the classical movement to which he and Chris had made love. How could he have mistaken it for hard rock?

The walls of the lab bent, until the corners of the room blended together. He could no longer distinguish the ceiling from the floor. The room had only one wall-ceiling-floor. But how was that possible? He couldn't see the laboratory. It had been replaced by a white vortex, spinning, sucking at him. He fell in. Bottomless, he kept falling.

His brain had slipped out of gear, his mind could no longer locate his body. Alone with distorted thoughts, no way to communicate. A dissociative anesthetic. Intramuscular. Distortion of reality. Hallucinations.

For a few terrifying moments, he found his body, collapsed on the floor, convulsing. He searched for the connection in his brain between his speech center, and his lips. "Damn you, Arens," he tried to say, "You've given me ketamine. Why didn't you just kill me?" A high pitched gurgle wailed from his throat. His pupils vibrated rapidly and his eyes rolled upwards.

Sucked into the churning vortex, images raced through his brain. All his life experiences surfaced together in one unintelligible rush. It felt like being torn apart and cast into Hell. Each thought locked itself in solitary confinement, with limitless despair and loneliness. And he fell, plunging down a white hot tunnel. Faster and faster. Accelerated beyond all tolerance, the charred ashes of his scattered soul dissolved into the light.

__CHAPTER 31__

WHIRLING PINK CLOUDS of cotton candy filled the air with a sickening, sweet smell. Paul floated through the soft, candy sky. Without a body, nothing weighed him down. Like a nervous housefly, he flitted from cloud to cloud, never staying in one place for more than an instant. He wished somehow he could stop the movement and grab hold of something. But how could he stop moving, if he had no body to stop?

Although his body had disappeared, he knew he'd find it, if only someone would show him where to look. But nobody lived in this lonely universe. Above him, he saw crowds of people, shoulder to shoulder, fighting for space. Had they squeezed him into this nothingness? Trying to swim for the surface, for the air and light, he realized he had no arms. Where was he? In a dark cocoon?

Undergoing metamorphosis? Into what was he changing?

Flecks of light began to permeate his universe, coalescing into a bright pair of overhead spotlights. Something covered his face. The scene revealed itself gradually, like a blurry picture coming into focus. An upside down face took shape. The face of Professor Arens.

Paul realized he had an anesthesia mask strapped to his face. He heard a steady beeping sound. The cold surface against his back felt like an operating table. Naked, except for a thin sheet, he discovered his arms taped securely to arm boards hung from the sides of the table. A leather belt fit snugly across his waist. Soft cloth restraints bound him at the ankles.

Paul fought the urge to scream. He remembered getting the ketamine anesthesia. Arens was now looking the other way, apparently unaware that Paul had regained consciousness. This was an advantage he intended to keep. He chose two spots to look at, alternating rapidly between the two, creating a vibratory movement of his pupils. Randomly, he contracted and relaxed different groups of muscles. He generated a slow, writhing motion, involving his entire body.

Two multifaceted operating room spotlights hung over his head. Rolling his eyes from side to side, he tried to assess the current situation. He felt sweat trickle down his cheeks. Glancing to his right, he saw a flat metal tray supported by a tall metal stand, a Mayo table. On the table, next to two syringes, he recognized two familiar drug bottles. One contained ketamine, the anesthetic drug he continued to mimic. The other bottle contained succinylcholine, a muscle paralyzing agent.

Parallel to the right side of the operating table, he saw a long table covered with blue paper sheets. It contained rows of shimmering stainless steel surgical instruments. Several large metal basins stood prominently next to the instrument table. Along the other side of the operating table was a cart filled with a generous supply of white Styrofoam coolers and open cardboard boxes of various sizes.

At the head of the table, Arens worked quickly, placing a plastic breathing tube on the Mayo table. Then, he tested the light on a metal laryngoscope blade that he would need to pass the breathing tube. As he set the laryngoscope upon the Mayo table, it made a loud clang and Paul shook.

In the back of Paul's left hand, he felt the sting of a plastic intravenous needle. He swallowed. Dangling above from a pole, a clear bag of intravenous electrolyte solution dripped ominously into the plastic tubing, the cold fluid entering his vein. Round paper pads, electrocardiogram electrodes, attached to his bare shoulders, with wires extending beyond his view.

The air pump of an automated blood pressure machine sizzled, inflating a blood pressure cuff, squeezing his upper right arm. Something connected to his left middle finger. Wiggling his finger caused the beeping in the background to falter. He no longer had any doubt, the device clamped to his finger was a pulse oximeter. It would look through his finger continuously, with infrared light, measuring the oxygen level in his blood during each beat of his pulse.

He couldn't detect a smell in the anesthesia face mask. With his eyes, he traced the twin corrugated plastic oxygen tubings from the mask, to an anesthesia machine beyond the head of the operating table. Even though it was an older style machine, the gauges and knobs were familiar. Automated monitors sat vigilantly on the shelf over the anesthesia machine, alive with red and amber lights. Paul realized he was breathing oxygen, and about to be paralyzed and anesthetized by Professor Arens.

Thousands of times, Paul had stood over his patients, watching the fear in their upside down faces as he prepared them for anesthesia. Anesthesia and surgery were necessary evils to which Paul expected he would submit, someday. Never before had he understood the terrifying reality of yielding total control of his body to a stranger.

Suddenly, all of the anxieties of his surgical patients made perfect sense. He'd seen the worried looks, the sudden crying, the elevated heart rates, the high blood pressures, the last minute need to urinate, a wad of tissue clutched tightly in the fist, irrational statements, and most of all, denial. *This can't be happening to me.*

Arens peered down at his patient. Paul continued to roll and vibrate his eyes, peeking when he could at the Professor's face over the lip of the plastic anesthesia mask. Upside down, the Professor's bald forehead hung in the air like the moon, and his half lens glasses sparkled.

"This is an historic moment, Dr. Powers," gloated the Professor, raising his bushy eyebrows. "You and I are pioneers. I wish you were aware enough to know the contribution you will be making. Your eyes will enable a blind twelve year old boy to see. Your heart will replace the heart of a generous benefactor. Your kidneys will enrich the lives of two of the most wonderful women I have ever known. Your liver will give life back to a dear, dying colleague. I can't thank you enough for your unselfish gift."

Paul's heart raced, his feigned movements turned into trembling. In a few minutes, he was to become an organ donor, even though he didn't meet the most important criteria. He was not dead!

Arens reached for the succinylcholine syringe on the Mayo table. Out of the corner of his eye, Paul watched the long needle pierce the rubber stopper of the intravenous tubing. He bent his left hand sharply upwards, kinking the vein into which Arens intended the paralyzing drug to flow. Since the medication couldn't travel down the intravenous tubing, it back flowed into the hanging bag of electrolyte solution. So many times Paul's patients had unintentionally kinked the intravenous line, hindering the induction of general anesthesia. He prayed Arens wouldn't notice.

The Professor carefully waited for the succinylcholine to take effect. Paul's eyelids abruptly shut. Violent muscle spasms began around his eyes, progressing down his neck and chest. His arms and legs twitched coarsely at first, ending with fine movements of the fingers and toes.

"Ah, the enchanting, paralyzing dance of the succinylcholine," said Arens, grinning.

Paul's breathing stopped. Satisfied, Arens lifted the heavy laryngoscope in his left hand. He unhooked the rubber straps that bound the anesthesia mask to Paul's face, and removed the mask. Paul's jaws relaxed, his mouth opened sightly. Arens used the thumb and forefinger of his right hand to pry Paul's teeth further apart. Hovering inches above Paul's head, Arens prepared to insert the laryngoscope.

Paul bit down on the Professor's thumb and forefinger, and didn't let go. Simultaneously, Paul threw his head upwards, smashing the metal laryngoscope into the Professor's face, connecting on his glasses with a loud snap. Arens reeled backwards, his bifocals clattering to the floor. He couldn't free his thumb from the tightly clenched jaws. After glancing toward the drip chamber of the intravenous line, he reached for Paul's left hand.

"So. You're awake. A little bit of paralysis will encourage you to release me."

The intravenous line began to drip again, as Paul struggled against his restraints. Arens nearly sat on Paul's left arm, to keep the intravenous flowing. Blood from Arens right thumb dripped down Paul's throat, but his jaws remained tightly clenched.

"Let go of me, boy, damn you!"

Three inch adhesive tape bound Paul's right forearm to the padded wooden armboard. Lifting his right shoulder off of the table, he slid the armboard out of the bracket by which it hung from the side of the table. Bending his arm at the elbow, he swung the heavy armboard.

Arens, tethered to the table by his trapped thumb, tried to dodge the flying armboard. It hammered the Professor's jaw. Struck in the head again, his iron grip on Paul's left hand grew stronger. Sweat beaded up on the Professor's red forehead. The tainted intravenous fluid poured into Paul's vein. But he knew the succinylcholine had been diluted into the large bag of intravenous fluid, delaying the onset of paralysis.

"Just a little more of this, son, and you won't have the strength to lift that arm."

He swung the armboard a second time. Arens turned his face away, offering his right shoulder to absorb the blow. Paul reached backward, over his own right shoulder, to the Mayo table. He grabbed the ketamine syringe, and plunged it into the upper arm of a very surprised Professor Arens.

"Good God! Christ! You young idiot! To the devil with you! You'll be a cadaver donor, now! I'll ... I'll ... hassssss ... ponn ..."

The Professor's curses became unintelligible and his grip on the hand with the intravenous line loosened. Paul released the bloody thumb from his mouth, and swung his clumsy right arm again. Sweeping past the hanging intravenous tubing, he ripped the plastic needle from his vein. The back of his left hand began to swell, blood oozing from the puncture site.

Arens collapsed on the floor, writhing and moaning, his pupils vibrating madly, a blur. Strange contortions twisted his lips into grotesque configurations.

Paul strained frantically against the remaining arm and leg restraints. In a few moments, the succinylcholine would start to work. He'd be paralyzed and unable to breathe. His life depended on getting some oxygen before the paralysis began. Three quick breaths would do it.

The oxygen tubing on the anesthesia machine hung tantalizingly behind him, beyond the head of the table. He reached for the tubing, batting the Mayo table out of the way, sending the table crashing to the floor with a deafening roar. Fighting against weight of the bulky armboard, he stretched his right arm toward the oxygen tubing. The ankle restraints pulled painfully, preventing him from reaching further. Squirming through the leather belt around his hips, he forced himself toward the head of the table. His joints stretched and the cloth ties bit into his ankles.

The tip of the armboard touched the plastic oxygen tubing. He pushed the hanging tube, like a child on a swing, setting it into motion. After a couple of pokes, the tubing swung into his open fingers. His eyelids began twitching.

"Oh God. Not Yet."

Hysterically, he pulled the long, corrugated tubing through his fingers. At last, he held the face mask in his hand, just beyond the head of the operating table. The skin over his face crawled, and then spasmed. The armboard suddenly weighed a ton, and he couldn't lift the mask up to his face. Before losing all strength, he dragged the smooth edge of the armboard over the lip of the operating table and dropped the mask to the right of his head.

The infinitely heavy armboard fell over the side of the operating table, taking his arm with it. With his last ounce of strength, he turned his head into the mask and tried to take three quick breaths. He only got two.

Muscle fibers fired violently in his face and neck, setting off excruciating spasms that marched from head to toe for what seemed like forever. He felt like a truck was running over him, in slow motion.

After the spasms ended, millions of tiny painful twinges danced all over his body. His skin shimmered like the early morning ripples on a quiet lake. One by one, the tiny twinges stopped, and then there was nothing.

Motionless, unable to open his eyes, he listened, without even the sound of his own breathing to comfort him. Only the steady beeping of the pulse monitor assured him that he was still alive. Far in the distance, he heard Arens moaning and the sound of thunder.

Paul had the will to breathe, but he didn't have the way. Concentrating on trying to breathe proved futile. He felt like a swimmer underwater, holding his breath, unable to surface. Air hunger in the pit of his stomach became a hellish ball of churning fire, threatening to consume him. His heart pounded furiously against his chest, and the beeping of his pulse now sounded like a desperate cry.

Drowning in a sea of air, he doubted he could stay conscious much longer. The frenetic beeping of the pulse oximeter changed in pitch from soprano to baritone, indicating the oxygen level in his blood had sunk below the danger zone. He figured four or five minutes remained until the death of his brain. The two initial breaths of oxygen might buy him a few more minutes.

The soft glow of light permeating his eyelids turned to jet black. He could no longer hear the beeping of his pulse, or feel his heart pounding. His panic transformed into calm, peaceful bliss, without pain, without hunger. His thoughts gave way to silence, as he slipped into unconsciousness.

Minutes passed. Paralysis continued. Brain cells shut down all nonessential functions, concentrating their efforts on staying alive just a bit longer. His young heart continued to pump without oxygen, his blood turning to acid. His internal environment deteriorated, nearing the point at which life can not exist. A few seconds more, and the damage would be irreversible. Powerful enzymes in his blood busily chewed the paralyzing drug to pieces.

Tiny contractions began in his diaphragm, the powerful muscle of breathing. The contractions grew rapidly into a coordinated movement, sucking air into his chest. His lungs filled with the life-giving gas. The pulse oximeter tone shifted from bass to treble, signaling the return of oxygen to the blood. Oxygen starved cells throughout his body feasted ravenously. Gradually, consciousness returned.

Paul opened his eyes and drew a slow, deep breath, savoring the stale laboratory air like fine wine. He thanked God the succinylcholine had worn off. That was the beauty of succinylcholine, it lasted less than ten minutes. Gradually, the strength returned to Paul's muscles. He swung the loose armboard to his left and used his right fingers to tear the adhesive tape off his left arm. With his left arm free, removing the remaining restraints was easy. Unbound, clothed in a sheet, he scanned the operating room. Arens still lay on the floor, anesthetized by the ketamine. On the far wall of the room, he spotted a closed door, the way out.

Exiting, he found himself back in the rear of Arens' huge laboratory. Everything looked just as he remembered it, except Jackey now occupied a gurney next to Chris. Both appeared to be heavily drugged. He had the eerie feeling of being watched. Whirling around, he saw, framed by the huge wooden doorway to the lab, a very angry looking Joe Tyce.

<u>CHAPTER 32</u>

"**YOU SHOULD NOT** be out here," said Joe, closing the laboratory door and then bolting it shut. He approached Paul, cautiously. "The Professor will be angry."

"Joe, listen to me. You've got to help me." Paul met Joe at the center of the lab. Covered only by a sheet, Paul felt exposed and vulnerable.

"Go back inside," Joe insisted, shoving Paul roughly.

Joe's unfocused eyes bulged with a far away look, he didn't blink. "Go back inside," Joe repeated, pushing Paul harder.

"Joe, you're sick. It's not your fault. I'm a doctor, I want to help you."

Joe shuffled toward the back of the lab. Paul walked backward, carefully staying out of reach. "Sure. A doctor," said Joe, "Like the other doctors. Like the ones who destroyed me." He ran after Paul. "A new life they said.

Now I need to kill. Always to kill. I will kill you. I will enjoy killing you."

Dodging the threatening giant, Paul ran in circles around the laboratory tables, keeping just out of Joe's reach. Joe had difficulty changing directions quickly, and it worked to Paul's advantage. As Joe rounded the lab tables, he scattered all manner of glassware and fluids across the room.

Barefooted, Paul stepped around the broken glass. Outrunning Joe became more and more difficult. After about a dozen trips around the lab, Paul could no longer avoid capture by circling the workbenches. He made a fast break for the laboratory door. Fumbling with the deadbolt, he released it and pulled hard on the inner handle. The door wouldn't budge. A large hand stretched over his head, with the palm flat against the door.

He turned around, his back against the cold door. "Joe, take it easy," he said, holding his hands up, signaling Joe to stop. "You don't need to take orders from Professor Arens, anymore. You've no reason to hurt me." As a signal of trust, Paul closed the distance between them. "You're sick, I can help you. You have increased pressure on the brain. There are ways to relieve the pressure. Let me help you."

Joe stood silently, a confused leviathan, towering over the doctor. A moment passed, as Joe considered his options. Then the answer came. He grabbed Paul by both of his upper arms, and carried him to the back of the lab. Joe kicked the door to the operating room open, and then tossed Paul across the room. Fortunately, Paul landed relatively softly on the Styrofoam coolers and cardboard boxes. Joe advanced, rapidly.

Paul kicked the packing materials into Joe's path to slow his progress. This worked surprisingly well, since Joe found it difficult to step around or toss away multiple objects. His dexterity was mildly impaired, probably from residual Parkinsonism. Rigid arm movements prevented the objects Joe threw from traveling far. Many of the boxes he attempted to hurl fell in front of his shuffling feet. But he kept coming.

By the time Paul got back on his feet, Joe was upon him. Paul threw his most powerful punch, impacting painfully on Joe's huge muscular jaw. But Joe didn't budge. Instead, he broke into a wide smile, peppered with missing teeth. One thick hand grabbed the doctor by his left arm, while the well trained iron fist of Joe's right hand swung freely.

Paul's face didn't take the pounding well. The vision from his left eye became blurred.

He felt like a rag doll, helpless in the hands of an overgrown two year old during a temper tantrum. The warm flow of fresh blood trickled from his nose.

Joe was a trained fighter, and Paul knew he didn't stand a chance to win a clean fight. Then he remembered that Joe's medical record had mentioned extensive reconstructive surgery on his left knee. Paul smashed his right heel into Joe's left knee. The unstable knee buckled slightly, and Joe screamed in pain. The bone crushing grip on Paul's left arm relaxed. Paul slipped behind Joe, reaching around his expansive waist. Struggling, Paul clasped his hands together tightly and thrust them into Joe's abdomen, directing the force upwards, toward the ribcage.

Paul had learned the Heimlich maneuver years ago, when he certified for cardiopulmonary resuscitation. The maneuver had been designed to create a sudden, enormous increase in abdominal pressure, enough to dislodge a piece of meat from the windpipe of a choking person.

The abdominal pressure wave transmitted instantly to Joe's brain. In most people, blood or spinal fluid could move out of the skull, to adjust for the pressure change. But Joe's brain, already under high pressure, would not be able to compensate. Paul continued the violent upward thrusts, the abdominal compressions raising the pressure inside of Joe's skull.

Joe's swollen brain filled his skull and then needed more room to expand. Like squeezing the last bit of toothpaste from a tube, Joe's brainstem forced its way through the hole at the base of his skull, the foramen magnum. His eyes, at the front of the brain, nearly dangled from their sockets. The brainstem slipped through the constricted orifice, crushing the few cells vital to the control of breathing and heartbeat.

A tortured expression formed on Joe's face, as his heart stopped beating. His right eye dilated widely, followed soon by the left. He jerked a few times, and then sunk to the floor. Paul released his grip, and then stood trembling, gazing at his hands, appalled by his sense of relief and satisfaction. *I've killed a man. God forgive me.*

A moment later, all his thoughts turned to Chris. Outside the operating room area, Chris lay motionless on the gurney, oblivious to the fight that had raged around her. He checked her pulse, not surprised to find it slow and regular. Jackey slept peacefully on the other gurney, a smile across her face.

"Chris. Chris. Wake up." Paul shook her violently, but with no effect. "Jackey. Somebody. Wake up." Jackey smiled with abandon. "I'll have to call the police to get you two out of here."

He spied his clothes under Jackey's gurney and dressed as quickly as possible. Pulling his undershirt over his head, his swollen face slid painfully through the hole. As his head popped out of the shirt, he spit old blood from his mouth.

Then he smelled alcohol. The odor came from the front of the lab, from the glassware shattered during the fight with Joe Tyce. Fluid dripped off the laboratory table nearest the main door, forming an expanding puddle on the floor. A Bunsen burner on the table flickered, and then the lab exploded in a blinding flash. Flames ate greedily at the old wooden floor and thick, black smoke billowed into the room.

Paul ran toward the laboratory door, but the fire had already blocked the exit. Through the smoke, he couldn't see the front wall. Looking to the balcony above, he once again noticed the metal ladder at the end of the circular staircase. In the darkness of the tower roof above, Paul couldn't see where the ladder ended, but he hoped it led to a fire escape. He realized he'd never be able to get

Chris and Jackey up the ladder, but he couldn't just leave them.

Keeping low, he ran back to the rear of the lab and opened one of the two freezer chests that stood against the back wall. He looked at the plastic packages and the grotesque shapes of the frozen organs inside. Emptying the contents of both freezers onto the floor, he tried not to think about what the packages contained.

The gurney, upon which Chris lay drugged, wheeled easily along side the open freezer. A wall of fire covered the front of the lab and the air was hot. He'd have to work fast. By removing the side rails of the gurney, he managed to slide Chris into the empty freezer chest. Protecting her head with his hands, she fell the short drop into the freezer. He smiled at the face cradled in his hands. "I love you, Chris," he spoke softly, then kissed her on the cheek before setting her head down gently on the bottom of the freezer.

The smoke grew thicker and tears poured from his eyes. After emptying the other freezer, he placed Jackey's limp body inside. Reentering the adjacent operating room, he stepped over the grey corpse of Joe Tyce. Moving through the piles of packing materials, he made his way to the anesthesia machine.

Arens remained on the floor, anesthetized, moaning, with jerky, purposeless movements.

Paul removed the two oxygen cylinders from the back of the anesthesia machine. Into his pocket, he placed the cylinder wrench. He threw one oxygen cylinder onto each shoulder, holding on to the valve yokes at the top. Stepping over the Professor, he looked down. The Professor's unseeing eyes stared back, rolling slowly from side to side. "I believe you will have to fend for yourself," said Paul.

Returning to the rear of the lab, he set the oxygen cylinders down by the freezers, and then put his ear near the valves. Using the cylinder wrench, he opened the valve on each cylinder slightly. He could barely hear the hiss of flowing oxygen over the sound of his own labored breathing. Into each freezer, he placed an oxygen cylinder, between the legs of his drugged friends. From the nearby ice machine, he gathered enough ice to surround, but not cover, Chris and Jackey.

After packing the freezers with ice, he hovered over Chris. "You'll have a much better chance this way," he said, as he closed and locked the freezer door. "See you soon, Jack," he said, lowering the heavy lid over Jackey, and latching it shut. "Believe me, I know how it feels."

The fire had advanced to within a few feet of the staircase to the second level. Paul charged through the scorching heat and jumped onto the stairs. The iron steps shook under the stress of his feet as he ran upwards. Reaching the balcony, he gazed up the iron ladder, still unable to see where the ladder ended. Paul didn't know if the ladder would lead to safety, but he had no other choice.

He looked down at the blazing inferno. Orange flames leaped toward the balcony. A huge wooden beam collapsed with an earsplitting shriek. Smoke scalded his throat. He reached for the iron ladder and the rungs began to writhe and hiss. Snakes struck at him from all directions, paralyzing him with venom, and he collapsed on the floor of the balcony. The snakes vanished as quickly as they had appeared.

Paul realized he'd had a ketamine hallucination. The drug was well known for producing bizzare hallucinations, even up to 24 hours after ketamine anesthesia. He might be able prevent the hallucinations by avoiding common triggers, like bright lights, loud noise, and pain. But in his current situation, that would be difficult.

With his pocket knife, he cut two small pieces of cloth off his shirt. After popping the cloth pieces into his mouth and wetting them, he rolled the cloth into plugs and stuffed them into his ears.

Testing the solidity of the rungs of the ladder, he grabbed them tightly and began his ascent up the stone wall of the tower. The flames below grew taller every minute, pursuing him as he climbed. He coughed in spasms. A high pitched screeching and a fluttering blast of wind almost knocked him off the ladder. A dozen dark shapes soared past and vanished. "Yech. Bats. I hate bats."

Resisting the temptation to look downward, he avoided staring into the bright fire. A ketamine hallucination now could be fatal. Above, he saw only unrevealing darkness. Higher and higher he climbed in the smoke filled tower, sweat draining from every pore, the air unbearably hot. More thick smoke drifted upwards. He wished he could see where the ladder ended.

The fire grew brighter until, at last, the golden glow illuminated a wooden ceiling. Above the last rung of the ladder hung a square, metal door. He tried to discover how to open the door, feeling all the edges. Dirt and spider webs brimming with the carcasses of dead bugs fell onto his upturned face. He spit. Finding a deadbolt, he slid it open, but the hatch would still not budge.

He felt like a bug, trapped against the hatch, unable to escape. Below lurked a creature with fiery breath that would suck out his vital juices, without remorse. Using the butt end of his pocket knife, he pounded on the overhead hatch, and a hollow metal sound resonated eerily through the thick smoke. The thin metal hatch marked the border between death and freedom.

Carefully, he reversed his position, hanging upside down, clinging tenaciously to the narrow ladder. Flames leaped up to his face and singed his hair. He closed his eyes. With his right foot, he pounded on the stubborn hatch. It opened a little and cold water poured in, drenching him. It felt good.

Upright on the ladder again, gasping for breath, he inspected the hatch. Sinuous asphalt bands prevented it from opening. Evidently, it had been tarred over many times. With his pocket knife, he cut through most of the asphalt strings, and then pried the door open wide. Rain pelted his face.

Emerging in the darkness, he took a deep breath of the cool, wet air. He stood in the cupola of east tower, peering over the edge of a short, stone barrier. Twenty feet below, he saw the main roof of the stacks, the roof over the fourth floor. At any moment, he expected flames to shoot through the wooden roof of the tower. The main roof of the Stacks would be safer, but he'd have to climb down.

The facade of the tower consisted of thick columns, interconnected with stone arches, ornate carvings, and ivy. Paul felt he could use the carvings and ivy for foot and hand holds. Ten feet below, halfway between the floor of the tower and the main roof, the griffin, a tiger-like beast with broad wings, projected from the rock wall. Paul thought if he could reach the stone beast, he could use it to check his progress and then swing down to the main roof.

Lightening flashed. Stepping over the short stone wall, he started down. The surface of the tower, worn smooth by years of wind and rain, proved more slippery than he'd expected. He dug his feet into the elaborate, continuous stone script on the columns, his fingers clinging to the wet edge of the low stone wall. Releasing his foot holds, he lowered his body further.

Rain pounded. Dangling, he found new foot holds in a tangle of stone vines carved between the pillars. The ivy couldn't support his weight and made finding new hand and foot holds difficult. After running his fingers over each crack and crevasse in the wall, satisfied he had achieved an acceptable grip, he reached downward with his left foot.

A piercing pain tore at his left shoulder, causing his left arm to lose it's grip. Unable to hold himself on the wall, he fell, his left hip crashing against the stone griffin. Careening off the beast, Paul landed on his right leg with a twisting crunch.

Crumpled on the main roof of the Stacks, immobile, neither leg would support his weight. Pain erupted from multiple places on his body. He surmised he'd broken his left hip and his right leg. His left arm hung limp, useless, but he was uncertain why. A wave of dizziness and nausea took hold. After feeling his left shoulder, his right hand returned covered with blood. Paul wondered if he was having another ketamine hallucination.

Above, he beheld the ghastly face of Professor Arens. Water poured onto his bald scalp, forming merging tributaries on his forehead, cascading off the tip of his bulbous nose. Over Paul's broken body the Professor towered, brandishing his old revolver. Reality struck Paul, this wasn't a ketamine hallucination, he'd been shot.

"Son, you should have taken the back door of the lab to the roof, and saved yourself the climb," said Arens, his thin lips puckering and twitching. "If you think, young man, that destroying the lab will end my quest, you are sadly mistaken. You'll perish in this fire, along with the others. There're other places where I can continue my research."

Paul observed the Professor's wild, wide eyed rage. Arens stood at the heart of the raging tempest, a thundering menace against a background of dark sky. Lightning and rain played at his feet. In the unsteady light of the storm, the Professor's dilated, black pupils flickered and his lips contorted as he spoke. Paul could see that the professor was still under the influence of the ketamine.

"Doctor Arens, do you remember the oath you swore to preserve life?" Paul shouted as loud as he could. "Do you remember your duty to heal the ills of your fellow men?"

Arens stepped over to the low stone barrier that marked the edge of the roof. He looked down. Turning his back on the short stone wall, he walked close to Paul. Ten feet overhead, the stolid griffin loomed, with stone teeth bared in a fixed expression of strength.

"My boy, how better can I serve my fellow men, than to offer immortality?"

"Professor, you already think of yourself as immortal. That's why you've lost your respect for human life. You no longer realize that death defines life. You've forgotten each living being is a unique creation, precious, and transient."

"How immature. You would outgrow that viewpoint, if you were immortal."

"Professor, God alone claims the right to immortality. He stands ready to punish men who would give the secrets of immortality to mankind."

Arens smiled, grasping the revolver in both hands, aiming it at Paul.

"Look at the lightning, Professor," Paul screamed. "The wrath of God is upon us. We will all pay for our sins."

Arens faced into the storm for a moment, his eyes squinted during a blinding flash of lightning. His smile vanished, as Paul's voice continued booming.

"Hear the thunder, Professor? It's the anger of God. Who can escape such anger?"

A deafening peel of thunder ripped the night. Arens shook. Paul drew his pocket knife with his only functioning arm. He opened the blade by pushing it against the roof.

"Hear the words of an angry God." Paul bellowed. "His punishment is worse than death. Beware you who are immortal, for you shall have eternal pain." Swinging the knife, Paul stabbed Arens' left ankle. The blade penetrated deeply and withdrew.

Arens jumped backward, out of reach. His face twisted, and he moaned unintelligibly, pupils vibrating madly, hands twitching, shaking the revolver. His body writhed.

o o o

Arens thought it strange. He knew that his left ankle should hurt, but he couldn't feel it. Raising his gun, he gasped. Paul Powers appeared like a distant speck, miles away. "A trick," Arens tried to say. But from deep within his throat came a low pitched moan. Staring at the wall above his head, he dropped his jaw in disbelief. The nostrils of the tiger-like beast flared, spouting plumes of moist vapor. The cold grey eyes of the creature blinked, and when they opened, blazed fiery red. Stone flesh on it's forepaws receded, revealing razor sharp claws. Saliva drooled through rows of viscously grinding carnivorous teeth. The beast yawned, displaying it's enormous mouth.

Arens watched as the creature wrenched it's forelegs free of the stone pedestal upon which it crouched. Stone crumbled, pieces tumbling downward. Muscles tensed in the powerful haunches of the beast and the huge wings flapped. The crazed beast recoiled, readying for the assault.

The Professor dropped his gun and clutched his abdomen. To his horror, his abdominal cavity was open. He felt the warm pulsations of his bowels as they slid out of the way of his exploring hands. Groping, he felt the smooth, slippery edge of his liver and the well defined capsule of his kidneys.

o o o

Paul thought Arens was trying to scream. Jaw open wide, the Professor made a high pitched whine, cocking his head upward toward the stone griffin.

Like lumps of dough, Arens kneaded the loose flesh of his abdomen. After jerking his hands away from his stomach, he raised them in front of his head, holding the palms outward as if to fend off the griffin. Backing away, the color ran from his face. Suddenly, he turned and leaped over the stone barrier, plunging to the pavement. The grey beast sat upon it's pedestal, silent and motionless in the pouring rain.

EPILOGUE

OPENING HIS EYES, Paul found himself peering over the lip of an anesthesia mask into bright lights. He felt the uncomfortable surface of an operating table beneath his back. Turning his head to the right, he saw rows of stainless steel instruments glistening on a long table draped in blue. Blood dripped into an intravenous tube ending in the back of his right hand. Reaching up, he ripped the mask off, breathing heavily. A dark face wearing a surgical mask came into focus.

"Hey, Pauley, leave the mask on."

"Benga?"

"It's me, Pauley. Put on the mask so we can fix you up."

Another face, gaunt with droopy eyes, appeared in a surgical mask, this time upside down. "When you recover," said Beck, "you're going to take all my call until the end of residency, understand?"

"Where's Chris?" said Paul. "I put her in a freezer."

"Don't you remember?" said Beck. "You told the firemen and they pulled her out, along with the policewoman."

"Are they all right?"

"They're both cold and drugged, but, hey, so are you. Don't worry, they'll recover. Smart thinking, putting 'em on ice. They'd never have survived the fire. There isn't much left of the Stacks."

"And the Professor?"

"Arens? He's dead. Jumped off the roof trying to escape the fire."

"No, not the fire," said Paul. "The griffin."

"What?" Beck shook his head. "Still loony from the ketamine."

Benga nodded. "Or the shock. Put him out, I've got to revascularize his arm."

"OK. Now, Paul. You've got to trust me," said Beck. "I need to put the mask on and give you a few quick breaths of oxygen before we get started. You of all people know how important it is."

"Believe me, I know."

"Good." Beck started to put on the oxygen mask, but Paul batted it away. "What is it, Paul? What's the matter?"

Paul bit his lower lip, shivering. He felt so cold. "Just one last request. And you've got to promise me."

"OK."

"Whatever happens, I don't want to be an organ donor."

"OK, I promise."

Beck put the mask on Paul's face. He didn't fight it this time. As the cool intravenous anesthetic ran into his veins, he yielded peacefully, clearing his mind and praying for pleasant dreams.

o o o

A painful muscle spasm in Paul's leg forced him once again to press the button on the control stick clutched tightly in his hand. The automated pump pushed a few more milligrams of morphine into his intravenous tubing. The bolus traveled quickly through the tube, into his vein. A few seconds later, the warm glow of the narcotic hit him, too little, and too late. He hated the drowsy feeling, a side effect of the pain killer, so he tried to minimize the dose and bear the pain.

Daydreaming out the window to the left of his hospital bed killed the pain better than morphine. He desperately needed distractions to help him forget his broken left hip and right leg, and his wounded left arm. The bandages nearly covered him from neck to toes, wrapping him tightly like a mummy. Only his right arm had been spared. He felt confined, suffocated. He tried to move his legs, but foam boots prevented most movement, as did the pain. For reassurance, he wiggled his left fingers. The tiny movements felt wonderful.

Given enough time, he hoped to recover fully. But passing time proved the hardest part of recovery. Less than two days in the hospital, and he was already going crazy.

On the little night table to the right of the bed, the phone rang. Eagerly, he picked it up.

"Hello?"

"Milton Freeman here, and I've got good news."

"Lawyers never bring good news."

"You obviously haven't read the paper."

"I'd read it, if somebody would bring one."

"Too bad. Why don't you ask the Federal Marshall outside to give you his?"

"Federal Marshall? Do they expect me to run away?"

"That's the government mentality. The FAA, FDA, and CDC are taking a beating in the press for allowing dangerous cargo to fly interstate. The airline's being criticized, too. On the other hand, you're a hero."

"That's the good news? I'm a hero?"

"It gets better. Since no one got hurt, the airline wants to drop the charges against you. If they do, the Feds will be under pressure to follow suit."

"No charges?"

"You can walk away."

"What's the catch?"

"Just one. Airwest airlines incurred certain expenses, and they're worried about the threat of future lawsuits from the passengers for pain, suffering, and pre-impact terror. Also, a rumor has it Airwest didn't have a good quarter, financially."

"So?"

"So they want the media rights."

"What?"

"You know. Books, movies, TV, tabloids. You've got a heck of a story."

"I don't believe this. You're telling me I can buy my way out of a felony."

"Doc, this is America."

"Milton, how come you're always counseling me to give up my worldly possessions?"

"It's a good deal, doc. I advise you to take it. Unless you'd rather be the richest man in prison."

"Go ahead, draw up the papers."

"You'll have them tomorrow. Just remember, Airwest owns you. No unauthorized interviews."

"Yeah, no problem. And thanks, you did good." Paul hung up the phone, wondering what had happened to all the heroes who didn't have good press and money to trade for freedom. At least he wouldn't lose his medical license or rot in jail. All he had to do now is recover.

The phone rang, again.

"Hello?"

"You can't know what it's like," a man said, "watching my career destroyed, my life stolen from me. Without knowing why."

Paul sat bolt upright. "You saved my life, didn't you. It was you all the time." He dropped the phone on top of the night table, reached down, and pulled open the top drawer of the table. He could still hear the phone.

"Yes, I needed to know the truth. And I thank you for leading me to it. Your services were too valuable for me to allow anything to happen to you."

From the drawer, Paul pulled out a plastic bag and fumbled with it, spilling the contents onto his bed. The bag contained his old clothes.

"Powers, are you still there?"

"Yeah, I'm still here," Paul shouted. "Don't hang up."

"The changes came slowly. The tremors, the sweats. And I wanted to hurt people, to kill. I couldn't help it. I tried drinking to stifle the violence. And drugs. But I couldn't fight it."

Paul found the paper he'd stuffed into his shirt pocket and unfolded it. The copy of Trudy Dobbs' operative report had faded with time. But now that he knew what to look for, the indistinct handwriting of the circulating nurse became legible. He picked up the phone. "I understand," he said. "My guess is a needle stick. Am I right?"

"Right, Powers. And they tested me. No AIDS, no hepatitis, nothing. I tried to fight it, you've got to believe me."

"Why didn't you get help?"

"Where? From whom? For what? They kept the information from me."

"Who did?"

"I followed people, threatened them, but they had a secret."

"You need help. There's still time. I'll do whatever I can."

"Ha! Powers, you don't understand. I don't need help anymore. I know the secret, too."

"What secret?"

"I don't have to fight it anymore. It's got as much right to live as I do. That's the secret. It's not evil. All it wants is to survive. A partnership. It's waited so long for a partnership. We're together now, stronger than before."

A motorcycle roared in the telephone receiver and outside the window. The phone went dead and Paul dropped it. Grabbing a metal triangle hanging overhead, he lifted his buttocks off the bed and swivelled his hips to the left. In one excruciating movement, his legs slid over the side of the bed, and he collapsed on the floor. Clutching at the windowsill, he pulled his body upward.

"Paul! What are you doing?" said Chris, running into the room. She circled around the bed and supported him under the bandaged arm, holding him in front of the window. He screamed in pain.

"There," he said, panting. "Outside." A motorcycle engine rumbled.

She looked. A man in a long overcoat and a cowboy hat wearing sunglasses sat on a motorcycle with a lion shaped seat and red flames painted on the front fender. He flipped a cellular phone closed, put it in his pocket, and revved up the bike. Then he removed his hat, shook off the drizzle, and tucked the hat into a saddlebag. Reaching into his leather boot, he pulled out a long, serrated knife, clenched it in his teeth, and looked up at the hospital room window. He appeared to be smiling.

"Rupp!" said Chris.

"Yeah. On Joe Tyce's bike. Rupp was junior surgery resident for Trudy Dobbs' kidney transplant."

"What?"

"Stuck himself with a needle."

"Oh, no. You mean he's infected? He's sick?"

"No, Chris. When I heard Trudy Dobbs came from Whitechapel, England, it rang a bell, but I didn't know why. Now I remember. Whitechapel was home to Jack the Ripper. That unsolved killing spree was probably the work of many people, an outbreak, an infection caused by a mutant strand of DNA passed along by a virus. Trudy must have been a carrier. She could have inherited it."

"Paul, wasn't that 100 years ago?"

"Yes, it was. That piece of mutant DNA was dormant for a century, until Arens accidently combined it with his genetic engineering virus. That was his big mistake, but he was too arrogant to realize the danger. All life forms want to live forever."

"In a way, Arens did achieve immortality," said Paul. "But not for himself. You see, Rupp's not sick anymore. Rupp and this monstrous evil, they're one now. A completely new form of life." Paul felt Christine's grip tighten, a good feeling, despite the pain.

The Harley roared, spraying wet gravel as it screeched away from the hospital, lion tail flying. Within seconds, the dark figure disappeared into the fog.

EXTRAS

Even your thoughts are not secure.

Dr. Paul Powers returns
in the acclaimed mystery

Secret Thoughts: A Medical Thriller

Something is rotten in Seattle, where seven innocent people are dead from tainted cold medicine and some of the country's wealthiest CEOs are targets of corporate espionage on an unprecedented scale. Dr. Paul Powers' search for the truth turns him into the prime suspect and an international fugitive desperate to clear his name. But how do you catch a killer who knows exactly what you're thinking?

H.S. Clark takes the reader on a wild ride along the cutting edge of medical technology and into the dark side of digital medicine.

Preview:

<u>CHAPTER 1</u>

AS DR. PAUL POWERS entered Lakeside Hospital, he noticed a difference right away. It was subtle to any casual visitor, but loud as a trumpet to him. It wasn't going to be an ordinary day. Perhaps it was the buzz of conversations in the hallway, or the cluster of whispering physicians and nurses around the espresso bar. The hum was a washing undercurrent that spelled trouble. And before he made it through the lobby, he got the story. One of Lakeside's own had been admitted to the ICU that morning.

Running late as usual, Paul hurried to the operating room. Today's surgery schedule was packed. If he didn't get the anesthetic for his first patient started within thirty minutes, there would be hell to pay with the surgeons and the nurses. Unlike in his anesthesia residency, the surgeons at Lakeside worshiped speed, hard work, and most of all, themselves. Paul reluctantly catered to their workaholism and bloated egos, even as he admired their technical skills.

The clientele of Lakeside, in Bellevue, a yuppified eastern suburb of Seattle, demanded the finest of medical care no matter what the cost. Residents of Bellevue displayed their wealth with pride, but Paul suspected that much of the city's opulence was a fragile illusion, with reality lurking one missed payment away.

He'd been lucky a few months back to land his first private practice job with the anesthesia group at Lakeside, a feat he owed primarily to Dr. Valdimire Zhazinsky, a staff radiologist. Zhazinsky had taught Paul at the University of Washington in both undergraduate classes and in the medical school. Efficiently known as Dr. Z, the Professor had left his prestigious post at the University of Washington, but not before achieving recognition as a brilliant research scientist. It was no wonder Lakeside Radiology used an outrageous first-year package to lure Dr. Z into private practice.

Pounding up the stairs, Paul banged the large silver button on the wall and ran through the double doors of the operating suite, panting, almost colliding with Ben Hinkley. An internist first, Ben specialized in intensive care medicine. Seeing him leaving the operating suite so early in the morning was a bad sign. Paul figured Ben had come to mooch off the donuts and coffee the hospital provided to the OR staff every morning.

Paul grabbed Ben by the tweed sleeve of his Armani suit. "I know you hate to eat and run, but what the hell's going on today, Hinkley?"

Ben's fat bulldog face wrinkled. "Look, I've had a long night, Powers. No games, now, please."

"Long night?"

"There's a VIP in ICU, and I'm losing the battle. It's crazy. And there's media coming." Ben tried to pass, but Paul blocked his path.

"Media? So what's happening and who is it?"

"Cyanide poisoning, from an over-the-counter pill. A radical cure for the common cold. I think you know him. A new doc here named Zhazinsky. Radiologist."

Paul froze.

"You OK? Were you close?"

Paul stared. "Is he dead?"

"Probably, just a formality now. Wait for the cyanide levels to drop, then run the EEG again. You know the routine."

"I'm going with you," said Paul.

"But, they're already looking for you in the lounge."

"Sorry, Ben, the OR will just have to wait."

On the walk to intensive care, Paul remembered the many fatherly encounters he'd had with Dr. Z. During medical school, they'd talked all night in the cozy confines of Dr. Z's private library, the musty smell of old volumes of wall-to-wall books mingling with the vapors of mint tea. Tchaikovsky played softly in the background as Tolstoy, Solzhenitsyn, and Chekov came alive. Dr. Z fancied himself a great student of Russian art and history. So often Paul had almost broken beneath the stress of becoming a physician, trying to understand his profession's awesome responsibilities. But Dr. Z was always there for Paul. Z had a way of making sense out of all the insanity of the world.

In intensive care, Paul looked on as Dr. Z lay motionless, eyes taped shut and his face dark blue. A breathing tube originated from his mouth and connected to a ventilator. Blood percolated intermittently from a smaller tube emerging from the right side of his nose. The high-pitched, rapid beeping of his pulse punctuated the slow, cyclical rush of air from the ventilator to his lungs. Paul held his hand to his face at the sight of the usually rosy-cheeked Dr. Z. Whatever Paul expected to see, it wasn't this. He'd never seen cyanide poisoning before, and he hoped never to see it again.

Dr. Z's wife, Natasha, sat at the bedside. When she saw Paul, she jumped up from the chair and embraced him.

"Paul, oh, Paul, I'm glad you're here." Tears streamed down her cheeks. "Val had a cold, a co..." She choked on the last word.

"I'm sorry, Natasha, I just heard. Ben's doing all he can."

She released her grip, nodding her head as her hair fell over her wet face. Bright, green eyes peered through the curly brown tangles of her hair. "I know, but who would do such a thing?" Reaching up, she parted her hair gracefully, sweeping it past her dark, red lips, over her cheeks and behind her shoulders. Above her nose, Paul noticed more wrinkles than ever before. Natasha seemed to have aged years overnight.

Paul stroked his mustache. "I wish I had something to tell you, to make sense of all this, but these kind of things never make any sense." Natasha sat back down, sobbing.

Ben approached the bedside. Speaking softly out of the corner of his mouth, without making eye contact, he said, "I'm working with a preliminary diagnosis of cyanide poisoning from a tainted acetaminophen pill, but I'm still waiting for toxicology and levels. We had to send the samples out."

"How do you know it's cyanide?"

"Oh. Well. Clinical history, presenting signs, and a mean smell of bitter almonds."

Paul moved closer, placing his hand on Dr. Z's cheek. To Paul's surprise, Dr. Z's cheek felt hot. His face had swollen like a balloon and his arms felt ridged. Lifting his eyelids revealed moderately dilated pupils.

"When did he come in?"

"About four a.m.," Hinkley said.

"I can't believe it."

"And there's more. At least six other cases reported so far. One's a little girl, DOA in our ER about an hour before Dr. Z."

"How come Z wasn't DOA?"

"Who knows? He's a big man, well over three hundred pounds. That could explain it."

"How'd you treat it?"

"You've got to realize, fourteen years in practice, I'd never seen a case before tonight. Of course, the ER passed a stomach tube and washed him out. Then I used a standard cyanide poisoning protocol, from a kit. Amyl nitrate inhalation, then sodium nitrite and sodium thiosulfate intravenously. And, of course, mechanical ventilation and one hundred percent oxygen."

"That treatment's the same as it was twenty years ago," said Paul. "You're using the blood itself to scavenge for cyanide. Isn't there something else you can do?" He felt Dr. Z's wrist. The pulse bounded rapidly.

"They've got a drug in Europe, a cobalt compound that mops up the cyanide and turns it into Vitamin B12," said Ben, "Not FDA-approved in the USA."

"Damn," said Paul. "Has he any brain activity?"

"First EEG was flatline, no brain waves at all. I'll do the next one tomorrow. I'm sorry."

A respiratory therapist, dressed in protective gown, mask, and gloves, disconnected Dr. Z's breathing tube from the ventilator. The therapist passed a plastic suction catheter into the breathing tube. Dr. Z didn't respond to the stimulation of the catheter entering the passages of his lungs. This was a bad sign; even a severely comatose patient usually has some response to poking in the lungs. Brain-dead patients, like patients under deep anesthesia, lack brain wave activity and don't respond to pain or other stimulation.

Paul detected a fruity smell coming from the breathing tube just before the therapist reconnected Z to the mechanical ventilator. Paul leaned in and sniffed.

"I wouldn't snort too much of that, if I were you," said Ben. "That's hydrogen cyanide gas. Smells like almonds."

"More of a fruity smell to me," said Paul. "A slight citrus tang, kinda like anesthetic gas, but not as sweet."

"Strange stuff," said Ben. "A lot of people can't even smell it, and those that do perceive it differently. All I know is, it's definitely not good for you." He left the bedside.

Natasha stood at the bedside, her slender torso bent over the bed rail, running her fingers through her husband's thin, sandy hair.

"Paul, why's he so hot? What's happening to him? Can he survive?"

"He needs a miracle, Natasha. But he's a strong man. It's a wonder that he's made it this far. The cyanide prevents his cells from using oxygen."

Her eyes widened. "You mean he's suffocating?"

"On a cellular level, internally, yes," Paul answered. "Some of his cells are using oxygen in a useless fashion, producing heat instead of energy. That's why he's hot."

"Paul," she said, grabbing his hands. "I love him."

"I know, he was like a second father to me. I wish there was something I could do."

"There is," she said. "I want you to find out who did this."

"What? That's for the police."

"I've no confidence in police, I want you. Most of my childhood, in the old country, I hid from the police. I can't rest until I know the truth. But if you won't do it for me, that's all right, Paul. Do it for him. Val helped you through school, residency, and got you this job. Although he'd never say it, I know he loved you like a son. I want his killer brought to justice."

Releasing her hands, Paul recoiled. "It's a random, serial murder. There are others..."

"That doesn't matter," she said, hanging her head, leaning over her husband. Clutching the bedrail, her pale hands turned red, matching her fingernail polish. Turning her head toward Paul, with eyes blazing green, she glared at him. He felt her desperation compelling him to obey. Now he realized Natasha had spoken the truth, that she'd never be whole again until the killer had been found. "Paul, I need this one favor."

The ventilator cycled, sending air rushing noisily into Z's congested chest. "All right, I promise I'll look into it. And if the police can't find the killer, I will."

Natasha smiled. Her hands relaxed their death grip on the bedrail, and her fine, white fingers flowed off the metal bar. "Thank you, Paul. You're a very special kind of friend." She wiped the tears from her eyes. They were cool, green, and bottomless.

Paul wondered just how deep he'd fallen into the abyss.

End of Preview

Get *Secret Thoughts: A Medical Thriller*

in eBook, audiobook, or paperback from

Amazon.com

Also in Spanish eBook